Frankie saw the blade coming at him...

"Banzai!" screamed Captain Sato, swinging downward with all the strength in his muscular arms.

Frankie La Barbara couldn't run and couldn't hide. His only option was to raise the ax for protection, and...CRACK! the samurai sword cleaved the handle of the ax in half. The samurai sword continued its downward rush, but Frankie leaned backward in time to save himself from being castrated.

Frankie looked down at half the ax handle in his two hands and the rest of the ax lying on the ground. Captain Sato smiled as he raised his samurai sword for the death blow, but Frankie wasn't going to stand there and get wiped out. All he had to fight with was that ax handle, and he threw it at Captain Sato's face...

Also in THE RAT BASTARDS series from Jove

Go For Broke

by
John Mackie

A JOVE BOOK

Excepting basic historical events, places, and personages, this series of books is fictional, and anything that appears otherwise is coincidental and unintentional.

The principal characters are imaginary, although they might remind veterans of specific men whom they knew. The Twenty-third Infantry Regiment, in which the characters serve, is used fictitiously—it doesn't represent the real historical Twenty-third Infantry, which has distinguished itself in so many battles from the Civil War to Vietnam—but it could have been any American line regiment that fought and bled during World War II.

These novels are dedicated to the men who were there. May their deeds and gallantry never be forgotten.

GO FOR BROKE

A Jove Book/published by arrangement with
the author

PRINTING HISTORY
Jove edition/May 1985

ISBN: 0-515-08189-2

Jove books are published by The Berkley Publishing Group,
200 Madison Avenue, New York, N.Y. 10016. The words
"A JOVE BOOK" and the "J" with sunburst are trademarks
belonging to Jove Publications, Inc.

PRINTED IN THE UNITED STATES OF AMERICA

Go For Broke

ONE . . .

It was June of 1944, and dawn came to the New Guinea jungle where the Twenty-third Regiment was digging in. Around them were trees and vegetation blasted by the artillery and mortar bombardment of the night. The air was filled with the smell of gunpowder and the curses of men as they hacked into the root-entangled earth. They had just captured the ground they were on, after fighting Japs all night long.

Lieutenant Dale Breckenridge, six feet four inches tall, weighing 260 pounds, gazed ahead at the jungle, expecting the Japs to counterattack at any moment. His left leg was covered with blood from a bayonet wound in his thigh, and his uniform was torn to shreds. He had cuts on his arms, chest, and shoulders from the brutal hand-to-hand clash that had just ended. The Japs had gone for broke in their big night attack, but the GIs stopped them cold and pushed them back.

Lieutenant Breckenridge looked at his watch: It was six o'clock in the morning. He couldn't understand why the Japs hadn't counterattacked yet. The men from the Twenty-third were tired, low on ammunition, and hungry. They were vulnerable, and surely the Japs knew it; but maybe the Japs were

1

tired, low on ammunition, and hungry too. Maybe they couldn't mount another attack after the beating they'd just taken.

Lieutenant Breckenridge lit a Lucky Strike and looked around. The battlefield was a nightmare of shell craters and devastated jungle. Bodies of Japanese soldiers lay everywhere, and here or there a stray arm or leg could be seen, blown off the body from which it had been attached. Lieutenant Breckenridge knelt on one knee, raised his binoculars to his eyes, and examined the jungle in front of him for the trembling of leaves or the sudden peculiar movement that would signal the onslaught of more Japanese soldiers.

Next to Lieutenant Breckenridge, Pfc. Craig Delane from New York City, a former socialite and playboy and now Lieutenant Breckenridge's runner, dug a hole for both of them in the ground. Delane was of medium height, built on the slim side, with blond hair and delicate facial features. His entrenching tool was bent into its *L* position, and he swung it like a pickax at a root as thick as his wrist that was hindering his progress.

Pfc. Delane gritted his teeth and perspiration streaked his face. He raised his entrenching tool in the air and brought it down with all his strength, but the blade of the entrenching tool merely bounced off the root.

"Son of a bitch!" he said.

Lieutenant Breckenridge turned toward him. "What's the matter with you?"

"I can't get through this goddamn fucking root!"

"Lemme try it."

Lieutenant Breckenridge stood and limped toward the hole, which had been a shell crater. He jumped inside and took the entrenching tool from Pfc. Delane, who stepped back out of the way. Lieutenant Breckenridge spread his legs far apart, gripped the entrenching tool tightly in his hands, and poised it over his head. He took aim and swung the entrenching tool downward.

Smack!

The root was cut in half. Lieutenant Breckenridge handed the entrenching tool back to Pfc. Craig Delane. "Here."

Pfc. Craig Delane took the entrenching tool, and Lieutenant Breckenridge climbed out of the trench. He lay on his stomach, because he didn't want to present too inviting a target to any

2

Jap snipers, and raised his binoculars again, scanning the tree-tops. Footsteps approached from his left.

"Sir?"

Lieutenant Breckenridge turned and saw lanky Sergeant Cameron kneel beside him. Sergeant Cameron's nose had been broken during the night and was covered with a bloody dirty bandage.

"Eight dead and twelve wounded," Sergeant Cameron said.

Lieutenant Breckenridge frowned. Before the battle last night, he'd had forty men and one officer. Now he was down to twenty men and one officer. "Shit," he said.

Sergeant Cameron shrugged and took a pinch out of his package of Beech-Nut chewing tobacco, placing the tobacco in his right cheek. He, too, was cut and torn by bayonets, and his eyes were half closed with fatigue.

"Tell the men to get ready, because I think the Japs are coming back any minute now," Lieutenant Breckenridge said.

"What about chow?"

"They can eat after they dig in, if there's time."

"Don't you think you should get that leg looked at, sir?"

"It's not that bad."

"I'll send the medic over."

Sergeant Cameron walked away. Lieutenant Breckenridge raised his binoculars to his eyes and scanned the jungle straight ahead. He wondered if the Japs had been beaten so badly last night that they wouldn't come back. He'd been told that the Japs had three divisions west of the Twenty-third Infantry Regiment's position, but he didn't know how much of that force was in the vicinity.

Lieutenant Breckenridge's cigarette dwindled to one inch, so he took out another one and lit it with the burning end of the butt. He knew he shouldn't smoke so much, that it cut his wind and made his mouth taste like shit, but his veins were full of adrenaline and he couldn't help himself. The battle had just ended and might start again at any moment. He couldn't calm down.

"Sir?" said a voice from behind him.

Lieutenant Breckenridge glanced behind him and saw Pfc. Dailey, the recon platoon medic, a scrawny fellow with sad eyes.

"Sergeant Cameron said you got a bum leg," Pfc. Dailey

3

said, kneeling beside Lieutenant Breckenridge.

"If I can still walk on it, it can't be that bad."

"Mind if I take a look at it, sir?"

Lieutenant Breckenridge wheezed as he rolled over onto his back. He took off his helmet and gazed up at the clear blue sky. A bird darted past overhead, and all around him he could hear the sounds of shovels and entrenching tools striking the earth.

Pfc. Dailey rolled up his pant leg and exposed the wound, which was one big mass of clotted blood. "How'd you get this, sir?"

"Bayonet."

"Ah." Pfc. Dailey upended his canteen and poured water on the wound, then dabbed it with gauze, cleaning away the dried blood. Gradually the true shape of the wound emerged, a red slit resembling a woman's vagina in miniature. "Looks deep."

"It's not that deep."

"You should go back to the battalion aid station and get it stitched up, sir."

"I'll go back when things settle down."

"If you move around a lot, it'll probably open up."

"Fix it so it won't."

"I'll do what I can."

Lieutenant Breckenridge puffed his Lucky Strike as Pfc. Dailey poured coagulant powder onto the wound. It stung, but the pain didn't particularly bother Lieutenant Breckenridge. He'd been wounded many times, in many places, and was used to it, but he could not overcome the onrushing fatigue so easily.

Pfc. Dailey tied a fresh bandage around the wound. "You really should go back to the battalion aid station, sir."

Lieutenant Breckenridge grunted. He wasn't going back to the battalion aid station because he expected the Japs to attack at any moment, and he didn't want to miss the action. This wasn't because he loved war and its bloody hand-to-hand combat but because he felt responsible for his men. He didn't think they'd get along well without him, and felt that his proper place was with them.

Pfc. Dailey rolled down Lieutenant Breckenridge's pant leg. "That's it, sir."

4

"Thanks."

Pfc. Dailey stood and walked away. Lieutenant Breckenridge rolled onto his stomach again and raised his binoculars to his eyes. The jungle ahead was still. There was no wind to trouble the leaves. It was going to be another hot, humid, horrible day.

"Sir!" said Pfc. Delane, holding up the walkie-talkie. "Captain Spode wants to talk to you!"

Lieutenant Breckenridge walked on his hands and knees to the hole and slid inside. He took the walkie-talkie from Pfc. Delane and held the instrument to his ear.

"Lieutenant Breckenridge speaking."

"How're you doing out there?" asked Captain Spode, the commanding officer of Headquarters Company.

"Eight dead and twelve wounded."

"The ammo truck's just come up. Send a detail of men over here to get whatever you need."

"Yes, sir."

"Any problems?"

"No, sir."

"Over and out."

Lieutenant Breckenridge handed the walkie-talkie back to Pfc. Delane.

"The hole deep enough now?" Delane asked.

"No."

Delane grumbled as he accepted the walkie-talkie and laid it on the ground. He tightened the nut that held the blade of his entrenching tool in place, then raised the entrenching tool high in the air. Lieutenant Breckenridge cupped his hands around his mouth.

"Sergeant Cameron!"

"Yes, sir!"

"Get over here!"

"Yes, sir!"

Lieutenant Breckenridge felt dizzy and sat on the ground. The day was becoming warmer and the humidity was rising. He'd lost blood from his various wounds and had a stomachache. Taking a deep breath, he wiped his mouth with the back of his hand. It seemed as though he had no strength left in his body. The adrenaline in his body had spent itself, and he was

5

coming down from the high of the fight.

Sergeant Cameron walked toward him, the bloody bandage on his nose making him appear ridiculous. "Yes, sir?"

"Captain Spode just told me he's got ammo at headquarters. Take a detail and get some for us."

"Yes, sir."

"Make it fast. The Japs might come back any time now."

"Yes, sir."

Sergeant Cameron walked away, his M 1 rifle slung over his shoulder. He had a ferocious headache, although he'd taken numerous aspirin. The medic had told him that his nose might be broken and that he should go back to the battalion aid station, but Sergeant Cameron thought he'd do that later. He didn't want to be back at the battalion aid station when the Japs attacked again. Like Lieutenant Breckenridge, he didn't think the recon platoon would survive without him.

In addition to his flattened nose, Sergeant Cameron had a bayonet wound on his right arm and a nick, also from a bayonet, on his right side. His uniform was torn and bloody, and his boots were rotting apart from the humidity. But he was an old war dog with a nasty disposition, and he wasn't stopped easily. A professional soldier, he'd enlisted in the Army in 1936, during the Depression, when his father had lost the farm to the goddamn fucking bank.

He approached a shell crater containing a machine gun mounted on a tripod. A soldier lay on either side of the machine gun, sound asleep, and Sergeant Cameron blew a fuse. He jumped into the shell crater and kicked one of the soldiers square in the ass.

"Get up, you son of a bitch!"

Moving around the machine gun, Sergeant Cameron bent over and smacked the other soldier in the mouth.

"On your feet, you fucking goldbrick!"

"Huh?" asked Pfc. Frankie La Barbara, blinking his eyes. "What?"

"On your feet, I said!"

Frankie La Barbara raised himself to a sitting position and looked up at Sergeant Cameron. Frankie had black hair and a swarthy complexion. He was from New York's Little Italy and was built like a tall light heavyweight. "What the fuck's the matter with you, Sarge?"

6

"On your feet, you son of a bitch!"

"What do I hafta get on my feet for? Are you nuts or something?"

"Yeah," said Pfc. Morris Shilansky, the other soldier in the shell crater. He was an inch taller than Frankie La Barbara and a bit slimmer. "Why don't you fucking relax, Sarge?"

"Relax?"

Sergeant Cameron lunged toward Shilansky and drew back his foot, then kicked at Shilansky's head. Shilansky calmly raised his hands and caught Sergeant Cameron's foot in his hands, twisting it around. Sergeant Cameron lost his balance and fell on his ass. Frankie and Shilansky laughed.

"You fucking clown," Frankie said.

Sergeant Cameron was spitting, pissing mad. He jumped to his feet, unslung his M 1 rifle, rammed a round in the chamber, and flicked off the safety switch, aiming the barrel at Frankie La Barbara.

"Whataya gonna do now?" Frankie asked. "You gonna shoot me? Okay, go ahead and shoot me. See if I care."

Frankie lay back on the ground and closed his eyes. Sergeant Cameron's lips and hands trembled violently. In his feverish mind he debated whether or not to shoot Frankie. He desperately wanted to shoot him, because Sergeant Cameron hated Frankie. Frankie always complained and never wanted to do anything. He was a lazy, worthless son of a bitch, a typical Yankee from New York, not worth the powder to blow him to hell.

"Relax, Sarge," said Shilansky, who had been a professional bank robber in the greater Boston area before the war. "If you shoot him, they'll shoot you in front of a fucking firing squad."

Frankie grimaced. "He ain't gonna shoot me. He ain't got the guts to shoot me."

That was the last straw for Sergeant Cameron. His head hurt, his arm hurt, and the night battle had taken its toll. He was thirty-five years old and didn't have the stamina of the younger men. He aimed his M 1 rifle at Frankie La Barbara and squeezed the trigger. Shilansky leaped to his feet and tackled Sergeant Cameron.

Blam!

The rifle fired, but Shilansky had upset Sergeant Cameron's aim. The bullet shot into the clear blue sky, and Sergeant

Cameron fell to the ground, Shilansky landing on top of him.

"Calm down, there, Sarge," Shilansky said soothingly.

"Let me go!"

"I'll let you go when you calm down."

"I said let me go!"

Frankie jumped to his feet and danced around, waving his fists in the air. "The son of a bitch tried to kill me! Lemme at him! I'll whip his fucking ass!"

Frankie dived on top of Shilansky and Sergeant Cameron, trying to punch Sergeant Cameron in the mouth, while Sergeant Cameron tried to kick Frankie in the balls. Shilansky was in the middle, and somehow all the blows were landing on him.

"Hey, cut it out, you two!" he yelled.

But they wouldn't cut it out. They punched and kicked each other, snarling and spitting, pummeling and mangling Shilansky in the process.

"Halp!" shouted Shilansky.

A powerful voice thundered above them. *"What in the hell is going on here?"*

It was a familiar voice, and the three men in the bottom of the hole froze. They swallowed hard and turned pale. Turning around and looking up, they saw Colonel Robert Hutchins, the commanding officer of the Twenty-third Regiment, standing above them, a Thompson submachine gun in his hands. He was five feet eight inches tall and had the jowls of a bulldog; his big potbelly hung over his cartridge belt.

"I said what the hell's going on here?"

"Nothing, sir," said Shilansky weakly.

"Nothing at all," agreed Frankie La Barbara.

Colonel Hutchins glowered down into the hole and wrinkled his nose. "Is that you down there, Sergeant Cameron?"

"Yes, sir."

"What is this, a circle jerk!"

The men disentangled themselves from each other and stood up. Sergeant Cameron smiled sheepishly. "Guess I musta slipped and fell, sir."

Colonel Hutchins snorted. It was an obvious lie and he knew it. The men had been fighting, and it looked like a court-martial offense had been taking place; but the Japs might attack again, and Colonel Hutchins had more important things to worry about.

"Where's Lieutenant Breckenridge?" Colonel Hutchins asked.

Sergeant Cameron pointed. "Thataway."

"You men cut out the shit here, understand?"

"Yes, sir."

"Carry on."

Colonel Hutchins walked away. Sergeant Cameron brushed himself off and picked up his rifle. "I shoulda told him the truth," he said, glancing at Frankie La Barbara. "You belong behind bars, you son of a bitch."

"Fuck you where you breathe, you bastard," Frankie replied.

"You wouldn't talk to me that way if I was Butsko," Sergeant Cameron said.

"Fuck Butsko and fuck his mother."

They were referring to Master Sergeant John Butsko, the platoon sergeant of the recon platoon, who was recovering from wounds at a hospital in Hawaii. Butsko had dominated the unruly recon platoon through sheer brutality and physical intimidation. His left leg had nearly been blown off during the last days of fighting on Bougainville, but his spirit and memory were still very much with the recon platoon.

Sergeant Cameron slung his M 1 rifle over his shoulder. "It seems to me I came over here for some definite reason," he said vaguely.

"You fucking dim bulb," Frankie replied. "Somebody ought to put you up against a wall and shoot you."

Sergeant Cameron stuck his finger straight up in the air. "I remember now. I need a detail to go to headquarters and pick up some ammo. You just volunteered for the detail, La Barbara."

"Fuck you in your ear," Frankie replied. "I'm busy."

"Okay," Sergeant Cameron said. "I'm not going to argue with you. I'm tired of arguing with you. I'm just gonna walk over there to Lieutenant Breckenridge's command post and tell him you refused a direct order. I'll let him take care of you personally."

"Fuck him too."

"I'll tell him that for you. I'm sure he'll want to know how

9

you feel about him." Sergeant Cameron grinned. "See you at the court-martial, wop, and I'm talking about *your* fucking court-martial, not mine."

Sergeant Cameron climbed out of the hole. He touched the bandage on his nose to make sure it still was there, and it was. Meanwhile, in the hole, Frankie La Barbara was thinking that he didn't feel like hassling with Lieutenant Breckenridge that morning. Lieutenant Breckenridge was a big bruiser, as tough as Butsko and mean as a bull once he got going.

"I'll go," Frankie said sullenly.

Sergeant Cameron stopped and turned around. "Kinda thought you'd change your mind. Follow me."

Frankie slung his M 1 rifle over his shoulder. He put on his steel pot and climbed out of the hole. "Hold the fort," he said to Shilansky.

"Hurry back with the ammo."

"Fuck you in your eyeballs."

Frankie La Barbara followed Sergeant Cameron across the battlefield. He passed two soldiers from a graves registration squad carrying a stretcher on which was the bloody, broken body of Private Jilliam, only sixteen years old, who'd been killed during the big fight. Frankie spit at the ground and took out an Old Gold cigarette. He lit it and blew smoke out the corner of his mouth. He felt nervous and crazy, as if he'd drunk four cups of coffee in a row, except that he hadn't drunk four cups of coffee in a row. His helmet was tilted on his head because he had a three-inch gash on his head and a big bloody bandage on top of it.

Sergeant Cameron stopped at a foxhole and looked inside. Pfc. Jimmy O'Rourke sat inside beside Pfc. Billie Jones, the biggest man in the recon platoon, known as the Reverend because he'd been an itinerant preacher in Georgia before the war.

"Jones," said Sergeant Cameron.

"Whataya want?" asked the Reverend Billie Jones, looking up from his handy pocket Bible.

"You just volunteered to go to headquarters and get some ammunition."

"I did?"

"Yeah, you did."

The Reverend Billie Jones groaned as he stood and stuffed his handy pocket Bible into his shirt pocket. He didn't argue because he was used to being assigned to all the details that required heavy lifting. The good Lord didn't make him big and strong for nothing. He was six feet two inches tall and weighed 285 pounds. He picked up his M 1 rifle and climbed out of the hole.

Sergeant Cameron looked down at Pfc. Jimmy O'Rourke, who had been a movie stuntman in Hollywood before the war and who always wanted to be a big star like John Wayne, Gary Cooper, and, most of all, Clark Gable. He wore a black mustache like Clark Gable's and had a tendency to tug his earlobes the way Clark Gable did.

"How you doing?" Sergeant Cameron asked.

Jimmy O'Rourke's pant leg was rolled up and he had an ugly purple swelling on his right shin. "I think my fucking leg's broken."

"Can you walk on it?"

"More or less."

"Then it's not broken. Go see the medic and get some APC pills."

"I already saw him and he gave me a bunch of them."

"You take 'em?"

"Yeah, but it didn't do no fucking good. I think my leg's broken."

"Your fucking head is broken, you bastard."

"Up your ass, Sarge."

"If I see the medic, I'll send him over."

"Up his ass too."

Sergeant Cameron walked away, followed by Frankie La Barbara and the Reverend Billie Jones. Sergeant Cameron looked east, the direction in which the Japanese had fled at the first glimmer of dawn, and wondered when they'd come back. He hoped to have the fresh ammo in time.

"Hurry up, you guys," he said.

"Fuck you," replied Frankie La Barbara.

The Reverend Billie Jones looked at Frankie. "Why do you always talk to him that way?"

11

"Fuck you too."

"My God," the Reverend Billie Jones replied, shaking his head in dismay.

"Fuck Him too."

The Reverend Billie Jones rolled his eyes and groaned. They approached a spot where two shells had landed almost on top of each other. The resulting crater was deep and wide, and inside it sat Pfc. Hotshot Stevenson, the former pool shark from Chicago, and Private Victor Yabalonka, a former longshoreman from San Francisco. Hotshot Stevenson was a wiry little man, full of fidgets and twitches, whereas Yabalonka, a relative newcomer to the recon platoon, was a big man, though not as big as the Reverend Billie Jones.

"Yabalonka!" said Sergeant Cameron.

Private Yabalonka looked up. "Whataya want?"

"You just volunteered to go to Headquarters Company and bring back some ammo."

"I never volunteer for anything."

"You just did."

"No I didn't. If you want me to do something, tell me to do it, but cut out the horseshit, will you?"

"Have it your way," Sergeant Cameron said. "Go to Headquarters Company with La Barbara and Jones, and bring back some ammo. Did I say it okay this time?"

"Yeah."

"Then get the fucking lead out."

Yabalonka covered his blond crew cut with his helmet and picked up his M 1 rifle. He climbed out of the hole and stood with Frankie and the Reverend Billie Jones.

Now Sergeant Cameron was faced with a dilemma. He should place one man in charge of the detail, but as far as he was concerned, each one was worse than the other. Frankie La Barbara was basically a criminal and refused to do anything right. Not much was known about Yabalonka, since he was new to the recon platoon, but he was only a private and you couldn't put a private in charge of two pfcs. Sergeant Cameron always figured Yabalonka was a bomb getting ready to explode, because Yabalonka wouldn't have been assigned to the recon platoon if he hadn't been in trouble someplace else before. The recon platoon got all the discipline problems, all the criminals,

12

all the men inclined to punch first and ask questions later. Sergeant Cameron had been assigned to the recon platoon because he was an alcoholic, although he was all dried out now.

Sergeant Cameron decided he'd have to appoint the Reverend Billie Jones, although the Reverend Billie Jones had demonstrated no leadership ability yet and was basically a religious fanatic who tended to go berserk on the battlefield.

"Jones, you're in charge," Sergeant Cameron said.

The Reverend Billie Jones was surprised. He touched his thumb to the middle of his chest and asked: "Me?"

"What'd I just say? Didn't I just say 'Jones, you're in charge'?"

"That's what you said."

"Then get the fuck going, and hurry back."

"Hup, Sarge."

The Reverend Billie Jones looked at the other two. "Let's go."

He stepped out in the direction of Headquarters Company, and to his amazement Frankie La Barbara and Victor Yabalonka followed him. They walked away and Sergeant Cameron looked at them as he took out a Pall Mall cigarette and lit it with his old trusty Zippo, which he'd carried onto the beach at Guadalcanal and had kept with him ever since.

I'm tired of dealing with these guys, he said to himself as he turned and walked back to his hole. *They're wearing me down. I'm no Butsko, and even Butsko had his hands full with the bastards. Maybe I should get myself busted down to private, and then some other poor son of a bitch'll have to be platoon sergeant around here.*

He trudged across the battlefield, puffing his cigarette and touching his fingers to the bandage on his nose to make sure it still was there.

Colonel Hutchins burped as he made his way across the battlefield toward the hole occupied by Lieutenant Breckenridge. The sun was rising in the sky and the heat intensified as if he were in an oven and somebody had turned up the knob all the way. He wore a bandage over his left eye, and another one could be seen on his chest through his open shirt. Like Sergeant Cameron, he was an alcoholic, but unlike Sergeant

Cameron, he was not dried out. He had a few bottles of Old Forester back in his tent, and when they ran out he could rely on his trusty mess sergeant, who had operated an illegal still in Kentucky before the war. Colonel Hutchins also had a flask in his back pocket that was half empty, the other half being in his body, producing a mild euphoria.

He came to the designated hole and saw Lieutenant Breckenridge sitting inside, looking at one of his maps. Craig Delane was nearby, taking a quick nap.

"Morning," said Colonel Hutchins.

Lieutenant Breckenridge looked up and nearly shit a brick. He pushed his hands against the muck in an effort to stand and salute.

"As you were," said Colonel Hutchins, hopping into the hole.

Craig Delane heard him land and woke up.

"Take a walk," Colonel Hutchins told him.

"Yes, sir."

Craig Delane grabbed his rifle and jumped out of the hole, walking away as quickly as possible, anxious to stay out of trouble. He thought he'd track down the medic and find out if the cut on his cheek would mean that he'd be scarred for life.

Meanwhile, inside the hole, Colonel Hutchins crouched down and lit a cigarette. "How's your leg?"

"I can walk on it."

"Can you go out on a patrol?"

"I think so."

"Good. Take a few men and find out what's in front of us out there. Use your walkie-talkie to stay in touch."

"When do you want me to go?"

"As soon as you can."

"Don't you think we should wait and see whether or not the Japs are gonna counterattack?"

"If they haven't counterattacked by now, I don't think they will this morning. Maybe they will tonight, but for the time being I think we're okay."

"Okay."

"Don't forget to stay in touch."

"Yes, sir."

Colonel Hutchins reached into his back pocket and took out

14

his flask. He unscrewed the top, tossed his head back, and took a swig. Then he held out the flask to Lieutenant Breckenridge.

"Want some?"

"Don't mind if I do."

Lieutenant Breckenridge accepted the flask and raised it to his lips. He eased his head back and let the mellow bourbon gurgle down his throat.

Just then there was a terrific explosion fifty yards away. The earth shook and two sago palms were blown to shit as tons of dirt flew through the air.

Lieutenant Breckenridge thought it was the bourbon. "Boy, this stuff has a helluva kick!" he said, passing the flask back to Colonel Hutchins.

But Colonel Hutchins was already on his stomach inside the hole. *"Hit it!"* he screamed.

A second explosion occurred one hundred yards away, demolishing a Jeep and the two GIs sitting inside it. Lieutenant Breckenridge dived toward the bottom of the hole, and when he landed, Colonel Hutchins snatched the flask out of his hand.

"I'll take care of that," Colonel Hutchins said, screwing the top back on.

Another Japanese artillery shell landed, and it was followed by another a few seconds later. Then the full weight of a Japanese barrage hit, artillery shells and mortar rounds exploding almost simultaneously up and down the Twenty-third Regiment's line. The ground shook as though an earthquake was taking place, and the remaining trees still standing were blown to bits. Rocks and earth flew through the air, some landing inside the hole where Lieutenant Breckenridge and Colonel Hutchins were lying.

"Sir!" shouted Lieutenant Breckenridge above the din. "I think this is the imminent attack you were referring to a few moments ago!"

"Where's your fucking walkie-talkie?"

"It's around here someplace!"

They searched around the bottom of the hole and Lieutenant Breckenridge found it near the spot where Pfc. Delane had been lying. He handed it to Colonel Hutchins, who pressed it to his face, hit the button, and called his headquarters. Static filled his ear, but then he heard the voice of his operations officer, Major Cobb.

"Cobb!" screamed Colonel Hutchins. "I'm with my recon platoon! If you haven't called for artillery support yet, I'm going to court-martial you!"

"I called!" replied Major Cobb. "It's on the way!"

"I'll stay where I am. You're in charge back there, understand?"

"Yes, sir!"

"Any questions?"

"No, sir!"

"Over and out!"

Colonel Hutchins placed the walkie-talkie on the dirt beside him. He wanted to raise his head over the edge of the hole and see what was going on, but was afraid a chunk of shrapnel would shear his head off. He knew the Japs would attack as soon as the artillery barrage ended. The big question was when the artillery barrage would end.

Lieutenant Breckenridge made sure his M 1 carbine had a full clip in it, and then he snapped his bayonet on the end. He rammed a round into the chamber and got set, because he knew the Japs were coming soon. Thinking about his men, recalling the position of each of them one by one, he realized that some were off on that detail to get more ammo. They probably were on open ground someplace, on their way to headquarters to get the ammo, when the barrage hit. And where in the hell was Craig Delane?

Lieutenant Breckenridge heard the whistle of artillery shells overhead. They were going from west to east, which meant they were American shells on their way to the Japanese lines. A few seconds later he heard a crescendo of explosions to the east in the jungle where the Japs had fled at dawn.

Colonel Hutchins smiled beside him. "Music to my ears!" he said.

TWO . . .

Pfc. Frankie La Barbara, Pfc. Billie Jones, and Private Victor Yabalonka were caught on open ground by the artillery barrage. They hit the dirt immediately as soon as the first shell landed, and then held their helmets tightly on their heads while pressing their faces into the dirt, their bodies trembling as the ground heaved underneath them.

"Them fucking Japs!" screamed Frankie La Barbara, baring his teeth in rage.

Next to him, the Reverend Billie Jones tried to figure out what he should do. He was in charge of the detail, and it seemed to him that he should do something, but he didn't know what. When in doubt, he prayed, and since he was in doubt just then, he closed his eyes and whispered an improvised prayer to God, asking for guidance and help in the Japanese attack that he knew was coming.

On the other side of the Reverend Billie Jones, Victor Yabalonka lay shivering, trying to overcome his fear. The night before had been his baptism of fire, and he'd wanted a reprieve so he could get his head together again, but now here was another battle; the Japs were coming back and he'd have to

17

fight for his life hand to hand, if a Japanese artillery shell didn't land on him first.

Victor Yabalonka was an unusual man, even for the recon platoon, which received all the lunatics, criminals, and trouble-makers in the regiment. Before the war he'd been a longshore-man in San Francisco, and he'd got involved with the far left political wing of the Longshoremen's Union. Although he'd never been a card-carrying Communist, he'd often been ac-cused of being one. He'd been jailed many times for militant union activity, and he'd beaten the shit out of numerous scabs during various strikes.

When the war broke out and he received his draft notice, he became a conscientious objector, because he thought the war was just another way for rich people to make money. But then people called him a coward, and he hated to be called that. In fact, it infuriated him, and he cracked the skulls of a few people whose mouths ran ahead of their common sense. Finally he decided to join the Army and organize the soldiers into a union so that they wouldn't have to fight rich men's wars.

Like many left-wing idealists, Yabalonka vastly misjudged the mood of average, ordinary people. He thought he knew how to talk to them, but he didn't, and wound up in a succession of barracks brawls, finally doing time in various stockades. In the early part of 1944, while a guest at the Lompoc Disciplinary Barracks in California, he decided to keep his mouth shut from then on, give up on his efforts to change the world, and attempt to get through the war as best he could.

That's what he'd tried to do ever since, but now, on a remote battlefield in New Guinea, with artillery shells and mortar rounds falling all around him, and his eardrums nearly bursting from the roaring god-awful explosions, he wondered whether or not he should have remained a conscientious objector.

Pfc. Frankie LaBarbara, lying next to him, chewed his gum ferociously and wondered what to do. He didn't like the idea of being exposed on open ground, without any protection, and realized that the Reverend Billie Jones was a follower, not a leader, which meant that Frankie La Barbara would have to take charge and do something quickly.

He glanced around and saw an artillery shell land on a big walled tent, engulfing it in an orange blast; then a big puff of smoke hid everything. Another shell hit a palm tree and obliterated it totally. In the distance, through the smoke and flames, he saw three soldiers running; but then a shell landed nearby, blowing them all into the air, arms and legs akimbo.

He spotted a shell crater straight ahead, about thirty yards away. He thought he'd be safe if he could get in that hole, and if a shell fell on him while he was trying to reach it, that would be better than lying on the ground like a sitting duck and getting killed that way.

He gritted his teeth, grabbed his rifle, and jumped up. *"Let's go!"* he shouted. He held his helmet on his head with one hand and clutched his rifle in his other hand as he sped toward the shell crater. A mortar round landed near him, the concussion wave pushing him to the side, nearly causing him to lose his balance, while shrapnel whistled all around him. But Frankie maintained his footing and kept going, chewing his gum like a maniac, huffing and puffing, snot dripping out of his nose.

Behind him came the Reverend Billie Jones and Victor Yabalonka. They were so accustomed to following orders that they were doing what Frankie told them, without questioning his rank. He sounded as though he knew what he was about, and that was enough for them.

Frankie approached the hole and dived in head first. He landed with a thud and his helmet fell off, but he put it back on as the Reverend Billie Jones and Victor Yabalonka dropped on either side of him. They burrowed into the soft, warm earth as artillery shells and mortar rounds detonated everywhere, transforming the battlefield into a nightmare holocaust, making the ground heave like the deck of a ship in a typhoon, while the smoke obscured the rays of the sun, transforming day into night.

Their ears pulsated with the cacophony of explosions. Their hearts were chilled by the fear that an artillery shell or mortar round might fall directly on them at any moment and blow them all to hell. They tried not to think of themselves being blasted to smithereens, but they couldn't ignore the bombardment. They felt every concussion wave along every inch of their nervous systems; dirt and rocks showered onto them; and they knew that the worst was yet to come, because when the bombardment ended, the Japs would attack.

• • •

To the east of the American position, long columns of Japanese soldiers streamed through the jungle, carrying rifles and bayonets, machine guns and mortars, pistols and samurai swords, moving toward their attack positions. The American artillery bombardment rained hell upon them, but still they came, showing no fear, determined to demolish the Americans facing them.

Many of the Japanese soldiers had lost comrades in the fight that took place during the night. Vengeance was on their minds; more than that, however, they wanted to wipe out the stain of defeat. For a Japanese soldier, defeat was a terrible humiliation. It was a betrayal of their Emperor, whom they considered a god. The defeat of last night must become the resounding victory of today.

No one felt this more strongly than Captain Yuichi Sato, leading his company through the fierce, tumultuous bombardment. He was twenty-nine years old, with an athletic, muscular build, and he had been a member of the Japanese Olympic team that participated in the Olympics in Germany in 1936. His specialty had been the decathlon, and he had placed eighth overall.

Dedicated to his Emperor and his country, convinced of the necessity for defeating the decadent West on the field of battle, he never flinched at artillery shells landing in his vicinity. He believed that a coward dies a million times, but a brave man dies only once. His head was shaved and he had high cheekbones. He wore no mustache or goatee, considering them ridiculous decorations, and his mouth was small and pursed, like a rosebud. He raised his samurai sword over his head and waved it around.

"Advance!" he hollered. "Follow me!"

The Twenty-third Infantry Regiment was part of the Eighty-first Division, and the commanding officer of the Eighty-first Division was Major General Clyde Hawkins, a graduate of West Point and a first captain while he was there. Hawkins had blond hair and a blond mustache, and his headquarters was in a large walled tent nearly two miles behind the Twenty-third Infantry Regiment.

The Japanese bombardment didn't reach his headquarters,

20

but he could hear it reverberating in the distance as he stood with his hands behind his back and gazed down at his map of the battlefield, trying to make rational decisions about how to proceed.

Beside him was his chief of staff, Brigadier General Bernard MacWhitter, a skinny, bony officer five years older than General Hawkins. But General MacWhitter had not been first captain when he was at West Point, and somehow he didn't have quite the commanding presence that General Hawkins had. It had taken General MacWhitter longer to become a general, and even he knew it was unlikely that he would rise much higher in the Army, unless he did something spectacular, which he had to admit was extremely unlikely.

General Hawkins puffed a cigarette in an ebony holder as he wondered how to respond to the Japanese bombardment. He knew that the bombardment was a prelude to something, but what? Was the activity in front of the Twenty-third Regiment a feint, or would the main enemy thrust come through there? General Hawkins had studied enough tactics and seen enough war to know it was extremely important to identify as soon as possible the point of the enemy's main thrust.

He examined his position, and it wasn't good. He and his division had landed on New Guinea only yesterday morning, and were attacked last night before they had a chance to dig in. Their mission had been to defend the Tadji airfields at Aitape, only a few miles west of his headquarters. He'd deployed his Twenty-third Regiment along the Driniumor River; one battalion of his Fifteenth Regiment on the northern beaches, to guard against a seaborne attack; and one battalion from his Eighteenth Regiment to the south, facing the Torricelli Mountains. Everything else was in reserve, to be shifted around to wherever they were needed.

A principle of offensive warfare was to fake your enemy out so he'd commit his reserves to a spot other than the main thrust. A principle of defensive warfare was to hold your reserves and not commit them until you knew where the main enemy thrust would be. Commanding officers suffered ulcer attacks and nervous breakdowns, trying to figure out where and when to commit the reserves.

However, General Hawkins had a cool head, as a rule. He'd learned long ago that a commanding officer had to have nerves

21

of steel. A commanding officer couldn't panic when reports of heavy casualties came in. A commanding officer had to remain calm and make sensible decisions. That was what separated great commanders, like General MacArthur, who was General Hawkins's idol, from mediocre officers who suffered nervous breakdowns and were relieved of command.

General Hawkins held his ebony cigarette holder in the air and made his decision. He would do nothing until the battle developed to a greater degree. He would not reinforce the Twenty-third until later in the game. He knew that no matter what he did he'd take casualties, but they would be less overall if he could counterattack at the right place.

General Hawkins puffed his cigarette, blew smoke in the air, and turned to General MacWhitter. "Direct all units to stay put and fight where they are," he said. "There will be no retreats without my authorization. All enemy activity must be reported to this headquarters immediately. Do you have any questions?"

General MacWhitter leaned forward and rested his fists on the edge of the map table. "You're not going to reinforce the Twenty-third, sir?"

"Not until the enemy's intentions become known."

"But, sir, the Twenty-third was badly mauled last night. They may not be able to hold up against a serious attack. The enemy might very well achieve a breakthrough across the Driniumor."

General Hawkins squinted, because smoke from his cigarette was getting into his eyes. He moved his cigarette holder away from his face and said: "If the Japs break through, we'll catch them farther back with one or more of our battalions in reserve."

"The Twenty-third will take a beating if that happens, sir."

General Hawkins looked down at his map table, his face showing no emotion whatever. "Casualties are unavoidable in war," he said.

The bombardment continued like roaring, swirling hell. The Twenty-third Infantry Regiment's position was raked from end to end by explosions, fire, and general destruction. Every tree that was standing was blown away. Logs and branches lay everywhere. The ground was pockmarked with shell craters. One shell landed on the ammunition that had been delivered to Headquarters Company, and the subsequent blast demolished Captain Spode's headquarters. The concussion burst Captain Spode's eardrums, and blood dripped out of his ears. His radio communications were destroyed. Headquarters Company was cut off from the rest of the world, and Captain Spode was in a daze. Master Sergeant Koch, the company's first sergeant, had taken over command of the company, but he didn't have anybody to order around except his clerk, Pfc. Levinson, who lay in a shell crater with his M 1 rifle and his Underwood typewriter, wondering how he'd replace all the records and Army regulations that had been blown to shit in the big explosion.

Casualties were mounting as artillery shells and mortar rounds fell on or near foxholes. GIs were blown into the air, dismembered, hacked apart by red-hot shrapnel with edges sharp as razors. The wounded hollered for their medic, and young Pfc. Dailey, his face covered with pimples, roved across the battlefield, braving the fury of the bombardment, tying tourniquets and bandages, shooting morphine into the asses of soldiers howling with pain, pouring sulfa and coagulant powder on wounds; but then, while running from one foxhole to another, he was hit in the chest with a chunk of shrapnel, and Headquarters Company was minus one medic when it needed him the most.

Colonel Hutchins didn't know that Pfc. Dailey was dead, or that Captain Spode was unable to snap out of his daze. He didn't know that ammo had been blown up, along with trucks, artillery emplacements, and machine-gun nests. But he did know that his regiment was in trouble. He knew that the bombardment was taking its toll. And he knew that the Japs would attack soon on the ground.

He picked up the walkie-talkie, held it against his face, pressed the button, but heard only static. He spoke the code name of his headquarters, released the button, but still heard static. He was cut off from his headquarters. All he could do was wait for the bombardment to end, like every other GI in the Twenty-third.

He pulled his flask out of his back pocket and took a swig, then held the flask out to Lieutenant Breckenridge, who took it and raised it to his lips. Colonel Hutchins looked at his watch and estimated that the bombardment had been going on for nearly twenty-five minutes, but it felt more like twenty-five hours.

Lieutenant Breckenridge handed back the flask and winked. "I thought you said the Japs weren't going to attack this morning!" he shouted.

Colonel Hutchins shrugged. "Guess I was wrong!"

Colonel Hutchins didn't mind being wrong. Everybody was wrong once in a while. The main thing was to try to minimize the damage. He wanted to contact General Hawkins and ask for reinforcements. It was clear to him that the Japs were about to mount a major attack, otherwise they wouldn't be wasting so much artillery ammunition. Colonel Hutchins didn't think his regiment could stand up to a major attack. They'd barely survived the last one; what's more, they were low on ammunition and hadn't slept all night, and many hadn't even had breakfast.

Colonel Hutchins's ears pricked up. The artillery bombardment was slackening. That meant it was going to stop at any moment. The attack was about to begin.

"Get ready!" he shouted.

Lieutenant Breckenridge also was aware that the artillery bombardment was diminishing. He lay on his side and held his carbine in both hands. Colonel Hutchins grabbed his .45-caliber Thompson submachine gun. As soon as the Japs attacked, he was going to lead his men in a counterattack. There was no point in waiting for the Japs to swarm over the Twenty-third Regiment. It would be much better to hit the Japs on the run.

The bombardment continued to slacken for several seconds, and then suddenly stillness descended on the Twenty-third Regiment. The men's ears continued to ring, but no more artillery shells or mortar rounds fell. A haze of smoke hung over the battlefield, while in the distance the American artillery bombardment continued its deadly work.

Colonel Hutchins raised his head over the edge of the shell crater and peered through the smoke at the jungle straight ahead. He couldn't see much, because there was no wind to blow the smoke away, but he knew the Japs were getting ready to charge.

"Any minute now," he said to Lieutenant Breckenridge. "How're you doing?"

Lieutenant Breckenridge was perched on his knees, holding

his carbine with fixed bayonet in his hands. "I'm as ready as I'll ever be, I guess."

Not more than three hundred yards away, Captain Sato lay on his stomach in a shell crater as the American bombardment continued. The din was so terrific that he didn't hear the Japanese shelling terminate, and his visibility was poor also, due to all the smoke and tumult.

His radio operator turned to him and poked his arm.

"What is it!" asked Captain Sato.

"The order has come down to attack, sir!"

Captain Sato stood and drew his long samurai sword out of its scabbard. American shells fell all around him, but he didn't acknowledge their presence. He raised his samurai sword high in the air and then pointed it forward toward the American lines.

"*Banzai!*" he screamed. "*Tenno heika banzai!*"

He bounded forward and began his long headlong dash toward the Americans. He swung his samurai sword in a circle over his head, and it caught a ray of the sun, glinting as if studded with a massive diamond. Dodging around trees, vaulting over shell craters, he sped toward the American lines with the vigor of an Olympic champion.

"*Banzai!*" he hollered. "*Tenno heika banzai!*"

"*Banzai!*" shouted his men as they surged out of their holes and followed him into battle. They shook their rifles and bayonets and bared their teeth as they charged through the flaming, churning jungle. They knew that the faster they ran, the sooner they would be free from the terrible bombardment. But they weren't out of the horror yet, and many were blown into the air by explosions.

Still, they charged with all the passion and determination that was part of their fanatical tradition. They streamed through the jungle, their tan uniforms soaked with sweat, their armpits stinking like raw fish that had been left in the sun too long. They elbowed bushes out of their way and jumped over fallen trees. They dashed through puddles of mud, splashing the muck in all directions, and plunged into thick, tangled vegetation, gritting their teeth, always pushing onward, anxious to close with the Americans and impale them on the ends of their bayonets.

25

Captain Sato was far in front of them, roaring at the top of his lungs. If the Americans shot him down, it would be a great honor to be killed while attacking the enemies of the Emperor. A shell exploded nearby and a small piece of shrapnel the size of an acorn blew a hole in the sleeve of his shirt, but it didn't even scratch his body.

"Banzai!" screamed Captain Sato, considering the near-hit as an omen that the gods were on his side. *"Banzai!"* he bellowed. *"Banzai!"* Ahead he saw a stretch of jungle that was receiving no shelling whatsoever. His heart leaped in his chest when he realized that was the American position. He was almost out of the bombardment area. "Charge!" he yelled. *"Tenno heika banzai!"*

He rushed toward the area receiving no shelling. His muscular legs carried him over the body of a dead wild pig and through a mangled bush, and then he was in the clear, away from the bombardment. Ahead, not more than one hundred yards away, he could perceive the outlines of American steel helmets inside holes.

"There they are!" he screamed, pointing his samurai sword toward the Americans. *"Banzai!"*

Colonel Hutchins narrowed his eyes as he watched the Japanese soldiers pouring out of the jungle ahead of him. American machine guns opened fire, cutting down Japanese soldiers like wheat before a scythe. Other American soldiers fired their M 1 rifles and carbines. A few fired BARs (Browning Automatic Rifles), but the American resistance was not nearly as stiff as it had been during the Japanese attack of the night before. Many American soldiers had been killed since then, and many machine-gun nests put out of action. Everyone was low on ammunition. The Japs were having an easier time now.

Colonel Hutchins waited for the Japs to get closer. He didn't fire his Thompson submachine gun because it wasn't worth a shit at long range. Lieutenant Breckenridge didn't have the same problem with his M 1 carbine. He rested it on the edge of the hole, lined up the sights on the chest of a Japanese soldier, and squeezed the trigger.

Blam! The Japanese soldier tripped over his feet and fell to the ground, a widening red splotch on the front of his uniform shirt. Lieutenant Breckenridge lined up the sights on another

Japanese soldier and squeezed the trigger again. *Blam!* That Japanese soldier lost his footing and collapsed onto the ground, a bullet through his throat. Lieutenant Breckenridge moved his carbine an inch to the right and aimed at a third Japanese soldier. *Blam!* He'd aimed too quickly and his bullet missed the Japanese soldier who was his target, but it hit the Japanese soldier beside him, and that Japanese soldier tumbled asshole over teakettle to the ground.

Blam! . . . Blam! . . . Blam! Lieutenant Breckenridge pulled the trigger as quickly as he could. The Japs were closer now and all bunched together; he couldn't miss. *Blam! . . . Blam! . . . Blam!* Japanese soldiers dropped to the ground, but others loomed up behind them and maintained the charge. They howled like wild animals, spitting and snorting, shaking their rifles and bayonets, thirsty for American blood. They rampaged across the jungle, and Colonel Hutchins felt a sickness in the pit of his stomach, because there were so many Japs and so few of his own men in comparison.

But he couldn't turn tail and run like a coward. It was too late for that now. The only thing to do was get up and fight. Colonel Hutchins took a deep breath, gripped his Thompson submachine gun tightly, and jumped out of the hole. Baring his teeth, he charged toward the Japanese, the butt of his machine gun tucked in against his waist. He was a middle-aged alcoholic with a potbelly, but so fucking what!

"Forward Twenty-third!" he hollered. *"Attack!"*

He pulled the trigger of his submachine gun, and it bucked and stuttered in his hands. Hot lead spewed out of its barrel and chopped down Japanese soldiers in front of him. Keeping his finger pressed against the trigger, he swung the submachine gun from side to side as he ran forward.

"Follow me!" he yelled. *"Up and at 'em!"*

His loud voice reverberated all across that sector of the American line; they didn't call him Hollarin' Hutchins for nothing. His men saw their squat potbellied commander charging the entire Jap army all by himself, and they came up out of their holes to follow him. The men from the South let out rebel yells, and the men from the West screamed cowboy cattle calls. The men from New York gave the Japs Bronx cheers, and the ones from New England just hollered like sons of bitches.

In a long line of tattered OD-green uniforms, they swept

27

across the jungle toward the Japanese soldiers, who in turn were charging them. Both sides drew closer and closer to each other. Each side could see the other's bloodshot eyes and white knuckles on hands that gripped weapons. Shots rang out on both sides, and Colonel Hutchins lunged into the midst of the Japanese soldiers, firing his Thompson submachine gun without letup.

Colonel Hutchins was surrounded by screaming hyped-up Japanese soldiers, and he dodged from side to side, spinning around, firing his submachine gun. He aimed at a Japanese soldier in front of him and shot his chest into sausage meat. The Japanese soldier was dead before he even had time to scream, and he collapsed onto the ground at Colonel Hutchins's feet.

Colonel Hutchins stepped over him and fired point-blank at another Japanese soldier, aiming a little high this time, and the burst of big fat .45-caliber bullets blew the Japanese soldier's head apart. Blood and brains splattered in all directions, and the Japanese soldier was hurled backward onto another Japanese soldier.

Colonel Hutchins got low and fired up into the belly of the next Japanese soldier, blowing his guts through his spine and out a massive hole in his back. Pivoting, Colonel Hutchins shot another Japanese soldier in the balls, the next Japanese soldier in the chest, and a third Japanese soldier in the lower jaw as the kick of his submachine gun raised the barrel progressively higher in the air.

Colonel Hutchins pulled the submachine gun down and fired at the stomach of a Japanese soldier who was charging toward him, aiming his rifle and bayonet at Colonel Hutchins's heart. The submachine gun fired two bullets that bored through the Japanese soldier's guts, and then the submachine gun went *click!*

Colonel Hutchins was out of ammo, and he didn't have time to load up. A Japanese bayonet sliced open his left arm, and then a Japanese rifle butt came out of nowhere and slammed him on the side of his helmet.

It was a good thing he was wearing that helmet, otherwise his skull would have been mashed in; but the force of the blow made him see stars anyway. He fell back on his ass, and when his vision cleared, he saw a Japanese bayonet streaking down toward his face.

With an angry, vicious snarl, Colonel Hutchins raised his hands quickly at the last moment and grabbed the barrel of the Japanese rifle, pushing it to the side. The Japanese bayonet continued its downward motion and buried itself four inches into the moist, warm ground, which had a consistency similar to human flesh.

Colonel Hutchins balled up his fists and jumped to his feet, putting all of his weight into a left hook. He caught the Japanese soldier flush on the mouth, knocking his teeth down his throat. The Japanese soldier dropped to his knees, and Colonel Hutchins spun around, pulling the Japanese soldier's rifle and bayonet out of the ground.

Before he could get set, a Japanese rifle butt whacked him on the shoulder, and the blade of a Japanese bayonet lay open his left cheek to the bone. Colonel Hutchins staggered to the side, hollering in pain, trying to get his bearings as blood poured down his cheek and onto his uniform shirt.

"You son of a bitch!" he screamed.

A Japanese soldier thrust his rifle and bayonet toward Colonel Hutchins's chest, but Colonel Hutchins parried the bayonet to the side, then swung his own rifle butt around and connected with the face of the Japanese soldier, splintering the bones in the Japanese soldier's face, fracturing his skull; blood squirted out of the Japanese soldier's nose, mouth, and ears. The Japanese soldier was slammed to the ground by the force of the blow, and Colonel Hutchins charged ahead, pushing his rifle and bayonet forward, burying the bayonet to the hilt into the stomach of the next Japanese soldier.

Colonel Hutchins stepped backward with his right foot and pulled the rifle and bayonet loose from the Japanese soldier's stomach. Then he raised the rifle and bayonet and saw another Japanese soldier directly in front of him, charging hard.

The Japanese soldier and Colonel Hutchins thrust their rifles and bayonets forward at the same time. They smashed against each other's hands, but neither let go of their weapons as their rifles and bayonets flashed toward each other's chest. Both men were approximately the same height and had the same reach. Colonel Hutchins twisted to the side at the last moment,

29

but the Japanese soldier was too excited to react intelligently. Colonel Hutchins's bayonet sank five inches into the Japanese soldier's chest, while the Japanese soldier's bayonet slashed across Colonel Hutchins's ribs but didn't penetrate deeply.

It was as if someone held a flaming torch to Colonel Hutchins's chest: The pain was so intense he blacked out for a few moments. When he opened his eyes he was lying face down on the ground, and it took another second or two before he realized where he was. In front of him he could see American combat boots and Japanese leggings close together, leaning toward each other. Men grunted and farted as they tried to stab each other and gouge out each other's eyes. Something glinted in the sunlight and Colonel Hutchins saw a machete lying in front of him, its handle in the hand of a dead American soldier on his back, his eyes wide open and staring. Colonel recognized the soldier as Sergeant Dolan from his own Headquarters Company.

Colonel Hutchins was half crazed with pain and covered with his own blood. He expected a Jap to harpoon him through the back at any moment, and he knew that his only chance for life was through the killing of others. He leaped forward like the old lion that he was and took the machete out of Sergeant Dolan's lifeless hand. Then Colonel Hutchins raised himself to his full height and looked around.

Men were locked in bloody hand-to-hand fighting all around him. There was barely room to move, and he couldn't put his foot down without placing it on a dead soldier. The fight was gritty and gruesome. Japanese soldiers outnumbered the GIs hugely, and Colonel Hutchins wondered when the reinforcements would arrive.

"Banzai!"

Colonel Hutchins turned to the sound and saw a Japanese soldier charging toward him, rifle and bayonet aimed at Colonel Hutchins's heart. Colonel Hutchins gripped the handle of the machete in both hands and raised it over his head, then darted to the side and swung down, chopping off the left arm of the Japanese soldier just above the elbow.

The Japanese soldier blinked in total abject horror as his arm fell to the ground, along with his rifle and bayonet. Blood gushed out of the stump of his arm as if from a fireman's hose, and Colonel Hutchins drew back the machete and swung again,

30

the blade slicing easily through the Japanese soldier's neck. The Japanese soldier's head, still blinking uncontrollably, flew into the air, falling onto the helmet of Frankie La Barbara, bouncing off, and dropping to the ground.

Frankie La Barbara felt something hit him but didn't know what it was, and didn't care anyway. The main thing was that it hadn't hurt him. In his bloody, gory hands he carried an ax that he'd found buried in the trunk of a tree that had been blown down during the Japanese bombardment. It was a lucky find, because an ax was a fabulous weapon to have in hand-to-hand fighting.

"YAAAAAHHHHHHHH!" screamed Frankie La Barbara as he raised the ax in the air.

"Banzai!" cried a Japanese soldier who charged him out of the great tumultuous melee of men struggling to kill each other.

The Japanese soldier thrust his rifle and bayonet forward, and Frankie La Barbara swung down with the ax. Its blade connected with the top of the Japanese soldier's rifle, and the power of the blow knocked the rifle out of the Japanese soldier's hands. Frankie La Barbara swung the ax to the side and buried it in the right shoulder of the Japanese soldier, who shrieked horribly as he was flung to the ground.

Frankie La Barbara stepped on his face and swung the ax in the reverse direction, hacking off the top half of a Japanese soldier's head. Blood and brains flew everywhere. Frankie raised the ax and brought it down, chopping a Japanese soldier's head in half lengthwise like a coconut, and more blood and brains fell on everyone nearby. Frankie swung to the side and cut off a Japanese soldier's arm just below the shoulder. On the backswing Frankie buried the ax in the chest of a Japanese soldier, and blood welled out around the head of the ax, along with bubbles of air from the Japanese soldier's lungs.

Frankie pulled the ax loose and spun around. He saw the back of a Japanese soldier who was fighting with an American GI. Frankie charged as he swung the ax back and then swung forward, cracking the Japanese soldier's spine in two. The Japanese soldier's torso bent backward at an impossible angle. Frankie raised the ax with the intention of cutting off the Japanese soldier's head, when something made him glance to the left.

He saw a Japanese officer charging toward him, holding a

31

samurai sword in both hands. The Japanese officer was none other than Captain Yuichi Sato, who had placed eighth in the decathlon competition at the 1936 Olympics in Berlin.

"Banzai!" screamed Captain Sato.

"Your mother's pussy!" replied Pfc. Frankie La Barbara, the former Mafia hoodlum from New York's Little Italy.

Captain Sato maintained his charge, holding his samurai sword over his head, the blade straight up in the air. Frankie drew back his ax and swung to the side, hoping to cut off Captain Sato's arm, but Captain Sato was an expert swordsman with excellent reflexes, and he merely hopped backward.

Frankie's ax whistled through thin air, and then Captain Sato lunged forward and swung down with his samurai sword. Frankie saw the blade coming at him and lurched out of the way, barely eluding the downward stroke of the samurai sword.

The American GI and the Japanese officer looked at each other, each realizing that the other would be no pushover. The Japanese officer was pleased to have found an adversary worthy of his steel, but Frankie La Barbara didn't like tough opponents, because tough opponents could kill you quicker than easy opponents.

Frankie wished he had a gun so he could shoot the Japanese soldier, because he didn't want to fuck around with him hand to hand. He looked down at the ground, hoping to find a spare rifle or pistol lying there—and in fact there were many ballistics weapons of all kinds on the ground—but Frankie didn't have time to pick one up, because the Japanese officer was charging again.

"Banzai!" screamed Captain Sato, swinging downward with all the strength in his muscular arms.

Frankie La Barbara couldn't run and couldn't hide. His only option was to raise the ax for protection, and . . . *crack*, the samurai sword cleaved the handle of the ax in half. The samurai sword continued its downward rush, but Frankie leaned backward in time to save himself from being castrated.

Frankie looked down at half the ax handle in his two hands and the rest of the ax lying on the ground. Captain Sato smiled as he raised his samurai sword for the death blow, but Frankie wasn't going to stand there and get wiped out. All he had to fight with was that ax handle, and he threw it at Captain Sato's face.

Captain Sato saw the ax handle coming and dodged out of the way. While he was dodging, Frankie La Barbara turned around and ran like a son of a bitch. A bunch of Japanese and American soldiers was in front of him, and he dived into their midst, pouncing on a rifle and bayonet in the hands of a Japanese soldier. Frankie pulled the rifle and bayonet, but the Japanese soldier wouldn't let go. Frankie pulled harder and lifted the short Japanese soldier off his feet, spinning him around so that he was between Frankie and Captain Sato, who had followed Frankie and was already in the midst of another deadly swing.

Captain Sato's eyes bugged out in horror as he saw his samurai sword slam into the head of the short Japanese soldier. Frankie La Barbara became covered with the blood and brains of the short Japanese soldier, whose hands went slack with his sudden demise.

Frankie yanked the rifle and bayonet out of the short Japanese soldier's hands and turned to face Captain Sato. *"I got you now, you son of a bitch!"* Frankie shouted, working the bolt of the Japanese Arisaka rifle. *"I ain't gonna fuck with you any more!"*

Frankie rammed a round into the chamber and pulled the trigger without taking careful aim. *Blam!* The Arisaka rifle fired, and Captain Sato felt as though his left shoulder had been hit by a truck. The force of the bullet spun him around and he fell to the ground.

Frankie stalked toward him to shoot him again, when suddenly three Japanese soldiers jumped in front of him. They'd seen their commanding officer fall and tried to protect him. In unison they pushed their rifles and bayonets toward Frankie's chest, and Frankie stepped forward, parrying one rifle and bayonet to the side, bashing the next Japanese soldier on the mouth with his rifle butt, and leaping beyond the range of the third Japanese soldier.

The third Japanese soldier turned toward Frankie and thrust his bayonet-armed rifle forward. Frankie parried the Japanese rifle and bayonet to the side, then pushed his rifle butt toward the Japanese soldier's nose, but the Japanese soldier leaned to the side and Frankie missed him.

They lined up against each other and tried again. The Japanese soldier feinted with his rifle and bayonet, but Frankie

33

didn't fall for it. Frankie feinted with his rifle and bayonet, but the Japanese soldier was not suckered out of position. They circled, trying to figure out how to kill each other.

The Japanese soldier was taller than most Japanese soldiers; in fact, he was nearly as big as Frankie La Barbara. He wore a black Fu Manchu mustache and goatee. On his collar was the insignia of a private first class, which was Frankie's rank. The protagonists were evenly matched. Within the next several minutes one would live and one would die. Both of them knew that as they sized each other up, looking for weaknesses and openings in the other's defense.

Close by, soldiers slammed each other over the head with rifle butts and stabbed each other in the stomach with bayonets. They kicked each other in the crotch and elbowed each other in the eye. The air was filled with screams and curses. Metal clanged against metal and fists slammed into noses.

"Hold fast!" shouted Colonel Hutchins, somewhere in the middle of the melee.

Frankie and the Japanese soldier continued to circle. They moved in one direction, and then the other. Each recognized in the other a tough, strong fighter, and each realized the least mistake could be fatal. They were being cautious—perhaps too cautious. Frankie felt the anxiety building inside him, because he had to do something about the Jap soldier in front of him. Frankie couldn't just walk away from the whole mess. He'd have to kill the goddamned Jap.

Frankie hated the predicament he was in, and it made him madder. He focused his hatred on the Japanese soldier, seeing in him the cause of all his troubles. Frankie would be back in New York City just then, wearing zoot suits and screwing chorus girls, if it wasn't for Japs like the one directly in front of him. They'd attacked Pearl Harbor and started the war, the sneaky, slant-eyed sons of bitches.

"You fucking bastard!" Frankie hollered, and then he charged. Clenching his teeth, he thrust his rifle and bayonet forward with all his strength. The Japanese soldier was ready for him, parrying the blow to the side; but Frankie's power was too much for the Japanese soldier at that particular moment, and Frankie's bayonet drank blood from the Japanese soldier's right pectoral muscle and right shoulder.

The Japanese soldier didn't cry out or register any other

reaction to the sudden pain. So concentrated was he on the fight, he barely felt the pain at all. Continuing the motion of his parry, he brought his rifle butt around and drove it toward Frankie's face.

Frankie saw the butt coming and ducked, his forward motion carrying him closer to the Japanese soldier. He collided with the Jap and pushed hard. The Japanese soldier staggered backward, off balance, and Frankie slashed diagonally, hoping to cut the Jap from neck to hip, but the Japanese soldier leaned backward to avoid the blow and lost his balance. He fell on his ass. Frankie lunged down with his rifle and bayonet, hoping to impale the Japanese soldier on the ground, but the Japanese soldier rolled out of the way, still clutching his rifle and bayonet, and jumped to his feet.

Frankie lunged again before the Japanese soldier could get set, and the Japanese soldier raised his rifle and bayonet to protect himself. The Japanese soldier hit Frankie's bayonet with the top of his rifle barrel, parrying it upward. An expression of horror came over the Japanese soldier's face when he realized that Frankie's bayonet was zooming directly at his throat. A split second later Frankie's bayonet pierced the Japanese soldier's jugular vein, cut his windpipe, and proceeded onward, brushing past the juncture between the Japanese soldier's skull and spine and finally protruding out the back of the Japanese soldier's neck.

"*Gotcha!*" screamed Frankie La Barbara in triumph as blood gushed out of the Japanese soldier's jugular, splashing onto Frankie's face.

Frankie La Barbara pulled his rifle and bayonet backward, and the Japanese soldier collapsed onto the ground, blood still spurting from his neck. Frankie spun around, and his flesh crawled at the sight of a Japanese officer standing there, aiming a pistol at him calmly, one eye closed and one eye open.

"*Yikes!*" cried Frankie as he dived to the ground.

Blam! The pistol fired and kicked up into the air. The bullet whistled over Frankie La Barbara's head, and then Frankie leaped forward to tackle the Japanese officer, who swung down with the pistol, clobbering Frankie on the back of his head as he was coming in.

Frankie felt pain for an instant, and then the lights went out, but his forward motion continued and he crashed into the

Japanese officer, hitting him at waist level, knocking him down.

The Japanese officer fell onto his back, and Frankie landed on top of him. The Japanese officer was a short man with a mosquitolike build, and Frankie weighed 193 pounds. The Japanese officer struggled to push Frankie off him. That didn't work, so he tried to crawl out from underneath Frankie; while he was doing that, Frankie came to consciousness.

Frankie reached out with both his hands and grabbed the wrist of the Japanese officer who was holding the pistol. The Japanese officer punched Frankie on the side of his head with his free hand, but Frankie had a thick head and could take a good punch. Still holding the Japanese officer's wrist, he elbowed the Japanese officer in the mouth, shaking loose a few teeth and causing the Japanese officer to become dazed.

Frankie plucked the pistol out of the Japanese officer's hand and leaped to his feet. *"Yeah!"* shouted Frankie La Barbara as he aimed the pistol down at the Japanese officer's head and pulled the trigger.

Blam! The Japanese officer's head exploded like a rotten cantaloupe. Frankie turned around and saw directly in front of him the back of a Japanese soldier fighting hand to hand with an American soldier. Frankie aimed and pulled the trigger of the Japanese pistol, and *blam!*—a black hole appeared on the back of the Japanese soldier's shirt, and then it became a red splotch. The Japanese soldier dropped to his knees; standing in front of him was Lieutenant Dale Breckenridge, his hands empty, blood dripping from a cut on his chin.

Lieutenant Breckenridge didn't know who had shot his Japanese opponent and didn't care. He'd lost his own carbine somewhere in the fighting, and now bent down to pick up the rifle and bayonet of the Japanese soldier who'd just been shot, when he saw something flash in the corner of his eye and turned in time to see a bayonet zooming toward his throat. He spun around and raised his hands reflexively, and the blade of the bayonet cut across both his forearms.

The pain was so sudden and intense, it made Lieutenant Breckenridge's eyes bulge out. He saw standing in front of him a Japanese soldier carrying a bayonet in each of his hands, with both of the blades pointing upward. The Japanese soldier was hatless and rangy, with a weird gleam in his eyes and a fiendish smile on his face.

36

He looks like a fucking homicidal maniac, Lieutenant Breckenridge thought as he took a step backward, wondering how he was going to deal with this new threat. He wished he had a weapon to fight with, but all he had were his bare hands. The Japanese soldier giggled as he lunged forward, slashing at Lieutenant Breckenridge's belly with the bayonet in his right hand, and at his throat with the bayonet in his left hand.

Lieutenant Breckenridge jumped backward and avoided both blows, but the Japanese soldier giggled again and lunged forward, slashing wildly with both bayonets. Lieutenant Breckenridge twisted, ducked, and jumped backward once more, but he wasn't quite fast enough, and the Japanese soldier sliced a thin piece of flesh the size of a silver dollar off Lieutenant Breckenridge's left shoulder.

The Japanese soldier paused a moment to assess the damage he'd done, and that was the last mistake he'd ever make in his life. Lieutenant Breckenridge kicked out with his long right leg, and his big foot buried itself in the Japanese soldier's groin. The force of the blow slammed the Japanese soldier's testicles into his intestines, mashing them like two soft plums. The Japanese soldier shrieked in terrible, excruciating pain, dropping both his bayonets and clutching his devastated crotch. The force of the blow also lifted him a few inches into the air, and when he landed he didn't have the strength or will to stand, so he crumpled onto the ground.

Lieutenant Breckenridge bent over and picked up one of the bayonets. He looked up and saw a Japanese soldier charging him, rifle and bayonet zooming toward Lieutenant Breckenridge's chest. Lieutenant Breckenridge timed the thrust and batted the barrel of the Japanese rifle to the side with his left forearm while punching upward with the bayonet in his right hand, sticking the bayonet into the stomach of the Japanese soldier.

The Japanese soldier's tongue stuck out, and Lieutenant Breckenridge's right hand became covered with blood pouring from the Japanese soldier's stomach. Lieutenant Breckenridge wanted to take away the Japanese soldier's rifle and bayonet, but before he could do that, he became aware that two Japanese soldiers were charging him from his left side.

Lieutenant Breckenridge grabbed the Japanese soldier collapsing in front of him and spun him to the side. The two

37

charging Japanese soldiers lunged toward Lieutenant Breckenridge with their rifles and bayonets, and suddenly the dead Japanese soldier was between him and them.

Both bayonets stuck into the dead Japanese soldier, who fell to the ground, dragging the bayonets with him. The two Japanese soldiers glanced upward and were horrified to see the big American officer coming at them, bayonet in hand. Lieutenant Breckenridge snarled viciously as he swung the bayonet at close range, ripping open the windpipe of the Japanese soldier on the right, then following up and dragging the blade of the bayonet across the face of the Japanese soldier on the left.

The cut opened the mouth of the Japanese soldier on the left a few inches wider, and Lieutenant Breckenridge raised his knee, crushing the Japanese soldier's balls. Both Japanese soldiers sagged to the ground, and Lieutenant Breckenridge dropped the bayonet in his hand, preferring to grab a rifle and bayonet on the ground. His fingers closed around it and he picked it up, but it was embedded in the back of the Japanese soldier whom Lieutenant Breckenridge had previously stabbed in the stomach.

Lieutenant Breckenridge pulled the stock of the rifle, but the bayonet was wedged securely in the back of the Japanese soldier. He pulled again, lifting the dead Japanese soldier off the ground, but still the bayonet wouldn't come loose.

"Son of a bitch!" he yelled.

His curse caught the attention of a short Japanese soldier with bowed legs, advancing nearby. The short Japanese soldier carried an Arisaka rifle and bayonet and charged toward Lieutenant Breckenridge, thrusting his rifle and bayonet forward, and then realized at the last moment that Lieutenant Breckenridge was a giant compared to him.

Lieutenant Breckenridge growled as he reached out and grabbed the bowlegged Japanese soldier's rifle, but the bowlegged Japanese soldier wouldn't let go. Lieutenant Breckenridge tugged, lifting the bowlegged Japanese soldier off his feet, but still the Japanese soldier wouldn't let go. Lieutenant Breckenridge swung around and slammed the bowlegged Japanese soldier into the bayonet of another attacking Japanese soldier, impaling the bowlegged Japanese soldier, who finally had to let go his rifle because he was damn near dead at that point.

Meanwhile the attacking Japanese soldier's rifle and bayonet were dragged toward the ground by the weight of the dying bowlegged Japanese soldier, and Lieutenant Breckenridge stepped forward, delivering a vertical butt stroke to the jaw of the attacking Japanese soldier, snapping his head back and putting out his lights.

The attacking Japanese soldier fell to the ground, and Lieutenant Breckenridge jumped onto his face with both combat boots, flattening the Japanese soldier's nose, cracking facial bones and cartilage.

Clang! Lieutenant Breckenridge's rifle and bayonet were whacked out of his hands in a sudden gleaming flash. Lieutenant Breckenridge looked up and saw a Japanese sergeant carrying a samurai sword, and the Japanese sergeant raised it for another go at Lieutenant Breckenridge.

Lieutenant Breckenridge jumped on the Japanese sergeant and grabbed his wrist in both his hands, at the same time kneeing the Japanese sergeant in the balls, but the Japanese sergeant twisted to the side at the last moment and received the blow on his hip. The Japanese sergeant raised his hand toward Lieutenant Breckenridge's face in an effort to claw out his eyes, and Lieutenant Breckenridge elbowed the Japanese sergeant in the chops.

The Japanese sergeant was momentarily dazed. He dropped his samurai sword and took a step backward. Lieutenant Breckenridge dived toward the sword, and the Japanese sergeant leaped on top of Lieutenant Breckenridge, wrapping his arms around Lieutenant Breckenridge's neck and torso and pulling him backward.

The Japanese sergeant fell onto his ass, still clutching Lieutenant Breckenridge, who landed on top of him. Lieutenant Breckenridge shot back his elbow into the Japanese sergeant's breadbasket. The Japanese sergeant said *"Oof!"* and scratched his fingernails across Lieutenant Breckenridge's face, hoping to gouge out an eye in the process.

Lieutenant Breckenridge rolled over and jumped to his feet, drawing back his left leg, kicking out at the Japanese sergeant's head; but the Japanese sergeant leaned to the side, avoiding the blow, and then he scrambled to his feet, too.

Lieutenant Breckenridge and the Japanese sergeant faced each other. Both were unarmed, but Lieutenant Breckenridge was several inches taller and approximately eighty pounds heavier than the Japanese sergeant, plus he had a much greater reach. All that should have given Lieutenant Breckenridge a clear-cut advantage, but it didn't. The Japanese sergeant was an expert in jiujitsu, judo, and karate, and he was quick as lightning. The Japanese sergeant spread his feet apart and bent his knees, raising the blades of his hands in the air. Then he proceeded to crab-walk sideways toward Lieutenant Breckenridge, with the intention of breaking up Lieutenant Breckenridge's body with judicious kicks to weak points and blows with the blades of his hands.

Lieutenant Breckenridge stepped backward, realizing the Japanese sergeant knew something about the Oriental martial arts. But Lieutenant Breckenridge had the confidence of a big, powerful man. He thought he could handle just about anybody hand to hand. He also knew that the Oriental martial arts were based on counterattacking off an opponent's lunges, using the opponent's strength against him. Lieutenant Breckenridge figured he could kill the Jap if he, Lieutenant Breckenridge, didn't make any mistakes.

Lieutenant Breckenridge raised his fists in the classic western boxer's defense and watched the Japanese sergeant crab-walk closer. Lieutenant Breckenridge feinted a left jab, and the Japanese sergeant swung the blade of his hand to block the blow that never came. But the Japanese sergeant saw his mistake immediately and pulled back, covering quickly, leaving Lieutenant Breckenridge no opening.

Lieutenant Breckenridge feinted a left jab again, and that time the Japanese sergeant didn't fall for it. Lieutenant Breckenridge stepped forward quickly in a fake attack, then stepped back. The Japanese sergeant let loose with a sudden ferocious roundhouse kick, slamming Lieutenant Breckenridge upside his head with the top of his foot, and Lieutenant Breckenridge saw stars.

The Japanese sergeant lunged forward with a punch toward Lieutenant Breckenridge's solar plexus, and it connected, sending waves of pain radiating out all over Lieutenant Breckenridge's body, paralyzing him momentarily.

Lieutenant Breckenridge was dizzy and racked with pain. He could barely move, had no offense and little defense. The Japanese sergeant drew back the blade of his hand, preparing to split Lieutenant Breckenridge's skull in half, when suddenly, out of the press of battle, the butt of a Browning Automatic Rifle crashed down on the top of the Japanese sergeant's head, caving in his skull, the violence of the blow causing the Japanese sergeant's brains to explode out of his ears, nose, and mouth.

The barrel of the BAR was in the mighty powerful hands of the Reverend Billie Jones, who had picked it up off the ground somewhere along the way. He was swinging it around like a baseball bat, lambasting Japanese soldiers all around him.

The Reverend Billie Jones had gone totally berserk, as he usually did in situations of hand-to-hand combat. Moreover a BAR was several inches longer than an ordinary M 1 rifle and weighed twice as much, making it a much more deadly weapon.

"Yaaaahhhhhhhhh!" screamed the Reverend Billie Jones, swinging the BAR to the side and slamming a Japanese soldier in the head, busting it apart, sending a shower of blood and brains flying into the air. On the backswing the Reverend Billie Jones smacked the butt of the BAR into the skull of another Japanese soldier, flattening that side of the Japanese soldier's head, forcing blood and brains through the Japanese soldier's nose.

"Yaaaaaaahhhhhh!" bellowed the Reverend Billie Jones, like a wild raging bull, swinging downward and burying the butt of the BAR in the skull cavity of another Japanese soldier, splattering blood and brains everywhere. A considerable amount of the cranial materials flew onto the face of the Reverend Billie Jones. Because his mouth was open, some of the salty stuff covered his teeth and tongue, but he only spit it out and swung again.

This time he connected with the shoulder of a Japanese soldier, and the force of the blow broke the Japanese soldier's arm and flung him to the ground. The Japanese soldier tried to get up, but the Reverend Billie Jones clobbered him on the head, destroying it utterly.

"I am the scourge of God!" shouted the Reverend Billie Jones, slamming one Japanese soldier on the shoulder, another Japanese soldier on the head, and a third also on the head. Rampaging forward, the Reverend Billie Jones whacked a Japanese soldier in the face, kicked the next Japanese soldier in

the balls, and slammed a third Japanese soldier in the neck, demolishing tendons and bursting blood vessels and nearly separating the Japanese soldier's head from his body.

The Reverend Billie Jones spun around and raised the BAR in the air.

"It's me!" screamed Sergeant Cameron, standing there horrified.

The Reverend Billie Jones was so insane at that moment that he didn't even recognize Sergeant Cameron. The Reverend Billie Jones swung down the BAR and Sergeant Cameron jumped backward.

"It's me!" he hollered again.

The Reverend Billie Jones still didn't know who he was and raised his BAR again. Sergeant Cameron turned tail and ran away. The Reverend Billie Jones lunged after him, when suddenly a foot came out of nowhere and tripped him up. The Reverend Billie Jones lost his balance and fell, like a big old elephant, to the ground.

The Reverend Billie Jones got to his knees and then leaped to his feet, looking around. He saw Pfc. Morris Shilansky pointing an M 1 rifle at him.

"Calm the fuck down!" shouted Shilansky.

"Yaaaahhhhhh!" screamed the Reverend Billie Jones, charging toward Morris Shilansky, who backpedaled as quickly as he could, because he didn't want to shoot the Reverend Billie Jones.

"It's me!" yelled Shilansky.

"I am the scourge of God!" replied the Reverend Billie Jones, and then suddenly he realized that he was attacking Pfc. Morris Shilansky, one of his buddies from the recon platoon.

The Reverend Billie Jones blinked and came to a stop just as Pfc. Morris Shilansky was about to blow him away. The Reverend Billie Jones realized he'd almost clobbered Pfc. Morris Shilansky and felt ashamed. His heart thundered in his chest, which heaved like that of a horse that just had run nine furlongs at the Santa Anita racetrack.

The Reverend Billie Jones looked around. In the distance he saw a few GIs fighting hand to hand with Japanese soldiers, but that was all. The ground was covered with dead and wounded soldiers from both sides. Lieutenant Breckenridge, hatless and

42

covered with blood, staggered toward Pfc. Shilansky and the Reverend Billie Jones.

"Take cover," he said hoarsely. "Most of the Japs passed us by. They're on their way to our rear now, but sooner or later more of them'll be by to finish us off."

"Finish us off?" asked Shilansky, beginning to see the light. "Does that mean we're cut off out here?"

"That's what it means," Lieutenant Breckenridge replied. He reached for his package of cigarettes and walked away to gather up the other survivors of the attack.

THREE . . .

Colonel Hutchins, cursing and swearing to himself, sat behind the wheel of a jeep and pressed the accelerator to the floor. The stub of a cigar hung out of the corner of his mouth, and the jeep bounced over holes and boulders as it sped toward the headquarters of the Eighty-first Division. Colonel Hutchins was covered with blood, and much of it was his own. He'd lost his helmet, and his hair was matted with dried blood. His only weapon was the machete that he'd been fighting with, and it, too, was covered with dried blood.

Colonel Hutchins had disengaged from the battle when he realized the Japanese vastly outnumbered his men. He remembered he was supposed to be the regimental commander, not a front-line private first class, and he pulled back to give direction to his soldiers and also to call for help.

Japs had tried to shoot him in the back as he ran away, but they missed and he found the jeep near the Driniumor River. The Engineers had constructed a pontoon bridge across the Driniumor, and Colonel Hutchins drove the jeep over the bridge, making his way to his own headquarters.

But no one was there. His headquarters tent had been blown

45

to shit. Confused, wondering what had happened to his reserves, he sped toward the headquarters of the Eighty-first Division to get some answers.

He drove around a palm tree and through a shell crater. He was rip-roaring mad because he could see no reinforcements on the way to the Twenty-third Regiment's lines, and the longer it would take reinforcements to arrive, the more of his men would become casualties. His heart ached with the pain of defeat as he barreled through a mass of bushes, ducking his head behind the windshield so that no branches would scratch him.

Soon he saw soldiers, jeeps, and trucks. He passed ammo dumps, artillery emplacements, and a field kitchen where beans and hot dogs were being cooked. Soldiers looked at the bloody apparition behind the wheel of the jeep and couldn't believe their eyes. Colonel Hutchins saw the Eighty-first Division command post and steered toward it. The MPs guarding the front of the tent saw him coming and didn't know what to do. They thought he might drive right through the entire goddamned tent, so they unslung their carbines, but Colonel Hutchins braked in front of the tent and hopped out of the jeep.

"Where the hell you think you're going?" said one of the MPs, who didn't recognize Colonel Hutchins underneath all the blood.

"You'd better say *sir* when you talk to me, young soldier!" Colonel Hutchins bellowed as he pushed the MP out of the way.

The MP recognized Colonel Hutchins's infamous voice and said: "Yes, sir!" but Colonel Hutchins already was inside the tent by then and couldn't hear him.

Seated behind his desk, Master Sergeant Abner Somerall, the sergeant major of the Eighty-first Division, looked up at the blood-soaked nightmare charging past him. "Who the hell are you?" he demanded.

"You better get your rifle ready," Colonel Hutchins growled, "because the Japs're gonna be here any minute now!"

"What!"

Colonel Hutchins pushed aside the tent flap and entered the office of General Clyde Hawkins, who was stroking his blond mustache and looking down at his map, still trying to figure

46

out where the main Japanese effort would be concentrated. Also in the office were General MacWhitter, Colonel Jessup, General Sully, and a few other Eighty-first Division staff officers, including General Hawkins's aide-de-camp, Lieutenant Jack Utsler.

General Hawkins looked up and saw Colonel Hutchins enter the office, the bloody machete rammed into Colonel Hutchins's belt.

"My God!" expostulated General Hawkins.

Colonel Hutchins marched toward General Hawkins, stopped in front of him, and saluted. "Sir, my men have been overwhelmed and probably overrun! Reinforcements are needed urgently and immediately to plug the hole!"

General Hawkins stared at Colonel Hutchins as if he were looking at a ghost. All he could say was *"What?"*

"Sir, my men have been overwhelmed and probably overrun! You'd better send reinforcements up there right away to plug the hole and maybe save them!"

When in doubt, General Hawkins looked at his maps, and that's what he did then. "Where is this attack taking place?" he asked.

Colonel Hutchins drew the bloody machete and brought its tip to rest on the spot where Headquarters Company of the Twenty-third Regiment had been. "Here!"

"Just in that sector?"

"That's all I saw, but I assume the attack was taking place on a broader front."

General Hawkins blinked. "You assume? I cannot commit thousands of men to a battle based on your assumptions! What about the rest of your regiment?"

Colonel Hutchins took a step backward, because he knew he was on thin ice as far as the rest of his regiment went. "I don't know, sir."

"Why not?"

"Because I happened to be up front with my reconnaissance platoon when the fight broke out. I've been out of touch with my headquarters. Have they been in touch with you?"

"We've been unable to raise them by radio or telephone."

"That's because the Jap bombardment must have blown up the telephone wires and fucked up radio communication as well.

47

Don't you know that we were under a shelling for a half hour?"

"Of course I knew," General Hawkins replied. "We're not deaf."

"But you must be dumb, you son of a bitch!" Colonel Hutchins could hold in his frustration and rage no longer. *"Why haven't you reinforced my regiment?"*

Everyone stared at Colonel Hutchins in dismay. His uniform was torn to ribbons and he was as bloody as a bull butchered in the Chicago stockyards.

General MacWhitter cleared his throat. "I think you'd better get ahold of yourself, Colonel."

"Fuck you, MacWhitter!" Colonel Hutchins replied. "You'd better get ahold of your own damn self!"

"At ease!" said General Hawkins, getting pissed off.

"Why haven't you reinforced my regiment?" Colonel Hutchins demanded.

"I don't have to answer your questions, Colonel! I realize you've been through an ordeal, but this is still the United States Army, and I still command this division!"

"There won't be a division left unless you plug that hole!"

Colonel Hutchins's eyes glowed like hot coals set in his blood-covered face. General Hawkins looked down at his map, because he was in doubt again. It certainly sounded as if there was a serious problem in the Twenty-third Regiment, but he didn't want to commit his reserves to that segment of the line just then, because if he did, it would appear as though he'd been coerced by Colonel Hutchins. But if he didn't, the Eighty-first Division might be split apart by the Japanese attack, and that would be a very undesirable thing. Also, he didn't know how many Japanese soldiers had broken through.

Colonel Hutchins's anger boiled over again. *"What the hell are you waiting for?"* he screamed.

"At ease!" said General MacWhitter.

"At ease yourself!" replied Colonel Hutchins, raising his sword in a threatening manner. "What is this, a goddamned debating society? The Japs are headed this way, and all you fucking bastards can do is talk! *The time has come to act!"*

"Now see here!" said General MacWhitter. "You're being insubordinate!"

Colonel Hutchins was so mad, he could have spit. "We're gonna be run over by Japs if somebody doesn't do something!

48

Wake the fuck up, you stupid bastards!"

"You're going too far!" General MacWhitter said.

Colonel Hutchins had lost a lot of blood, and now, on top of that, his agitation was making him dizzy. "I need to sit down," he said, looking around for a chair, but he couldn't see one. His knees buckled and he fell to the ground.

Colonel Jessup rushed toward him and knelt down. "We'd better get a medic in here," he said.

"Call a medic!" General Hawkins yelled.

Just then they all heard sounds like a popcorn machine in the distance.

"What the hell is that?" General Hawkins asked, his eyes widening.

"Sounds like gunfire," General Sully replied.

A phone rang and a clerk picked it up. The clerk listened a few moments, then held out the phone to General Hawkins. "It's for you, sir!"

General Hawkins raised the phone to his face. "What the hell's going on?" he yelled.

It was Captain Tracy from George Company of the Fifteenth Regiment. "Sir," he shouted, "all I can see are Japs in front of me, and they're swarming toward my headquarters right now!"

"How many?" asked General Hawkins.

"Lots!" Captain Tracy calmed himself down and tried to be more precise. "Maybe a battalion!"

General Hawkins swallowed hard, because he knew that George Company of the Fifteenth Regiment was right in front of him, and that meant that Japs were headed toward General Hawkins's headquarters, just as Colonel Hutchins had indicated. General Hawkins could hear gunfire and explosions over the telephone connection.

"Sir!" said Captain Tracy. "I think you'd better send reinforcements up here! We can't hold off all these Japs for long!"

General Hawkins thought quickly and reached a fast conclusion. He was, after all, an American general and not a retarded birdbrain. "Don't try to hold them off!" he ordered. "Conduct a fighting retreat! Help is on the way! Any questions?"

"No, sir!"

"Over and out."

General Hawkins hung up the telephone and strode toward his map. He looked down and decided what units to bring up on the line. "General MacWhitter!"

"Yes, sir!"

"Direct the first two battalions of the Fifteenth Regiment to deploy here and here." General Hawkins pointed to two spots on the map. "Move the first battalion of the Eighteenth Regiment here." He pointed to another spot. "That ought to stabilize our line. Hurry."

"Yes, sir."

General MacWhitter rushed to the phones and made the calls. General Hawkins continued to gaze down at the map, although now his doubt was gone. He believed he knew where the Japs' main effort was coming now. They were coming through where they had first been reported to be coming. They were attempting no complex double-envelopments or other fancy tactics. It was just an all-out, go-for-broke frontal attack, typically Japanese, and the first thing to do was stop it.

General Hawkins glanced toward the corner, where the radios and telephones were set up. He saw General MacWhitter talking on one of the telephones. General Hawkins hoped the replacements would arrive before the Japs took too much ground. General Hawkins now wished he'd acted sooner, but he still believed he'd behaved properly, from a military point of view. It had been necessary to wait until the enemy's full intentions were clear. Then and only then could the appropriate response be made.

General Clyde Hawkins stroked his blond mustache as he looked around at his subordinate officers, who in turn were looking at him. He saw Colonel Hutchins still lying on the floor, a medic bending over him. In the distance, rifle and machine-gun fire could be heard, and it wasn't that far away. It was possible that the Japs would advance much farther before they were stopped by the reinforcements that had been called up.

General MacWhitter, his face pale, hung up the telephone. "Your orders have been passed down, sir."

General Hawkins knew it was important for him to act calmly and decisively, so that he could instill confidence among his subordinates. "Excellent," he said in an ordinary conversational tone, without any trace of panic or even excitement.

50

"Now I suggest that we all arm ourselves and pull back toward Aitape, just in case."

The medic looked up at General Hawkins. "What should I do with him?" he asked, indicating Colonel Hutchins.

"Have him taken to the field hospital." General Hawkins turned to Lieutenant Utsler. "Call for transportation."

"Yes, sir."

Lieutenant Utsler picked up a telephone, but the line was dead. He picked up another, but could get no dial tone there, either. Meanwhile, officers filed out of the office, so they could round up their men and prepare to move them back toward Aitape. Only General MacWhitter and a few others remained with General Hawkins.

"Sir," said Lieutenant Utsler, "I can't get through on the telephone. Evidently the wires have been cut."

General Hawkins held his Colt .45 in his hand and was checking it to make sure it was loaded and ready to shoot. "See if you can find a spare jeep and a driver to carry Colonel Hutchins to the field hospital."

"Yes, sir."

Just then everyone heard a peculiar tearing noise. They looked around and saw the blade of a knife sticking through a wall of the tent. The knife made a quick downward stroke five feet long, and then a Japanese soldier burst through the hole.

"*Banzai!*" screamed the Japanese soldier, carrying a rifle with a bayonet attached. He thrust the bayonet toward General Hawkins.

General Hawkins raised his Colt .45 and pulled the trigger. *Blam!* The pistol kicked violently in General Hawkins's hand, and the bullet struck the Japanese soldier in the chest, hurling him backward toward the hole he'd cut in the tent. Just then a Japanese hand grenade came flying through the hole. It bounced off the Japanese soldier's back, which was a mass of blood and gristle, due to the passage of the .45-caliber bullet. The hand grenade dropped to the ground, and the dead Japanese soldier collapsed on top of it.

"*Hit it!*" hollered General Hawkins.

Everybody inside the tent dived to the ground, and two seconds later the hand grenade exploded underneath the dead Japanese soldier, blowing him into thousands of bloody little chunks. The interior of the tent filled with smoke, and the concussion blew out the walls of the tent.

General Hawkins's ears rang with the sound of the explosion. He knew that if the body of the Japanese soldier hadn't muffled the worst of the blast, he, General Hawkins, might have been killed. Covered with dirt and some of the Japanese soldier's blood, General Hawkins staggered to his feet.

"Let's get out of here!" he said.

He lurched toward the exit, holding his Colt .45 at the ready, in case more Japs were in the vicinity. He was beginning to realize that maybe he'd waited much too long before responding to the Japanese attack. Next time he'd take action sooner, and he hoped he'd be alive when the next time happened.

Outside he saw GIs running in all directions, but no Japs. Evidently the Japs who'd attacked his tent had been infiltrators, not part of the main Japanese advance. Colonel Jessup jogged toward him, his Colt .45 in his right hand.

"Are you all right, sir?"

"I'm all right!" replied General Hawkins, reaching for his canteen. "Be on the lookout for Jap infiltrators! Where's my goddamn jeep? Let's get the hell out of here!"

The medic and Lieutenant Utsler carried Colonel Hutchins out of the devastated tent. General MacWhitter followed, and then came Sergeant Somerall, carrying a tin box full of important documents in each of his hands. A jeep headed toward them, and a symphony of mortar explosions could be heard in the distance.

General Hawkins sipped from his canteen and returned it to its case as he waited for the jeep. Now he realized that he'd fucked up badly by not stopping the Japs sooner. His heart sank when he realized he'd be called on the carpet to answer for his mistakes, and maybe he'd even be relieved of command—if he lived that long.

FOUR . . .

It was a hectic morning, and the tides of battle rolled back and forth many times. The screen of GIs in front of the Japanese soldiers conducted a fighting retreat, slowing down the Japanese soldiers, but some Japanese soldiers broke through in several spots and raised hell behind American lines, blowing up ammunition dumps, cutting wires, and shooting cooks and quartermasters, in addition to a few high-ranking officers.

Meanwhile, over a period of two hours, General Hawkins's reserves moved into the area, slowing down the Japanese advance; but they couldn't stop it. General Hawkins was forced to call General Hall for help, and finally one more battalion from the Persecution Task Force reserve solidified the line. The Japanese soldiers were stopped cold approximately one mile west of the Driniumor River. The Japanese soldiers found that they were unable to advance farther, but neither could the Americans push the Japanese back. For the time being, a stalemate between both sides existed in the jungle west of the Driniumor.

Meanwhile, pockets of GIs had been left behind by the Japanese advance. They were cut off, isolated from each other, and faced the grim prospect of being annihilated by the Japanese once the Japanese decided to get rid of them.

One of these pockets of resistance was the recon platoon, or what was left of it, along with a few stragglers from the headquarters company of the Twenty-third Regiment. They huddled behind a wall of devastated trees and tangled vegetation, where the Japanese could not easily see them, while Lieutenant Breckenridge roamed alone through the area, trying to figure out how bad their situation was.

Frankie La Barbara sat cross-legged on the ground as Pfc. Gotbaum, a medic from Headquarters Company, knelt behind him, touching his fingers to the back of Frankie's head. "How does that feel?" Gotbaum asked.

"It hurts!"

Pfc. Gotbaum poked again.

"Ouch!" yelled Frankie.

Sergeant Cameron turned toward him. "Keep your voice down!"

"Suck my dick!"

"You're gonna get us all killed!"

"Fuck you," Frankie said in a voice barely above a whisper.

Pfc. Gotbaum continued to feel the back of Frankie's head. "I don't think anything's broken," he said, "but it's impossible to tell for sure without an X ray."

"I know something's broke back there," Frankie said. "It wouldn't hurt so much if it wasn't broke. Gimme another shot of something, willya?"

"I just gave you a shot, Frankie."

"Well, it wasn't enough. Gimme another one."

Pfc. Gotbaum didn't know what to do, because he didn't want to shoot up Frankie with too much morphine. Pfc. Gotbaum looked toward Sergeant Cameron, who winked at him. The wink seemed to say *Give him a shot and maybe then he'll be quiet.*

"Okay," Pfc. Gotbaum said. "Take down your pants and lay down on your stomach."

"What're you gonna do, fuck me?"

"I'm gonna give you a shot in your ass."

"Why don't you gimme the shot in my arm."

"Because it'll go to work faster in your ass."

"I ain't in that much of a hurry."

"Suit yourself."

Frankie La Barbara's sleeve was rolled up and his shirt was tattered. Pfc. Gotbaum had no difficulty finding a place to jab the ampule. He cleaned a patch of Frankie's bloody, filthy skin with a swab of cotton dipped in alcohol and stuck the ampule into Frankie's bulging round biceps.

"I don't feel nothing," Frankie said.

"It'll take a few minutes."

Pfc. Gotbaum pulled out the ampule and tossed it over his shoulder. He gathered up his things and moved to the next wounded man, Private Victor Yabalonka, whose hands were wrapped with his shirt.

Yabalonka, the former left-wing radical from San Francisco, had fucked up his hands during the big fight. A Jap had tried to stab him with his bayonet, and Yabalonka grabbed the bayonet in order to protect himself. He'd saved his life, but his hands had been cut to ribbons in the process.

Pfc. Gotbaum unwrapped the shirt, and when he got close to the actual wounds, the shirt stuck to the torn flesh.

"This'll hurt a little," Gotbaum said.

"Do what you gotta do, pill-roller."

Pfc. Gotbaum yanked the shirt loose, causing blood to flow freely again. He hoped Yabalonka hadn't got blood poisoning from the dye in the shirt. Sprinkling on sulfa powder to disinfect the deep cuts, he knew Yabalonka would have difficulty moving his hands for the next few weeks.

Yabalonka was in a state of deep depression, because he knew what Gotbaum knew. He'd have difficulty fighting Japs because of his damaged hands. He wasn't even sure he could hold a rifle, but he'd have to try if he wanted to stay alive, and he'd learned during the big fight that he desperately wanted to stay alive.

That had come as a surprise to him. He hadn't wanted to kill Japs, because he had no reason to hate them. He believed Japanese soldiers were brainwashed by their own ruling class's bullshit propaganda, just as American GIs were, and that Japanese soldiers were just workers and farmers for the most part, like American GIs. But when the shit hit the fan and Japanese soldiers attacked him, trying to cut open his belly, Yabalonka

55

had fought back with all the strength in his powerful long-shoreman's body, because more than anything else he wanted to live.

"Make a fist," said Pfc. Gotbaum.

Yabalonka tightened his fingers around the bandages, but couldn't move them into a tight fist. "I can't do it any more than this."

"You probably cut some tendons in your hand. Under ordinary circumstances I'd have you put on light duty, but you know how things are."

"I know how things are."

Pfc. Gotbaum waddled away to look at the nose of Sergeant Cameron, who'd lost his nose bandage in the scuffle. Sergeant Cameron's nose was an ugly mass of dried blood, torn flesh, and exposed cartilage. The morning became dark suddenly as a thick cloud passed in front of the sun, blotting it out. Sergeant Cameron glanced up at the sky.

"Looks like we might be getting some rain," he said.

Pfc. Gotbaum touched his fingers gently to Sergeant Cameron's nose, and Sergeant Cameron jumped three inches into the air. *"Ouch!"*

"That nose is real bad," Gotbaum said. "I can't do anything for it except put another bandage on."

"Don't bother," said Sergeant Cameron, who didn't want to go through the pain. "I don't need no bandage. Let the air get at it. Maybe it'll do some good."

"A bandage'll keep the bugs away, and help if it starts bleeding again."

"Gimme the bandage. I'll put it on myself if I have any trouble."

"Okay."

Pfc. Gotbaum reached into his haversack for a bandage, and just then Lieutenant Breckenridge broke through the foliage surrounding the survivors from the recon platoon. They looked up at him as he knelt in their midst and took out his very last cigarette, lighting it with his Zippo.

Lieutenant Breckenridge looked as horrendous as the rest of them, with fingernail scratches all over his face, and his uniform covered with blood and gore. He drew smoke out of his cigarette and savored it, because he didn't know where he'd get another one.

"See any Japs out there?" asked Morris Shilansky.

"A few, but not too many," Lieutenant Breckenridge said, cocking his ear and listening to the sounds of battle farther west. "Most of the Japs are that way." He pointed west, toward the sound of the fighting. "All we can hope for is that our people push their people back, so we'll wind up behind our own lines again." He puffed his cigarette. "We'll be safe here as long as the Japs don't see us, and we're going to be real quiet so that we don't attract their attention. Got it?"

Nobody said anything.

"If we do happen to attract their attention," Lieutenant Breckenridge continued, "we'll have to fight them, and if we have to fight them, we'll need something to fight them with. The jungle around here is full of rifles, bullets, machine guns, and hand grenades on the bodies of casualties. I even saw a couple of bazookas."

"Why didn't you bring one back?" asked Frankie La Barbara, who was stoned on morphine now and seeing blinking lights and dancing colors.

"I'll ask the questions, La Barbara," Lieutenant Breckenridge replied. "If I want any shit out of you, I'll knock it out of you."

"Big talk," said Frankie.

"Shut up."

"Make me."

Lieutenant Breckenridge glowered at Frankie La Barbara, wondering if he should kick his ass thoroughly to establish who was boss.

"Sir," said Pfc. Gotbaum, "I just gave him a shot of morphine. He doesn't know what he's saying."

Frankie turned to Pfc. Gotbaum. "I do, too, know what I'm saying. What the fuck are you talking about, pill-roller?"

"Shut up, Frankie," said Lieutenant Breckenridge. "We're cut off behind Jap lines and I don't have time to play games with you."

"Fuck you," said Frankie.

"Fuck me?"

"That's right."

"Okay."

Lieutenant Breckenridge stood and walked toward Frankie La Barbara, who tried to stand, but Frankie was so whacked out of his head he couldn't get ready in time. Lieutenant Breckenridge drew back his leg and kicked Frankie with all his might in the head. Frankie's back arched and he flew through the air, landing on some uprooted bushes. Lieutenant Breckenridge puffed his cigarette and sat down again.

"I'm not taking any shit from you guys," he said. "I don't have the time for it. Any man who doesn't do as he's told will get his fucking head kicked. Got it?"

Nobody said anything, but they all looked at each other, raising their eyebrows. They realized that Lieutenant Breckenridge was adopting the same tactics that Butsko used to keep them in line: sheer physical brutality and intimidation.

"Okay," said Lieutenant Breckenridge, "where was I? Oh, yes. I need three volunteers to go out and bring back weapons and ammunition, especially automatic weapons. Sergeant Cameron, Pfc. Shilansky, and Pfc. Billie Jones. Get going."

Pfc. Morris Shilansky was confused. "But I didn't volunteer!"

"I just volunteered you," said Lieutenant Breckenridge.

"Oh."

"And if you can find any cigarettes out there, bring 'em back."

"Yes, sir."

"Get going."

"Yes, sir."

A bolt of lightning shot across the sky above the Torricelli Mountains, and a few seconds later a peal of thunder reverberated across the jungle. General Hawkins adjusted his helmet on his head, because he knew the downpour would begin at any moment. He sat in a jeep that bounced and rocked over a dirt road that had been constructed by the Corps of Engineers. His driver, Pfc. Joseph Buxton from Spencer, South Dakota, sat behind the wheel and steered toward a big walled tent in a jungle area covered with camouflage netting. In the jump seat to the rear, General MacWhitter hung on while his bony ass bounced up and down on the bare metal.

Pfc. Buxton parked among the other jeeps and three-quarter-ton trucks in front of the tent. General Hawkins jumped down from the jeep and walked toward the tent, followed by General MacWhitter. He entered the front office area of the tent and was waved through to General Hall's office. General Hawkins's legs felt wobbly and he had an acid stomach as he pushed aside the tent flap.

General Hall stood in front of his wall map with several other officers. When he saw General Hawkins and General MacWhitter, he narrowed his eyes. "Leave me alone for a few moments with General Hawkins and General MacWhitter," he said, his voice laden with malevolence.

The staff officers filed out of the office, glancing at General Hawkins and General MacWhitter, whom they knew were being called on the carpet for their big fuck-up, letting the Japs break through their lines.

When the last staff officer was gone, General Hawkins snapped to attention. "If you want my resignation, sir, you've got it!" General Hawkins declared.

"That goes for me, too, sir," General MacWhitter replied.

The corners of General Hall's mouth turned downward. "Don't tempt me," he said. He placed his hands behind his back and looked them up and down. The Japanese attack had upset his defense system and imperiled the Tadji airfields. The failure of the Eighty-first Division to stop the Japanese attack at the Driniumor made him look bad to his superiors. He was expecting to get chewed out by General Krueger and General Eichelberger, and maybe even General MacArthur.

But he had to be prudent. He had to work with what he had, and what he had was General Hawkins and General MacWhitter. It was his responsibility as their commanding officer to get the best out of them and train them to be better than they were.

"I can't accept your resignations," he admitted, "because I need the both of you. Perhaps if we can focus on what went wrong, we can figure out how to prevent it from ever happening again." He forced himself to smile, although he didn't have anything to be happy about. "Come over here by the map with me and we'll analyze the situation."

General Hawkins and General MacWhitter joined General Hall near the map. Both were relieved to know they weren't being fired.

"Basically it boils down to this," General Hawkins said, his confidence returning. "The Japanese attacked my Twenty-third Regiment on the Driniumor, here"—he pointed at the map—

59

"at approximately oh-four-hundred hours. Colonel Hutchins, who commands the Twenty-third, asked for help. I refused, because I thought the attack might be a feint, with the enemy's main effort coming from another direction. I waited to see how events would develop, and I suppose I waited too long. The Japanese broke through the Twenty-third, crossed the Driniumor, and made a deep penetration into my area before we stopped them approximately here." General Hawkins described a line on his map with his forefinger.

General Hall pinched his lips together and nodded. "I see. Do you think you have the resources to push the Japs back to where they were?"

"Yes, but it would mean thinning out my lines in other places, and perhaps the Japanese will attack those weakened places. You see, sir, the situation is very fluid right now, and we don't know exactly what the Japanese are up to."

"I know what they're up to," General Hall replied. "They want our airfields."

"I understand that, sir, but I'm not sure at this point how they mean to achieve that objective."

"Hmmm." General Hall crossed his arms and wondered what to do. He had a virtual 360-degree ring around the Tadji airfields and the town of Aitape, because he didn't know where the Japs might attack next either. His predicament, in fact, was not very different from General Hawkins's. If he thinned out his defense somewhere to strengthen the line on the Driniumor, he might be attacked through one of the weakened sectors.

Finally he reached a decision. In war, as in most other fields of endeavor, it is sometimes necessary to gamble. The threat posed by the Japanese attack east of the Driniumor was more dangerous than anything happening west of Aitape. He would thin out a section of the line west of Aitape and beef up the defenses to the south along the Torricelli Mountains.

"All right," said General Hall. "This is what you'll do." He pointed to the Torricelli Mountains. "Which of your regiments do you have here?"

"My Eighteenth, sir."

General Hall looked at his watch. "Pull them back at eleven hundred hours and build up your defense in depth along the line you hold now. Then, tomorrow morning, I want you to attack the Japs and push them back to the Driniumor."

60

"Who'll cover the southern approaches along the Torricelli Mountains, sir?"

"I haven't figured that out yet, but I'll let you know later in the day." General Hall stepped back from the map and gazed into the eyes of General Hawkins. "Now, let's have an understanding between us right now. I know you've only been in this area a few days, and you've never served under me before. That's why I'm being lenient with you *this time*. But if you let the Japs push you around again like they did this morning, I'll relieve you of command so fast, it'll make your head swim. Is that clear?"

General Hawkins swallowed hard. "Yes, sir!"

"In the future," General Hall continued, "when you're attacked, I don't want you to wait until your lines are a shambles before you do anything. You'd better act *before* your lines fall apart. It is my opinion that the commander who waits too long before taking action lacks a proper fighting spirit. I don't like overcautious commanders. I want commanders who are like wild animals and who attack at the slightest provocation. Understand me?"

"Yes, sir."

"Good. Return to your headquarters. If I have any further instructions for you, I'll contact you there."

Captain Yuichi Sato opened his eyes and saw the roof of a tent. His left shoulder hurt so much, he nearly passed out again. The Japanese army had few painkilling drugs, considering them unmanly. Real men should overcome pain through the sheer force of their wills, the Japanese high command believed.

Captain Sato rolled his head to the side. He was in a hospital tent full of wounded men. They moaned, groaned, and vomited blood all around him. Orderlies carried wounded men on stretchers.

"Orderly!" shouted Captain Sato. "Where am I?"

"Shut up and lie down," the orderly replied.

"*What!*" screamed Captain Sato, a vein on his forehead bulging out. "*How dare you talk to me like that!*"

Captain Sato raised himself to a sitting position, and the orderly could see the insignia on his collar.

"I'm sorry, sir!" the orderly spat out. "Please forgive me, sir! A thousand pardons, sir!"

61

Captain Sato felt dizzy and lay down again. The orderly ran toward him and dropped to his knees. He felt for Captain Sato's pulse, looked at his wound, and pressed his palm to Captain Sato's head to take his temperature.

Captain Sato looked up at the orderly. "What happened?"

"I do believe you've been shot in the shoulder, sir. The bullet's still in there. I expect it will have to come out."

"I know all that," Captain Sato replied in a weak voice. "I mean, did the attack succeed?"

The orderly smiled. "Oh, yes, sir. We've crossed the Driniumor and advanced quite a good distance into the American defense perimeter."

"How much of a distance?" Captain Sato asked.

"I couldn't tell you exactly, sir. I'm only an orderly, you know. I'm not really up on those things."

"Idiot," Captain Sato said, and closed his eyes.

He heard the orderly move away. The wound in his shoulder throbbed wickedly and radiated pain throughout his body. Captain Sato forced himself to overcome the pain and think back to the battle in which he'd received the wound. He remembered the American soldier picking up the rifle and shooting him. Everything had been going so well, and a freak shot had put him out of the battle.

He understood that war was a haphazard affair. Despite all your skill and stamina, and no matter how well your body was conditioned, a bullet could come out of nowhere and finish you off. Skill could keep you alive to a certain extent, and good physical condition could help you, too, but anything could happen in a pitched hand-to-hand battle, and it had happened to Captain Sato.

He wondered what his men were doing, and hoped they were all right. He wished he could have shared in the victory with them, but instead, here he was, in a hospital tent far behind the main advance, surrounded by other men who'd been in the wrong place at the wrong time. He hoped the wound wouldn't keep him out of the war for long. He wanted very much to get his strength back, so he could return to the front.

Two orderlies approached him, carrying a stretcher.

"Time to have that bullet taken out, sir," one of them said.

"Steady, now," said the other.

They rolled him onto the stretcher and carried him away.

Captain Sato thought it was undignified to be carried on a stretcher, bouncing up and down, without being in control of himself. He entered the operating room and was assailed by the odors of blood and disinfectant. Turning his head, he looked at a bucket containing arms and legs that had been amputated. Blood was all over the ground. Leaning to the other side, he saw surgeons with their white aprons soaked with blood.

Normally, Captain Sato had a strong constitution, but he felt uneasy and helpless in the operating room with all the blood around. In fact, he even felt scared. He wondered what the doctors were going to do with him. The orderlies laid him on one of the operating tables, and a kerosene light above his head nearly blinded him. One doctor appeared to his left and another on his right.

"I hope," Captain Sato said, trying to affect a genial, jovial manner, "that you're not going to cut my arm off."

"Oh, no," said one of the doctors. "We're only going to remove the bullet. Hang on, now."

Captain Sato closed his eyes. He heard the doctors moving around, increasing his apprehension. He heard metal instruments being touched to each other. A soldier screamed on the next operating table. A fierce pain struck his shoulder as the doctor inserted a sharp instrument and probed for the bullet. Captain Sato squinched his eyes shut and clenched his teeth, resolved not to cry out.

A Japanese officer had to set a good example, but the pain was so brutal that Captain Sato passed out.

"Is he dead?" asked one of the doctors.

The other doctor stopped probing and felt Captain Sato's pulse. "Not yet," he replied, then resumed his grisly exploration.

"Here comes the Reverend," said Craig Delane.

Everybody turned in the direction of the crashing smashing sound. Then Private First Class Billie Jones appeared, carrying on his shoulder a .30-caliber machine gun attached to a metal bipod. He steadied the weapon with his right hand; in his left hand was a box of ammunition.

"Look what I got," he said happily.

"Set it down right here," Lieutenant Breckenridge said, "and see if you can find more ammo for it."

"Yes, sir."

The Reverend Billie Jones dropped the box of ammunition and lowered the machine gun to the ground. His face was red and sweaty from exertion, and he took out his canteen and sipped some water. Removing his helmet, he wiped his forehead with the back of his forearm, then returned his helmet to his head, squared his shoulders, and left the little sanctuary, trudging back to the battlefield.

A few minutes later, from another direction, Morris Shilansky returned, carrying M 1 rifles slung over both shoulders. Countless bandoliers of ammunition hung from his neck, and his pockets were stuffed with hand grenades, which also hung from his lapels.

"Good work," said Lieutenant Breckenridge. "Go get more and be on the lookout for Japs."

"Yes, sir."

Not far away, in a jungle clearing carpeted with bodies of dead Japanese and American soldiers, Sergeant Cameron found another .30-caliber machine, which he thought would be a real prize. It appeared to be in excellent working condition, and when he worked the bolt, it was smooth and slick. Nearby were crates of .30-caliber ammunition. Evidently the jungle clearing had been the site of a machine-gun nest.

Sergeant Cameron breathed through his mouth, because no air could pass through his blood-clotted nostrils. He bent over the machine gun to pick it up, when he caught movement in the corner of his eye. Turning in that direction, his hair stood on end when he saw a bloody Japanese soldier lying on his stomach and holding a pistol in both shaking hands, trying to take aim at Sergeant Cameron.

Blam!

The bullet whistled past Sergeant Cameron's ear, and he dived toward the ground. He wished he had a hand grenade to throw at the Jap, but he didn't have one. On top of that, the Jap was too close anyway; Sergeant Cameron would be killed by his own hand grenade.

Blam! The Japanese soldier fired again, and the bullet passed over Sergeant Cameron's head. Sergeant Cameron realized he was in a troublesome predicament. The Jap was less than ten feet away, and at any moment he might fire the lucky shot that would transform Sergeant Cameron into another casualty of the war.

Sergeant Cameron knew he had to do something, and all he could do was try to shoot the Jap before the Jap shot him. He unslung his M 1 rifle while trying to stay low to the ground, rammed a round into the chamber, and clicked off the safety. Then he took aim, but he couldn't see the Japanese soldier. There were too many bodies lying in the way, and they were starting to stink. If Sergeant Cameron rose up for a better view, the Jap would shoot him.

Sergeant Cameron ground his teeth together. *How did I get into this mess?* he asked himself. Then he saw the top of the Japanese soldier's head emerge from the melange of bodies on the ground. The Japanese soldier was trying to elevate himself so he could shoot Sergeant Cameron more easily, but Sergeant Cameron stayed where he was, lined up the sights of his M 1 on the Japanese soldier's forehead, and squeezed the trigger.

Blam! The bullet struck the spot where it was aimed, and its force blew the top of the Japanese soldier's head off. The Japanese soldier collapsed onto the ground, and Sergeant Cameron lay still, looking to his right and left and then behind him to see if any other Japs were sneaking up on him. He couldn't spot any, so he slowly rose to his knees, swiveling his head around as he searched for Japs, then stood.

He slung his rifle and bent over to pick up the machine gun. Balancing it on his shoulders, he headed back toward the place where the rest of the recon platoon was hiding out.

When Morris Shilansky heard the first shot, he dived to the ground. He had his pliers in his right hand and had been pulling a gold tooth from the mouth of a Japanese officer. Lying low, he heard more shots, but none seemed to be headed his way. Raising his head slightly, he couldn't see anything except demolished jungle, broken trees, and uprooted bushes everywhere. An eerie silence pervaded the area, because birds and monkeys had fled long ago. There were no more shots. Shilansky wondered what the commotion was all about.

He raised himself up on his knees and held the Japanese officer's hair with his left hand while working the pliers with his right. He tightened the jaws of the pliers around the Japanese officer's gold tooth and worked it loose. If Lieutenant Breckenridge saw what he was doing, Breckenridge would kick him in the ass, but Lieutenant Breckenridge was nowhere around, and fuck him anyway.

Finally the tooth came loose. Shilansky held it up; it was covered with blood. Just then a drop of rain *ping*ed on the top of Shilansky's helmet. He looked up. The sky was dark and oily: A rainstorm was on the way. He dropped the tooth into his shirt pocket and buttoned the flap. It would be a nice little souvenir that he could sell someday, but now it was time to do something for his buddies in the recon platoon.

He looked around and saw a BAR lying a few feet from a dead American soldier who had a belt of BAR ammunition around his waist and more BAR ammunition in bandoliers around his neck. Shilansky figured an automatic weapon was better than a semiautomatic weapon, like an M 1, so he picked up the BAR and slung it over his shoulder.

Reaching for the belt of ammunition, his hands froze at the sound of an engine. Silently he dropped to the ground and lay flat, wondering if it was an airplane coming to strafe his ass. Thunder rolled across the mountains to the south, and then he heard the engine again. It sounded like a vehicle engine, and it was headed in his direction. He twitched his nose and sniffed, gradually becoming aware of the direction of the sound. Turning in its direction, he lay still and peered ahead under the brim of his helmet.

Then he saw it coming through the jungle. It was a weird, spindly truck with spoke wheels and a maroon meatball painted on the door. It was a Japanese truck, and a Japanese soldier sat behind the wheel, bouncing up and down, wearing a soft cap with a visor. Shilansky couldn't see a Japanese soldier sitting next to the driver, but assumed one was there. The truck looked like something that had been manufactured in America thirty years earlier by a company that had gone out of business because it was fucked up, but evidently the Japanese truck had been manufactured recently.

Fucking Japs can't even make a truck right, Shilansky thought. He waited until the truck passed out of sight, then stood and picked up the BAR again. He slung it over his shoulder, gathered up the ammunition, and headed back toward Lieutenant Breckenridge and the others.

• • •

The rain began as a mild shower, but soon became a torrential downpour. Raindrops large as a man's thumb lashed trees and bushes, forming into brooks and streams where the ground had been dry before the storm. Roads became impassable, and the Driniumor overflowed its banks after only an hour.

But war doesn't stop just because of a rainstorm. Japanese soldiers dug fortifications into the mud, although the walls kept collapsing and they had to start all over again. Weapons were covered with canvas to help keep them dry. The Japanese soldiers sat in puddles of water up to their waists, stoically tolerating the discomfort. Some ate canned fish and rice out of the little metal canisters they carried around them. Their recently dug latrines overflowed, and turds floated everywhere, creating a colossal stink.

The Japanese really weren't in that good shape. The rain made it difficult to resupply their front, and they were worn out. They'd won a minor victory but were in a vulnerable position.

Meanwhile, on the other side of the line, the US Army restructured its deployment. Reserve battalions slogged through the mud to the positions of the Fifteenth Regiment along the Torricelli Mountains to the south, and the Fifteenth Regiment pulled back and shifted direction, moving in behind the shattered and bleeding Twenty-third Regiment.

This front-line shuffle was messy and confused. Companies got lost and fell out of radio contact. Roads became rivers, and trees bowed under the weight of the rainstorm. Leeches and ticks bit the skin of GIs and drank their blood, and clouds of insects surrounded every man, sucking their blood constantly.

Morale plunged to zero on both sides of the line. Everybody wanted to be under a dry roof and wearing dry socks. Nobody wanted to fight, but a battle was looming and they had to get ready.

Throughout the day, in the face of the howling thunderstorm, the recon platoon survivors, plus the stragglers from Headquarters Company, built up their little bastion. Weapons, ammunition, food, and cigarettes were brought back by teams of "volunteers." The jungle clearing became stacked with crates

67

and piles of stuff. By midafternoon they had two .30-caliber machine guns, three BARs, and countless rifles, pistols, and bazookas. Defensive walls had been constructed from fallen trees, and bushes were used for camouflage. Lieutenant Breckenridge left the position to examine it from a distance; it looked like just another portion of the blasted, twisted jungle.

He returned to the position and knelt in the midst of his men, lighting a cigarette and blowing the smoke out of the side of his mouth. "Okay," he said, "we're all set, or at least as set as we're likely to get. The Japs won't be able to see us, but we'll be able to see them. But that doesn't mean we're gonna start shooting at them when we see them, because if we shoot at them, that'll give our position away. The main thing is that we don't want to give our position away. We don't want the fucking Nips to know we're here. Does everybody understand why?"

They all nodded or grunted in the affirmative.

"Good," Lieutenant Breckenridge said. "If we spot any Japs, we're going to be still and not give any indication whatever that we're here. Our fire discipline must be flawless. We don't fire until they're right on top of us and we can't avoid the bastards. Does everybody understand that?"

Again they nodded or made sounds that they understood.

"Okay," said Lieutenant Breckenridge. "We've got plenty of ammo and enough chow for a few days. If the Japs don't stumble onto us, we've got a good chance of surviving. Sooner or later our people are going to attack the Japs and push them back to where they were before they attacked us. When that happens, we'll be behind our own lines again. Everything will be hunky-dory if we just stay calm and don't fuck up while we're out here. Does everybody still know what I'm talking about?"

"Yes, sir," said Sergeant Cameron, and the rest appeared as though they knew.

"Any questions?"

"Yeah," said Shilansky. "When the Japs retreat, they'll retreat right over us at some point. What'll we do then?"

"Just what I said before," Lieutenant Breckenridge replied. "We're gonna keep quiet and maintain strict fire discipline when the Japs retreat through this area."

Pfc. Craig Delane raised his forefinger in the air. "What if they don't retreat back through this area?"

"They will," said Lieutenant Breckenridge.

"But what if they don't?"

"Where else can they retreat through, Delane?"

"My point, sir, is, what if they don't retreat?"

Lieutenant Breckenridge puffed his cigarette and looked Delane in the eye. "I know General Hawkins and Colonel Hutchins personally, and I know General Hall by his reputation. All three of them were thrown for a loss last night, and they'll counterattack the Japs as soon as they can, with whatever is necessary to push them back. The Japs on New Guinea are cut off and cannot be resupplied from the outside, but we can be. The Japs are going to be wiped on New Guinea sooner or later. The only question is when. Do you get the picture?"

"Yes, sir," said Craig Delane, but he perceived a flaw in Lieutenant Breckenridge's presentation. It was probably true that the US Army would defeat the Imperial Army of Japan on New Guinea sooner or later, but there was a very real and horrible possibility that Delane and the others caught behind enemy lines might be detected by the Japs and wiped out before that happened.

Delane didn't give voice to his thoughts, though. He didn't want to demoralize the other men, and besides, Lieutenant Breckenridge would probably kick his ass if he opened his mouth again.

The rain continued into the afternoon, and the jungle became a mess. Many units were bivouacked in areas that had become swamps, and a rumor spread across the American lines that a GI had been attacked and killed by a crocodile. This rumor made all the GIs jumpy, and many fired at shadows and floating logs, thinking they were crocodiles looking for a meal.

Colonel Hutchins returned to the Twenty-third Regiment, his chest bandaged and his mind in a whirl, due to the various drugs and medicines that had been administered to him. He located his headquarters and marched into the tent. Sergeant Koch was studying morning reports, trying to get an accurate fix on the casualties the regiment had suffered, but some companies hadn't even sent in their morning reports yet because they'd lost typewriters, records, and forms in the retreat that had taken place that morning.

Sergeant Koch noticed Colonel Hutchins and jumped to his feet. "Ten-*hut!*" he shouted.

On the other side of the tent, Pfc. Levinson, the regimental clerk, scrambled to attention and stood with his arms stiff at his sides.

"At ease!" said Colonel Hutchins. "As you were! Where can I find Major Cobb?"

"He's in your office, sir."

"Carry on."

Colonel Hutchins entered his office and saw Major Cobb seated behind the desk. Major Cobb was a dumpy man in his forties, with sloping shoulders and glasses perched on the end of a tiny pug nose set in a round meaty face. He looked up from the correspondence he'd been reading, then jumped to his feet.

"At ease," said Colonel Hutchins. "Get out of my chair."

Major Cobb stood and walked to the front of the desk, dropping into one of the folding wooden chairs. Colonel Hutchins sat behind the desk and opened a drawer. "Where's my goddamn orange juice!" he screamed, referring to his Old Forester bourbon.

"It's been left behind, sir."

"It has?"

"Yes, sir. Your whole headquarters has been left behind. We've obtained this tent from division supply."

Colonel Hutchins opened the drawers to the desk and saw that his personal papers and various pens and things were gone. He'd been fooled because the tent, desk, and chairs were exactly the same as his tent, desk, and chairs that had been left behind. Everything in the Army looked the same.

Colonel Hutchins was out of whiskey. Even his pocket flask had been drained of every drop. Colonel Hutchins was a full-blown alcoholic, and he knew he'd start undergoing withdrawal discomfort very soon. Somehow he had to get some booze, and he directed his thinking toward that end, letting his alcoholism eclipse the huge offensive that was to take place in the morning.

"Where's Sergeant Snider?" he asked, referring to the Headquarters Company mess sergeant, who in civilian life, had been a moonshiner in the South someplace.

70

"I don't know where he is, sir."

"Find out."

"But, sir, don't we have more important matters to discuss?"

"No."

"Very well, sir. I'll see if I can find him."

"Make it fast."

"Yes, sir."

Major Cobb walked toward the door and put his helmet on, disturbed that an officer of his stature had to track down an ex-moonshiner in a rainstorm because Colonel Hutchins needed a drink. "Fucking Army," he muttered.

"You say something, Cobb?"

"No, sir."

Major Cobb left the office, and Colonel Hutchins lit a cigarette with trembling fingers. His mind felt weird, as if he were going nuts, and he felt sick to his stomach. The medicines and drugs he'd been taking were messing up his mind. He felt certain he'd be okay if he could just have a drink.

Then suddenly he remembered something, and his eyes lit up with delight. "Sergeant Koch!" he yelled.

"Yes, sir!"

"Get in here!"

"Yes, sir!"

A second later Sergeant Koch ran into the office and saluted.

"As you were," Colonel Hutchins said. "Tell me something: Is Lieutenant Rabinowitz around anyplace?"

"I don't know, sir."

"Well, find out and tell him I need a big bottle of GI gin right away. You bring it back to me right away, got it?"

"Do you have a cold, sir?" Sergeant Koch asked, because GI gin was the nickname given a cough syrup made primarily of alcohol and codeine.

"What's that to you?"

Sergeant Koch was flustered. "Well, sir, GI gin is for colds, isn't it?"

"Don't try to be Dr. Kildare. Just get me the medicine. Get going."

"Yes, sir."

Sergeant Koch turned and ran out of the office. Colonel Hutchins rubbed his hands together. His nose tingled and his

71

teeth chattered. He looked down at the maps on his desk, but his vision was blurry. *Maybe a cup of coffee will straighten me out.* "Who's out there?" he yelled.

"Pfc. Levinson!" a voice replied.

"Get your ass in here!"

"Yes, sir!"

Pfc. Levinson dashed into the office. He was a gawky youth with a long neck, a prominent Adam's apple, and a gigantic nose. He snapped to attention and saluted in front of Colonel Hutchins's desk.

"Levinson," said Colonel Hutchins, "get me a cup of coffee."

"A cup of coffee, sir?"

"You got a hearing problem, Levinson?"

"Where should I get a cup of coffee, sir?"

"That's for you to figure out, and if you can't, you're not smart enough to be the regimental clerk. I'll have to send you back to the line and get somebody else."

Pfc. Levinson smiled nervously, because the last place in the world he wanted to be was back on the line. "I'll get you a cup of coffee right away, sir."

"Now you're talking."

Pfc. Levinson sped out of the office. Colonel Hutchins searched through the desk again for something to smoke, drink, or chew, but there was nothing. A peal of thunder sounded like kettledrums over his head, and rain poured onto the tent. A fatigue came over Colonel Hutchins and he leaned back in his chair. His heart slowed and he was afraid it would stop. His breathing became shallow. *What's the matter with me?* he wondered.

The telephone on his desk rang, snapping him out of his torpor. He waited for somebody to pick it up in the outer office, but then realized he'd sent everybody away. He had to pick up the phone himself.

"Colonel Hutchins speaking," he said into the mouthpiece.

"What the hell are you doing there?" Colonel Jessup screamed into his ear.

Colonel Hutchins drew himself to attention in his chair. "I am leading my regiment!"

"You left the field hospital without authorization!"

72

"My place is here with my regiment, Colonel!"

"The doctor said you're not fit for duty!"

"What the hell does *he* know about duty! All he does is look down people's throats and up their assholes all day long!"

Colonel Jessup tried to calm himself down. "You're not supposed to leave the hospital without authorization."

"I left under my own authorization," Colonel Hutchins replied. "There's a war going on out here, and I don't have time to waste on doctors."

"I don't know what we're going to do about this. I'll have to speak with General Hawkins."

"Speak to whoever you want. Over and out."

Colonel Hutchins tried to hang up the telephone, but his hands were shaking so much, he couldn't put the receiver into its cradle. He gnashed his teeth as sweat poured off his face. His balls itched and he scratched them. He felt as though he were covered with ants, and scratched all over his body.

Major Cobb entered his office and stopped suddenly when he saw his commanding officer scratching like a maniac. "Are you all right, sir?"

"Did you find Sergeant Snider?"

"He's missing in action, sir."

"No!"

"I'm afraid so."

"Why does he have to be missing in action now? Why couldn't he be missing in action some other time?"

"Beg your pardon, sir?"

"Never mind."

"You're not looking so well, sir."

"Neither are you."

"Me?"

Colonel Hutchins lit a cigarette and puffed furiously. Major Cobb stared at him and thought seriously of calling General Hawkins and telling him that Colonel Hutchins was going berserk.

"What're you staring at?" Colonel Hutchins demanded.

"I think you'd better lie down, sir."

"What the hell for?"

"You're looking a little overwrought, sir."

Colonel Hutchins glowered at Major Cobb. "Keep your

goddamned personal opinions to yourself. I've been wounded but I'm not overwrought. Let's get down to business. What's happened while I was gone?"

"Well, sir," Major Cobb said, sitting down, "the division is going to attack first thing in the morning."

"We are?" Colonel Hutchins asked, astonished.

"Yes, sir."

"Why didn't you tell me before?"

"Because you ordered me to go out and look for the mess sergeant!"

At that moment Sergeant Koch exploded through the tent flap, carrying a bottle of clear liquid that looked like water. "Look what I got, sir!" he said, holding the bottle up.

"Is that what I think it is?" Colonel Hutchins asked.

"Yes, sir!"

"You're a good man, Crotch—I mean Koch. Give it here."

"Yes, sir!"

Sergeant Koch handed the bottle to Colonel Hutchins. It contained about a half a pint of GI gin. Colonel Hutchins plucked the bottle out of Sergeant Koch's hands, unscrewed the top, upended the bottle, and drained it dry.

"Good grief," said Major Cobb as Colonel Hutchins's Adam's apple bobbed up and down and a ferocious gurgling sound issued from his throat.

Colonel Hutchins tossed the empty bottle back to Sergeant Koch. "Go get more."

"More?"

"That's what I said. About a quart should hold me until tomorrow."

"A quart!"

"Get going!"

"But, sir," Sergeant Koch pleaded, "I don't think Lieutenant Rabinowitz will give me a quart!"

"Why not?"

"Because he doesn't like to give out too much . . . ah . . . medicine."

"What the hell does he think the medicine is for?" Colonel Hutchins asked in his booming bass voice. "Tell him I want to see him right away, and say that I want him to bring a quart of that shit with him!"

"Yes, sir!"

Sergeant Koch turned around and fled from the office, passing Pfc. Levinson, who was on the way in, carrying a canteen in his hands.

"What the hell you got there?" Colonel Hutchins asked.

"Canteen full of hot coffee, sir!"

"Just what I need! Toss it over here, young warrior!"

Pfc. Levinson lobbed the canteen to Colonel Hutchins, who unscrewed the top and gulped some down. He wiped his mouth with the back of his hand and screwed the top back on.

"Thank you very much, Pfc. Levinson," Colonel Hutchins said. "You may return to your desk now."

"Yes, sir!"

Pfc. Levinson walked out of the office. Colonel Hutchins leaned back in his chair and relaxed. Lazily he took out a cigarette and lit it up, blowing a smoke ring into the air, where it hovered like a halo between Colonel Hutchins and Major Cobb. Colonel Hutchins felt much improved. The alcohol, codeine, and caffeine had returned him to a state of relative normalcy.

"What was that you were saying about an attack?" Colonel Hutchins asked.

"In the morning, sir. The division is attacking then, sir."

"I see. Do you have the particulars?"

"Some of them. I was going to get the rest at a meeting with General Hawkins at sixteen hundred hours."

"Can you tell me what you know now?"

"Certainly, sir."

Major Cobb rose and walked around the desk to point out the various positions on the map, when suddenly the phone rang. Colonel Hutchins lifted it with a steady hand. "Yes?"

Sergeant Koch's voice came to him: "General Hawkins wants to speak with you, sir!"

"Put him through!"

"Yes, sir!"

The earpiece buzzed and popped, and then General Hawkins's foice resonated in the receiver. "Is that you, Hutchins?"

"It is indeed, sir."

"What's this I hear about you leaving the hospital without authorization?"

"I felt well enough to leave, so I did. I thought I belonged here with my men."

"You didn't look so well when you were at my headquarters earlier today," General Hawkins said. "In fact, you passed out. Are you sure you're all right now?"

"Absolutely, sir. I wouldn't lie about something like this. All I needed were a few bandages and some medicine."

"I must say that you sound pretty good to me, Hutchins."

"Thank you, sir. You sound fine yourself."

"You've heard of the meeting at my headquarters this afternoon?"

"Found out about it just now. I'll be there."

"You sure you're well enough to carry on with your duties?"

"I think so, and besides, who've you got to take over my regiment?"

"I'd rather not open that can of beans, if you don't mind."

"I don't mind."

"Well, I do. I'll see you at my headquarters later?"

"You will indeed, sir."

"Very fine. Over and out."

Colonel Hutchins hung up the phone.

"Who was that?" asked Major Cobb.

"That horse's ass up at division headquarters," Colonel Hutchins replied.

FIVE . . .

Frankie La Barbara moved across the blasted jungle with his knees close to the ground and his shoulders hunched. He carried a pair of pliers in his right hand. He was looking for gold teeth. Shilansky showed him the teeth he'd pulled, and now Frankie wanted some for himself.

The rain poured incessantly as Frankie opened the mouths of Japanese soldiers, and as he looked inside for gold the mouths filled up with rainwater. Some of the mouths were filled with maggots, and Frankie slapped them shut, moving on. A foul stench arose from the jungle as the bodies putrefied.

Visibility was poor. Frankie was surrounded by shattered trees and uprooted bushes, all twisted and gnarled together by the maelstorm of explosions. Bodies of dead American and Japanese soldiers littered the nightmare landscape, and there were the usual scattered limbs disconnected from bodies.

Frankie didn't bother looking into the mouths of American soldiers. He was low, but he wasn't that low. He couldn't steal from dead American soldiers, but Japs were the enemy. They were fair game.

Soaked with rain, unaware of a leech on his left leg, Frankie opened more Japanese mouths but found no gold. It occurred to him that Shilansky had been lucky, and these Japanese soldiers must have been poor in civilian life. Some had empty gaps between teeth, but no gold.

Frankie was getting discouraged. The macabre aspect of what he was doing was not lost on him. He was starting to feel like a ghoul, and shivered at the thought. *What the hell am I doing this for?* he wondered. *What good is this gold going to do me out here?*

He took out a damp cigarette and put it into his mouth. Then he shielded his Zippo with his hands and lit the cigarette. It took a lot of puffing to get it going. He squatted down and sat on his haunches near a Japanese soldier whose head had been hacked off in the hand-to-hand fighting. Maggots squirmed in the ragged stump of neck, and the stink of the battlefield was getting to Frankie. *Fuck this,* he thought, *I'm getting out of here.*

As he raised himself he could barely make out an unusual movement straight ahead. Quickly he ducked down and lay on his belly. The rain made a constant roar all around him, obliterating other sound. Through the network of foliage ahead he saw Japanese soldiers moving about. Creeping forward for a clearer look, he saw that it was the Japanese version of a graves registry detail: The bodies of Japanese soldiers were being tossed into a wheelbarrow. The Japanese soldiers were spread out all over the jungle, and Frankie was afraid that some might have worked around behind him.

I've got to get out of here, he thought. Turning around, he kept his head low as he made his way back to the spot where the others were, pausing every few moments and looking around for Japs, the soggy cigarette dangling out of the corner of his mouth. *What an asshole I am,* he told himself. *I should've stayed where I was safe instead of coming out here for gold teeth.*

Something compelled him to look down. He saw a Thompson submachine gun lying on the ground next to the body of Sergeant Jake Krock from Baker Company. Sergeant Krock was turning green, and his mouth was twisted permanently into an expression of pain. A haversack full of ammunition clips hung from his neck and shoulders.

Frankie threw down his M 1 and picked up the Thompson

submachine gun. He worked the bolt; it handled smoothly. Sergeant Jake Krock had been an old battle-seasoned GI, and he'd kept his weapon coated with oil. There wasn't a speck of rust on it.

"Good old Sergeant Krock," Frankie muttered, pulling the haversack off the dead man's body. "I'll remember you in my prayers." He slung the haversack over his shoulder and cradled the Thompson submachine gun in his arms. It was loaded and presumably ready to fire. The only way he'd know for sure would be when he pulled the trigger.

He took a step forward and saw movement in front of him. Freezing, holding the submachine gun ready to fire, Frankie discerned Japanese soldiers carrying dead bodies through the jungle on the other side of the vegetation that separated them. *The Japs are behind me,* Frankie thought. *Now what'll I do?*

He crouched down and eased himself into the knotted vegetation, so that it covered him completely. His left foot sank up to the ankle in a puddle of mud, and he cursed under his breath. Glancing around, he saw Japs everywhere, clearing away dead bodies. He counted twenty live Japs, all armed. Frankie checked his watch: It was three o'clock in the afternoon. He realized with dismay that he might have to hide out until dark before he could return to the others.

Fucking gold, he thought. *I'm liable to get killed out here, just because of some fucking gold.* Then he became aware of a vague itching ache on his left leg. He pulled up his fatigue pants and saw the slimy black leech. "You son of a bitch bastard," Frankie mumbled. He pulled the cigarette out of his mouth and held the lit end near the leech, which cringed and loosened its bite on Frankie's flesh. Frankie pulled the leech away and threw it as far as he could.

"Get down," Sergeant Cameron said softly, pushing the palm of his right hand toward the ground.

The other men dropped down onto their stomachs, and the ones who'd been lying on their backs rolled over, holding their weapons tightly. Lieutenant Breckenridge crawled forward and joined Sergeant Cameron.

"Japs," said Sergeant Cameron.

Lieutenant Breckenridge peered through the leaves and saw Japanese soldiers moving into view. "Looks like a patrol," he said. "Remember what I said about fire discipline, you guys. We don't fire unless we have to, and I'll give the order."

Morris Shilansky lay behind one machine gun. Craig Delane lay behind the other. Victor Yabalonka had been given one of the BARs, and the Reverend Billie Jones had wound up with the other one. All the other men were armed with American M 1 rifles, and they had plenty of ammunition. Everyone had grenades stuffed into his pockets and more grenades hanging from his lapels.

Lieutenant Breckenridge narrowed his eyes and strained to see what the Japanese soldiers were doing. He became aware that they were bending over and picking up bodies.

"Looks like a graves registry detail," he said.

"That's what it is, all right," Sergeant Cameron replied, brushing a mosquito away from his nose, or what was left of his nose.

"Everybody sit tight," Lieutenant Breckenridge said. "Don't anybody make a sound, and there'll be no smoking until I say so."

"I gotta take a shit," said Pfc. Jimmy O'Rourke, the former movie stuntman.

Lieutenant Breckenridge shook his head. "He's gotta take a shit now, of all times."

"I can't help it, Sarge."

"Go out back someplace and do what you gotta do, but if you get shot, don't come crying to me." Lieutenant Breckenridge craned his neck around and watched Jimmy O'Rourke slip through the jungle while farting outrageously. Lieutenant Breckenridge checked over his men and realized somebody was missing. "Where's Frankie?" he asked.

Shilansky was supposed to be covering for Frankie. "He went out to take a shit too," Shilansky said.

"What are we getting here—mass diarrhea?" Lieutenant Breckenridge asked. "When did he leave?"

"I don't remember."

"Was it a long time ago?"

"I don't remember."

"I hope the Japs don't get him," Lieutenant Breckenridge said. Then he added: "On second thought, maybe that's not such a bad idea."

· · ·

Frankie crouched behind the dense foliage and watched Japanese soldiers carry away their dead, plus the dead American soldiers. They searched the pockets of the GIs, handing all documents to a sergeant but keeping gold rings, wallets, money, crucifixes, and various other souvenirs. They gazed at the photographs in American wallets and giggled. Frankie wanted to raise his submachine gun and blow them away, but Frankie wasn't that crazy. His desire for survival far outweighed his hatred of the Japanese.

The Japanese soldiers were all around him, tossing bodies onto wheelbarrows. Sergeants barked orders, and soldiers reluctantly carried them out. Frankie was struck by how much they behaved like American soldiers. Frankie had never observed a Japanese work detail at close range before, and he thought they appeared almost human.

Two Japanese soldiers approached Frankie La Barbara, and he tried to make his breathing shallow so they wouldn't hear him. They bent down six feet in front of him, picked up a dead Japanese soldier, and carried him away. Frankie's heart pounded like a tom-tom. Another Japanese soldier walked by, peering into the bushes where Frankie La Barbara lay. Frankie was sure the Japanese soldier saw him, but the Japanese soldier walked away, and Frankie was able to breathe again.

Frankie was angry at himself. He knew he was in a fix because of his own greed. It was frustrating not to be able to blame anybody. He couldn't pray to God and promise to go to church every Sunday for the rest of his life if God would save him, because he'd promised that before many times and had yet to go to church once.

I'm a bad egg, Frankie thought. *No doubt about it.* He thought grimly that everybody was always telling him he was no good, and for the first time he began to think that maybe they were right. He was afraid the Japs would discover him in their midst. He deserved to die for his greed, but to his amazement the Japs cleared his area of bodies and moved on without spotting him.

Frankie crossed himself and kissed his thumb. "I'll go to church first chance I get," he muttered. "This time I really mean it."

81

• • •

The steady roar of rain filled the air. Wind lashed the wide leaves of palm trees and made the trees bow before the storm. A jeep rumbled through the jungle behind the American lines; it had no canvas cover to protect its occupants from the rain. The driver was Pfc. Nick Bombasino from Philadelphia, and beside him was Colonel Hutchins, soaking wet, his chest thickly bandaged. Colonel Hutchins was heavily medicated. His canteen was full of GI gin.

The jeep stopped in front of division headquarters, and Colonel Hutchins jumped out of the jeep, slipped in the mud, and fell on his ass. Major Cobb climbed down more cautiously from the jeep and helped Colonel Hutchins to his feet.

"Easy, there," Major Cobb said.

"Ground's as slick as rat shit," Colonel Hutchins replied.

They entered the tent, shook themselves off like dogs in the vestibule, and entered the war room of General Hawkins. Most of the top officers from the division were already there, and they fell silent when Colonel Hutchins answered. Many of them had been present when Colonel Hutchins had cursed and insulted General Hawkins earlier that day and then passed out. Colonel Hutchins had a reputation for being a drunk, a reputation that he'd done much to earn. It would not be an exaggeration to say that he was the most notorious officer in the division.

Hutchins was aware of his reputation, and walked across the office itching for a fight. Approaching the map table, he looked down at the red line that described the current front-line situation. The Japanese attack had made a long salient into the American line. The salient was where the Twenty-third Infantry Regiment had been. Many of the officers in the room blamed Colonel Hutchins for the loss of ground. They thought the Japanese had kicked his ass because he was a worthless drunk, and he knew how they felt. That's why he was anxious to redeem himself.

Finally, General Hawkins entered the office, followed by a retinue of aides, staff officers, and flunkies. He approached the map table and called the meeting to order. Using a captured Japanese samurai sword as a pointer, he touched various segments of the line as he explained the attack that would begin in the morning.

Two battalions from the Eighteenth Regiment would hit the Japs on their left flank. Two battalions from the Fifteenth Regiment would attack on the right. The Twenty-third would go right up the middle. The objective of the attack would be to pinch off the Japanese salient and annihilate the enemy soldiers inside it. A heavy artillery bombardment would precede the attack, beginning at four o'clock in the morning. General Hawkins ordered the commanders to move their troops into attack positions overnight. He added that they'd be resupplied during the night, so they'd lack nothing.

A lengthy question-and-answer period followed General Hawkins's talk. Numerous details were discussed. Time allowances were made to compensate for the difficulty of movement in the rain. The problem of rusting weapons was discussed, along with that of rotting combat boots. Finally there were no more questions.

"Meeting dismissed," General Hawkins said. "I'd like Colonel Hutchins to stay behind for a few minutes, please."

"Uh-oh," mumbled Colonel Hutchins, and then he burped. The sweet odor of alcohol and codeine infused the air around him. "Wait for me outside, Cobb."

"Yes, sir."

The officers filed out of the office. It took a while because there were a lot of them. They all were wet and filthy, in need of shaves, and their bodies stank of sweat. Finally Colonel Hutchins and General Hawkins were alone, facing each other across the map table, a kerosene lamp flickering overhead.

General Hawkins spoke first. "Are you sure you're well enough to lead your regiment, Colonel Hutchins?"

"Yes, sir."

"Are you drunk right now, Colonel Hutchins?"

"No, sir."

"Will you be drunk tomorrow when the attack begins?"

Colonel Hutchins scowled. "Your questions are an insult, you bastard."

General Hawkins's eyes glittered with rage. "What was that?"

"You heard me, you bastard."

"How dare you call me a bastard!"

"How dare you call me a drunk!"

"But you *are* a drunk!"

"And you're a goddamn bastard!"

The war room became silent. In the vestibule Sergeant Somerall and his clerk, the bespectacled Corporal Howard Bamberger, glanced at each other in alarm. They could hear every word. So could the officers outside. The walls of a canvas tent are awfully thin.

General Hawkins still held the samurai sword in his right hand as he stared with unconcealed malevolence at Colonel Hutchins, whose hand was near the handle of the Army-issue Colt .45 in the holster attached to his cartridge belt.

"You're a disgrace to the Army," General Hawkins said, trying to keep his voice under control.

"You don't have the brains of a piss ant," Colonel Hutchins countered.

"You give me more trouble than anybody else in the division, and I'm transferring you out of here first chance I get."

"That's fine with me."

"Good. I'm glad we understand each other."

"Me too."

"You can go now," General Hawkins said.

"I'm not going until I'm ready to go. I got a few things to say to you, you pompous, fancy-pants, son of a bitch!"

General Hawkins's eyes bulged and his face turned a deep shade of purple. "I ought to have you shot!" he said.

"You're the one who should be shot!" Colonel Hutchins replied, pointing at him with his forefinger. "Half my regiment got wiped out because you didn't have the sense to back us up this morning! I may be a drunk, but you got blood on your hands, you prick! I just want you to know that!"

Colonel Hutchins turned and walked toward the exit.

"Now you wait a minute!" General Hawkins screamed.

"Fuck you!" Colonel Hutchins replied.

"I just gave you an order!"

That stopped Colonel Hutchins. He may have been a drunk and a madman, but he was still a soldier underneath it all. He turned around and faced General Hawkins, who was practically foaming at the mouth. General Hawkins stomped around the map table and approached Colonel Hutchins, stopped a foot in

84

front of him and bending forward so that their noses almost touched.

"I hate you," General Hawkins said in a sinister, menacing tone, "and I know that you hate me, but I've got two stars on my collar, and you'd better respect them. This is still the Army, you know."

"Yes, sir!"

"Any more insubordination from you and I'll have you court-martialed on the spot!"

"Yes, sir!"

"And don't give me any more shit about who'll command your regiment if you're relieved of command, because there are plenty of officers in this division who could take over and do a better job than you!"

"Bullshit!" said Colonel Hutchins.

Sparks shot out of General Hawkins's eyes. "I dare you to say that again!"

"Bullshit!"

General Hawkins was so pissed off, he thought he'd have a heart attack. "I'm losing my patience with you!"

Spit from General Hawkins's mouth flew all over Colonel Hutchins's face, but Colonel Hutchins didn't flinch

"Your problem isn't patience," Colonel Hutchins said. "Your problem is that you don't have any guts!"

General Hawkins's jaw dropped open as Colonel Hutchins did a smart left-face and marched out of the war room, through the vestibule, and out of the tent. General Hawkins stood alone next to the map table, shaking all over, wanting to run after Colonel Hutchins and chop him up with his samurai sword.

The survivors from the recon platoon, plus several other assorted survivors from Headquarters Company, lay quietly in their camouflaged jungle hideout and watched sullenly as the Japanese soldiers roved closer, clearing the area of dead and wounded. The Japanese soldiers pushed wheelbarrows full of dead soldiers back and forth to a rickety old truck, while other Japanese soldiers loaded dead men onto the wheelbarrows that had returned.

A sergeant was in charge of the detail, and he strutted around giving orders, his hand resting on his samurai sword. The Japanese soldiers were lazy as the soldiers from any other country, and they tended to gather the dead that were easy to reach. The sergeant continually had to order them into the thickest, most thorny part of the jungle to look for more dead. The sergeant knew that dead bodies lying around in a tropical climate can cause disease, and his job was to make sure that didn't happen.

The Japanese soldiers moved closer to the thicket where the American soldiers lay. The rain had slackened off, but mud and muck was everywhere. The GIs sweated in the heavy humidity and brushed away mosquitoes and flies. Each GI had his weapon in hand, ready to go to war as soon as the Japs spotted them.

The Japanese soldiers surrounded the thicket, clearing the area of dead men, while the truck waited fifty yards away, its driver napping behind the wheel. The Japanese soldiers avoided the thick, tangled vegetation, but the sergeant didn't. He hollered at a Japanese soldier and pointed to the spot where the GIs were hiding. The Japanese soldier headed for the thicket, and all the GIs inside the little stronghold tensed up. They knew that the sergeant had ordered the soldier to look for bodies inside.

"I'll take care of him," Lieutenant Breckenridge whispered, silently drawing his bayonet out of its scabbard.

The Japanese soldier happened to be a fuck-up, otherwise he wouldn't have been on the corpse detail. His name was Koike, and before the war he'd been an actor in pornographic films. He was a lowlife and a scumbag and wouldn't do a good job unless watched carefully. His uniform fit him poorly and he had a stomachache, because the steady parade of dead men was making him sick.

He cut through the dense vegetation with his machete, stopped to look around, and saw nothing. He shouted a few sentences back to the sergeant, who replied with a harsh guttural remark. Koike frowned and proceeded to cut his way into the wall of bushes. He climbed over a tree trunk and looked around, seeing nothing. Then he heard something that sounded like a twig snapping in front of him. He paused and leaned forward, narrowing his slanted eyes, trying to see, but the foliage was so thick his vision only penetrated a few feet. He figured the noise must have been made by a rat or some other jungle creature, and raised his machete for another swing.

Slicing through the bushes, he stepped forward, then noticed a blur out of the corner of his right eye. It was the last thing he ever saw. Lieutenant Breckenridge rose up and slashed Koike's throat with his bayonet. Blood spewed out, and Lieutenant Breckenridge's big hand closed around Koike's mouth, muffling the death rattle. Lieutenant Breckenridge held on to Koike and gently eased him toward the ground, then slowly dragged him the few feet to where the other GIs were hiding.

They all looked at the dead Japanese soldier. He was skinny and reminded them of a rodent. Lieutenant Breckenridge raised his forefinger to his lips, to indicate they should all be quiet. He knelt down and then lay on his stomach, watching the Japanese soldiers, wondering when they'd realize the dead one was missing.

At first the Japanese soldiers didn't seem to notice. They continued to clear the area of dead bodies. The Japanese sergeant swaggered around, giving orders. Then suddenly he turned toward the thicket and wrinkled his nose. He shouted something, waited a few seconds, then shouted again. His forehead became creased. He walked toward the thicket and stopped at its edge, leaning forward, trying to peer within. Then he shouted something again. Evidently he was calling out to the Japanese soldier he'd ordered inside the thicket, and of course he received no answer. The Japanese sergeant didn't know it, but fourteen American gun barrels were pointed at him. The Japanese sergeant took off his soft cap and wiped his forehead with a handkerchief. He spat into the mud, took out a cigarette, and lighted it up. A light rain fell on him as he turned around and shouted an order to his men.

Three of his men stopped gathering corpses and picked up their rifles. They held the rifles in both hands and entered the thicket where Koike had gone. The Japanese sergeant continued talking to them in a loud voice as they penetrated more deeply into the thicket.

The three Japanese soldiers didn't know how close to death they were, but they were aware that something had gone wrong somewhere. Slowly and cautiously they pushed their way through the bushes and branches, looking to their left and right, searching for their friend, not realizing that he was now with his ancestors.

The rain continued to slacken. Bugs buzzed around their

heads. The sergeant asked if they saw anything suspicious yet, and they replied that they didn't. The path they were treading upon came to a halt. Ahead was a solid wall of bushes. The lead Japanese soldier pulled his machete out of his scabbard while the second Japanese soldier happened to look down. The latter Japanese saw a drop of ruby red blood on a dark green leaf.

"Look!" he said, pointing to it.

"Look at what?" asked another Japanese soldier.

"I see blood!"

"Where?"

"There!"

The three Japanese soldiers knelt down to look at the blood. One touched it with his finger and wondered whose blood it was. Then he heard a rustling sound next to him. He turned around and saw the legs of American soldiers. He opened his mouth to scream, but a big hand clamped over his lips and nose. A second later he felt a terrible rip in his stomach, followed by the severance of his windpipe.

Lieutenant Breckenridge let the soldier fall to the ground. Pfc. Morris Shilansky and Pfc. Jimmy O'Rourke had dispatched their men with ease and speed also. Lieutenant Breckenridge nodded his head sideways, indicating that they should return where they had come from, then got down on his belly and crawled away from the gruesome scene.

The Japanese sergeant standing outside the thicket heard movement in the bushes and looked in the direction of the sound. "What's going on in there?" he yelled.

There was no answer.

"I said what's going on in there?"

Again there was no answer. He called out the names of the three Japanese soldiers, but they'd never respond to his questions again. The Japanese sergeant knitted his eyebrows together. A chill passed over him. He got down low and shouted for his men to take shelter. He crawled away from the thicket, and when he was at a safe distance he sat behind a tree to think things over.

His name was Takayuki, and he was a veteran of numerous battles on the Huon Peninsula, as well as other battles in China. Despite all his experience, he was confused about the current situation. Something in those bushes over there was silencing his men. Was it a jungle animal of some grotesque proportions, or American soldiers? And why hadn't his men sounded an alarm?

It was a very perplexing situation, and he had no radio with which to call his headquarters for guidance. Neither could he walk away as if nothing had happened, because four of his men were missing. He'd have to investigate.

He bent to the side and gazed around the tree. The thicket didn't appear to be too big. If he had artillery, he'd blow it to shit, but he had no artillery or even mortars. He could order his men to charge it, but the foliage appeared impregnable. The charge would bog down. He'd have to be more subtle.

Finally he decided on a plan that seemed sound from a military point of view. He'd gather his men together and circle the thicket, then move inward toward its center and probe for whatever was in there.

He cupped his hands around his mouth and shouted the orders. All his men would participate in the attack, even the truck driver. He told his men to circle the thicket and move in toward its center when he gave the command. He also told them to be careful, but that was an unnecessary order. His men already knew that something dangerous was inside the thicket, because it had done something terrible to four of their comrades.

The Japanese soldiers hunched low to the ground as they moved through the jungle and formed a ring around the thicket.

"Uh-oh," said Lieutenant Breckenridge.

"They know we're in here," replied Sergeant Cameron.

"No they don't. All they know is their buddies have been disappearing. You stay here and face front. I'll deploy the rest of the men. When I give the order, we throw grenades and then open fire. Get it?"

"Got it."

"Good."

Lieutenant Breckenridge crawled through the foliage, passing along the same orders to each of his men. As he did so he heard the Japanese sergeant order his men to move out. Seconds later Lieutenant Breckenridge heard the Japanese soldiers coming through the bushes, talking among themselves. Lieutenant

Breckenridge finished his rounds and returned to a spot near Sergeant Cameron, who had his grenade in his hand with the pin loosened so that it could be pulled out easily. Lieutenant Breckenridge tore a grenade off his lapel and also loosed the pin. Now he was ready. He glanced around at his men: They all had grenades ready to throw.

The Japanese soldiers advanced slowly and cautiously through the jungle. They hacked branches with their machetes, paused, looked around, and hacked more branches. Other Japanese soldiers held fingers on the triggers of their rifles and followed the ones with the machetes. All were apprehensive. They didn't know what to expect in the gnarled, uprooted thicket. What had silenced their comrades? Who was in there?

One of the lead machete men saw blood on the ground. "Sergeant Takayuki!"

"What is it?" replied Sergeant Takuyaki, who was in another part of the thicket.

"I see a lot of blood!"

"I'll be right there!"

Sergeant Takayuki, his Nambu pistol in his hand, crashed through the foliage, sounding like an elephant on a rampage. He reached the machete bearer who'd called him and looked down at the blood. Kneeling, he touched it; it was sticky and warm. The foliage in the area was matted down. He could see trails leading from where he was, and there were streaks of blood on the trails. Perhaps the bodies of his men had been dragged down those trails. But by what?

He heard something pass through the leaves over his head and looked up. An oblong gray metal object the size of an apple was falling toward him. Sergeant Takayuki's eyes bugged out of his head.

"Grenade!" he screamed.

He jumped up to catch the grenade and throw it back, but it exploded before he could grasp it, blowing off his head and arms. He flew through the air like a rag doll, and seconds later more grenades exploded throughout the thicket, blowing up Japanese soldiers. Those who weren't blown up were horrified by the sudden turn of events. They fled from the thicket, but the GIs opened fire with their automatic and semiautomatic weapons, shooting down most of them. Several managed to get away. They ran out of the thicket and headed toward the truck. Shots continued to ring out, and they dropped to the ground. Finally only one Japanese soldier was left. Bullets flew around him like angry gnats as he jumped up onto the running board of the truck. The truck had no door, and he found himself face to face with the barrel of a Thompson submachine gun held in the hands of an American soldier with a big smile on his face, sitting behind the wheel.

Frankie La Barbara pulled the trigger, and the submachine gun rumbled in his hands. Bullets flew out the barrel and tore up the head of the Japanese soldier, who fell off the running board and dropped to the ground. Frankie slid across the seat and stood on the running board, waving his submachine gun in the air.

"Hey guys, it's me!" he yelled.

Lieutenant Breckenridge walked out of the bushes, carrying his carbine. "Where the hell have you been?"

"Out here."

"What are you doing out here?"

"I was looking for a nice Thompson submachine gun, and see—I've got one." Frankie held the weapon in the air.

"I didn't give you permission to go wandering around out here."

"It's a good thing I did, though, because if that Jap got away"— Frankie pointed to the dead Japanese soldier on the ground—"he might have brought back the whole Jap army with him."

Lieutenant Breckenridge gazed at the truck. Sergeant Cameron came out of the thicket, followed by Private Yabalonka and Pfc. Craig Delane.

"I wonder," said Lieutenant Breckenridge, "if that truck works."

"Sure it works," Frankie said.

"Start it up."

Frankie sat behind the wheel and looked at the levers and switches. He'd never driven a Japanese truck before, but the controls looked more or less like the controls of an ordinary American truck. Depressing the gas pedal with his foot, he flicked a few levers, and finally one of them made the engine turn over. Frankie stomped on the gas pedal and the engine roared to life.

Lieutenant Breckenridge wondered whether they should use

the truck to drive back to their own lines. He decided it was worth a chance.

"Everybody out here!" he said. "Bring your weapons with you!"

The others pushed through the foliage and carried their rifles and machine guns into the open. The rain had just about stopped, and the dead bodies stank more than ever. Lieutenant Breckenridge stepped away from a wheelbarrow full of dead Japanese soldiers in advanced states of rigor mortis, their arms and legs stiff and outstretched. The GIs gathered around Lieutenant Breckenridge.

"Everybody find a Japanese uniform and put it on," Lieutenant Breckenridge said. "Then load onto the truck. Frankie will drive, and I'll sit in the front seat with him. The rest of you get in back. We'll try to drive to our lines. Any questions?"

Pfc. Morris Shilansky raised his forefinger. "What'll we do with the dead Japs in back of the truck?"

"Unload them, and hurry up!"

SIX . . .

It was late afternoon, and dusk fell over New Guinea. The rain had stopped, but the sky still was cloudy. Frankie La Barbara sat behind the wheel of the truck, wearing a Japanese uniform several sizes too small for him, because Japanese soldiers tended to be smaller than American soldiers. A Japanese army soft cap was perched on top of his head.

Seated next to him was Lieutenant Breckenridge, similarly attired, carrying Frankie's submachine in his hands below window level, so that Japs couldn't see it. In back of the truck were the other men, also wearing Japanese uniforms, sitting in the stink of the dead bodies that had filled the space. Blood stained the wooden floor of the truck and the wooden slats that served as its walls. The GIs were crowded together. On the floor of the truck lay their automatic weapons and ammunition. Hand grenades were in their pockets. There were serious doubts in all their minds that they'd be able to break through the Japanese line without at least one major problem.

The body of the truck rocked from side to side on its suspension system as Frankie steered along the jungle trails. He passed groups of dead Japanese soldiers lying on the ground, and when he couldn't drive around them, he drove over them. Finally he came to a dirt road and stepped on the accelerator so that the truck could mount the shoulder of the road. Pistons clattered inside their cylinder walls as the nose of the truck rose in the air. Frankie looked to the left and right and could see no traffic. The road wound through the jungle, and he couldn't see very far in either direction.

The truck climbed the steep shoulder and then leveled off on the road. Frankie spun the wheel in the direction of the American lines and pressed the accelerator to the floor.

"Easy, now," said Lieutenant Breckenridge. "We don't want to get any speeding tickets out here."

Frankie eased off on the pedal. The truck slowed down. Frankie glanced at the gas gauge; the needle indicated that the gas tank was half full. The road curved sharply to the right and Frankie steered around the corner. Thick, tangled jungle lined both sides of the road, which then turned to the left. Frankie cut the wheel in that direction, and when he was halfway around the corner he saw a column of Japanese soldiers straight ahead, marching in a column of twos to the front.

"Uh-oh," said Frankie.

"Be calm," Lieutenant Breckenridge said, "and just keep driving."

The truck approached the column of Japanese soldiers. Not one of the Japanese soldiers turned around to look at what was coming. Frankie eased the steering wheel to the left so that he could pass the Japanese column. Lieutenant Breckenridge held the submachine gun tightly. In the back of the truck the other GIs inclined their heads downward so the visors of their Japanese caps would hide their Caucasian features.

The truck passed the column of Japanese soldiers, and some of the Japanese soldiers looked at the GIs in back of the truck. Several Japanese soldiers shouted greetings, and a few of them waved. Pfc. Morris Shilansky waved back. The truck moved on without incident, leaving the Japanese soldiers behind, slogging over the muddy road.

Frankie held the wheel tightly, because the truck was sliding all over the place. The mud on the road was slippery and had numerous deep puddles. Frankie wanted to drive faster, but he knew he was liable to go off the road if he did. He turned a corner and saw a group of soldiers sitting in the jungle beside the road, eating rice out of canisters. The Japanese soldiers waved and said hello, and a few of the GIs waved back.

Frankie steered around another corner and saw up ahead a truck like the one he was driving, towing a Japanese field howitzer. In the back of the truck was the gun crew, six Japanese soldiers, with boxes of ammunition.

"Don't get too close," Lieutenant Breckenridge cautioned.

Lieutenant Breckenridge examined the weapon, a Type 94 mountain gun that fired a 75mm shell. It was one of the principal infantry support artillery weapons in the Japanese army, and had a camouflage paint job. The big barrel of the gun was pointed directly at the truck in which Lieutenant Breckenridge was seated.

The truck towing the howitzer turned a corner, and Frankie followed at a safe distance. He steered around the corner, too, and his heart missed two beats when he saw Japanese soldiers all over the place. They were cooking around fires, digging fortifications, carrying crates around, and running back and forth with pieces of paper in their hands. It was a major Japanese staging area, and ahead was a US Army Corps of Engineers pontoon bridge spanning the Driniumor River.

"Just stay calm," Lieutenant Breckenridge said. "Keep on driving."

Frankie nodded. His heart had resumed beating, and it sounded like the drummer in the Jimmy Dorsey Orchestra. His face blanched and his knuckles turned white on the steering wheel. He was a tough guy, but even a tough guy can get scared shitless. The difference between a tough guy and a coward is that the tough guys keep going, despite their fear, and that's what Frankie did. He held his foot steady on the gas pedal and looked straight ahead. If the Japs realized that American GIs were in their midst, a quick, bloody fight would ensue, with a predictable end. All Frankie wanted to do was take as many Japs with him as he could before he got blown away.

In the back of the truck the mood was basically that of Frankie's. The men were scared, but they didn't let their fear destroy them. They glanced about at the huge Japanese encampment and held their weapons ready to fire. They expected the shit to hit the fan at any moment.

Lieutenant Breckenridge took out a cigarette and lit it with a hand that was shaking slightly. He puffed the cigarette and looked ahead. The truck pulling the howitzer rolled down the sloping incline toward the pontoon bridge. Another truck full of crates was already on the bridge. A third truck drove off the bridge on the far side; it also was full of crates. More Japanese soldiers were on the far side of the river. The whole area was infested with Japs.

Lieutenant Breckenridge noticed groups of Japanese soldiers at both ends of the bridge. They carried rifles slung over their shoulders and appeared to be guards. Four of them were on each end, and they were very lackadaisical about their work, or so it seemed. They didn't expect a truckload of American soldiers to pass their way.

"Listen to me," Lieutenant Breckenridge said to Frankie La Barbara. "If there's any trouble, just keep driving. Don't stop for anything. Your job is to drive and that's all. Got it?"

"Got it," Frankie replied.

In the back of the truck, Sergeant Cameron muttered orders to the men. "Don't fire unless I tell you to," he said. "Don't nobody try to be cute, okay?"

They all nodded as they looked down at the floor of the truck, trying to keep their American faces from being seen by the Japs. They could smell cooking odors and hear Japanese soldiers shouting back and forth to each other. Some Japanese soldiers shouted at them in a friendly manner, but the GIs behaved as if they were dozing off, fatigued after being on the road all day.

The truck pulling the howitzer rumbled onto the bridge, which was approximately forty feet long. Beneath the bridge the Driniumor surged and foamed as it rushed toward the sea. Frankie followed the truck pulling the howitzer, drawing closer to the Japanese guards on both sides of the bridge. The guards chatted with each other, laughed, and smoked cigarettes. Their morale appeared high, because they were safe behind their lines and had just won a victory against the Americans.

The two Japanese soldiers on Frankie's side looked at him as his front fender came abreast of them. One smiled and said something to Frankie, and Frankie smiled back, looking straight ahead. The Japanese soldier said something again. It sounded like a question to Frankie, but he just smiled again and waved.

The Japanese soldier stopped smiling. An expression of suspicion came over his face as Frankie rolled alongside him.

The Japanese soldier asked the question again, and Frankie waved once more. The Japanese soldier said something to his comrade, and both of them unslung their Arisaka rifles.

In the back of the truck, Sergeant Cameron was watching them. "Get ready to shoot those sons of bitches," he said to Private Yabalonka, who carried a BAR.

Yabalonka raised the BAR. The Japanese soldiers held their rifles in both hands and touched their forefingers to the triggers. One of the Japanese soldiers shouted at Frankie, but Frankie was past him now. The Japanese soldier looked at the men in back of the truck, and saw the blond hair underneath the cap of Pfc. Craig Delane.

The Japanese soldier screamed out an alarm and raised his rifle higher in the air. Yabalonka stood up in the back of the truck and opened fire with the BAR, spraying the two Japanese soldiers with hot lead. The two Japanese soldiers were spun around by the hail of the bullets. Blood spurted from holes in their flesh, and they fell to the ground.

There was a moment of silence, and then all hell broke loose. Japanese soldiers screamed and hollered, running back and forth. Other Japanese soldiers dived into holes, fearing that they were under attack. The truck pulling the howitzer sped up, to get away from all the trouble, leaving the bridge wide open.

"Move it out!" Lieutenant Breckenridge yelled, raising his submachine gun and pointing it out the window. Japanese soldiers ran along the riverbank straight ahead, and he mowed them down.

In the back of the truck the GIs fired their rifles and BARs at Japanese soldiers. Sergeant Cameron threw hand grenades as fast as he could pull the pins. A Japanese officer ran out of a tent to see what was going on and received a bullet in his stomach, doubling him over, flinging him back into the tent. A Japanese sergeant drew his Nambu pistol and fired a wild shot, but before he could fire another one, an American bullet hit him in the hip, shattering the bone and hurling him to the ground.

Meanwhile, Japanese bullets whizzed all around the truck and slammed into its sides. One bullet punctured the left rear tire. Japanese machine-gun bullets raked the door next to Frankie La Barbara, and he slammed the accelerator down to the floor.

The engine of the truck coughed and then stalled. A wave of horror came over Frankie. Japanese bullets whacked into the truck, and all the soldiers in the back dropped to the floor. But there wasn't much room in the bed of the truck, and they crashed into each other, bumping heads and elbows.

"Get this truck going!" Lieutenant Breckenridge screamed, firing the Thompson submachine gun wildly, trying to stop the entire Japanese army in the area.

Frankie turned the lever and tapped the gas pedal. The engine rattled but wouldn't kick to life. The unmistakable odor of gasoline came to Frankie's nostrils.

"You've flooded the engine!" Lieutenant Breckenridge yelled.

Lieutenant Breckenridge emptied his clip of .45-caliber bullets, ejected the empty clip, and slapped in a new one, resuming his fire. In the back of the truck the GIs shot back at the Japanese soldiers swarming toward the truck. Frankie worked the ignition lever and kept his foot off the gas pedal, so the engine would clear. The engine grumbled and growled as it turned over; it sounded as though the battery were running down.

Frankie bit his lower lip so hard, it bled. He prayed to God that the engine would start, but it wouldn't. A big bullet hole shattered the windshield in front of him, and the flattened nose of the bullet struck the seat an inch from Frankie's shoulder.

The engine coughed and sputtered. Frankie gave it some gas, and it turned over! He let up the clutch and the truck lurched forward. Another bullet made a hole in the windshield, and Frankie ducked. Japanese machine-gun bullets raked the radiator, and water spouted out through the holes. But the truck gathered speed and crossed the bridge. Sergeant Cameron held a grenade in his right hand and pulled the pin. As soon as the truck was on the other side of the river, he was going to throw the hand grenade onto the bridge and blow it to smithereens.

Then he realized that one hand grenade would not destroy the entire bridge. There would have to be more hand grenades. *"Everybody, grenade that bridge when I say the word!"* he screamed.

The GIs pulled out hand grenades and yanked the pins. The truck sped across the bridge. The Japanese soldiers in the vicinity didn't dare throw their own grenades at the truck, because they were afraid of blowing up the bridge themselves. All they could do was shoot at the truck, denting the fenders and shooting out all the tires in an effort to pin the GIs down.

The truck rumbled off the bridge, and Sergeant Cameron could feel solid ground underneath the wheels. *"Now!"* he hollered.

Sergeant Cameron raised himself up and drew back his arm. He threw the hand grenade, but before he could get down, a Japanese 6.5mm bullet from an Arisaka rifle pierced his throat and blew out the back of his neck. The gallant old sergeant fell backward as the other GIs tossed their grenades out the back of the truck, not exposing themselves as much to Japanese gunfire. Sergeant Snider, the mess sergeant from Headquarters Company, caught a bullet in his wrist, and he screamed in pain, blood spurting out of the hole.

Sergeant Snider fell on top of Sergeant Cameron. The other GIs plastered themselves against the bed of the truck, sticking their fingers in their ears, waiting for the big explosion.

Barrrrrooooommmmmmm! The grenades detonated one after the other in one long, pulsing, earth-shaking roar. The wooden planks on top of the pontoon bridge, and two of the pontoons, were blown apart. The bridge became wreathed with smoke; nobody could see the extent of the damage.

The Japanese soldiers in the area jabbered and screamed. Some rose up and continued to fire at the truck. Frankie wished he could speed up and get around the truck in front of him, but that truck was going so slow it appeared to be stopping. Frankie's mind filled with horror when he realized it was drawing to a halt, blocking the road in response to an order shouted from an officer in the vicinity.

Now Frankie was really scared. *"What'll I do now?"* he bellowed.

"Drive into the river!" Lieutenant Breckenridge replied.

"Drive into the river?"

"You heard me!"

Frankie didn't have time to think it over. He cut the wheel to the left, and the truck skidded sideways on the muddy road. Stomping on the accelerator made the truck skid more. Now it pointed backward toward the demolished end of the bridge.

Lieutenant Breckenridge stuck his head out of the window and roared, *"Jump in the river and swim for it!"*

"Are you serious?" screamed Frankie.

"You got any better ideas?"

Whang! A Japanese bullet hit the side of the truck near Lieutenant Breckenridge's head. He pulled back into the truck and fired one more burst from his submachine gun, then ducked down and slung the weapon across his back. Frankie cut the wheel to the right so he could drive down the riverbank instead of toppling the truck over the end of the bridge. The bank was muddy and Japanese soldiers lay on it, firing at the truck. Frankie drove the truck over their bodies and accelerated hard at the last moment. The truck smashed into the water and kept going until water came into the cab.

"Everybody out!" yelled Lieutenant Breckenridge.

He pushed open the door and dived into the fast-moving current. The weight of his body and all the equipment on it dragged him beneath the surface, but he kicked his feet and rose up again. Japanese bullets zipped into the water near his head, so he took a deep breath and dropped beneath the surface again.

On the back of the truck, all the GIs leaped over the sides except Sergeant Cameron, whose jumping days were over. Smoke from the blast still made visibility murky, and it was difficult for the Japs to get clear shots. The GIs splashed into the swollen current, which swept them up in its relentless gush through the jungle. Some of the wooden slats had come loose from the truck when it hit the water, and the GIs held on to them. Frankie La Barbara hit the water a few seconds after Lieutenant Breckenridge, and the straw seat followed him out. He clutched the seat and watched Japanese soldiers running along the riverbank in front of him, waving their arms and shouting. Some stopped to fire shots, but the GIs were low in the water, and the current was swift.

The jungle was thick and tangled, and the Japanese soldiers couldn't run far on the riverbank. They had to stop and watch helplessly as the American soldiers floated around a bend in the river, out of sight—gone.

SEVEN . . .

Dusk came to New Guinea, and the US Army prepared for its morning attack. The rain had stopped and it was hoped that the morning would be clear, so the Air Corps could support the troops on the ground. Supplies and reinforcements continued to move to the front. Commanders adjusted their lines and hooked up with units to their left and right. The Signal Corps laid new wires for telephone communications, and Engineer units strung concertina wire in front of the American positions. Listening posts were set up in no-man's-land to make sure the Japs didn't pull a nighttime sneak attack.

Colonel Hutchins sat in his tent near the front lines, smoking in the light of the kerosene lamp that hung over his head. He was heavily medicated, feeling little pain. A weaker man would have been knocked out by all the medication, but not Colonel Hutchins. He'd built up a high tolerance to medication over the years.

Puffing a cigarette, he studied the personnel records of First Lieutenant Samuel Porter from George Company, who'd been recommended to Colonel Hutchins by Major Cobb. Colonel Hutchins wanted to send out patrols to find out what the Japs were doing, but he didn't have his recon platoon to do this kind of dirty work anymore. Therefore he needed a substitution.

The recon platoon had always been Colonel Hutchins's pet project, and most of the regiment resented it, but Colonel Hutchins never let the disapproval of others dissuade him from doing what he thought was right. He wanted his recon platoon to be completely reliable, comprising the toughest, meanest men in his regiment, who could do the toughest, meanest jobs.

Unfortunately the toughest, meanest men in his regiment proved to be the most troublesome. When they didn't have any Japs to fight with, they fought among themselves. Many had been criminals in civilian life. Most had spent time in Army stockades. Few had any talent for barracks soldiering, but that wasn't Colonel Hutchins's forte either. He wanted tough brutal men with nerves of steel, and his recon platoon had never let him down.

Colonel Hutchins read the sheets of paper in Lieutenant Porter's file and could see why he'd been recommended by Major Cobb. Porter had been trained as a paratrooper but had transferred out of the Eleventh Airborne Division, for which no reason was given in his records. He'd been a pfc, when he went ashore on Guadalcanal, and had won the Silver Star and a battlefield commission during the fight for the Gifu Line on Guadalcanal. He'd joined the Army in 1938 and was from Spanish Fork, Utah. A Mormon, he'd joined the Army immediately after graduating from high school.

Porter had never been in any trouble, and Colonel Hutchins held that against him. He didn't see how a man could be worth anything if he'd never been in any trouble. A man who'd never been in any trouble lacked imagination and daring, Colonel Hutchins believed, but if Lieutenant Porter had won the Silver Star and a battlefield commission, he couldn't be all bad.

Colonel Hutchins sipped lukewarm coffee from his canteen cup. Sergeant Koch stuck his head through the tent flap. "Lieutenant Porter is here, sir!"

"Send him right in."

Sergeant Koch drew his head back, and two seconds later a short, well-built man marched into the office, carrying his helmet under his left arm. His hair was prematurely gray and clipped short, and his jaw was square with a cleft in the middle. He stopped in front of Colonel Hutchins's desk and saluted,

102

stating his name and rank in a firm, metallic voice.

Colonel Hutchins looked the lieutenant up and down a few times. He'd expected somebody taller. Flicking through Lieutenant Porter's records, he saw that Porter was five feet six inches tall. Colonel Hutchins hadn't noticed that particular bit of information before.

Yet, despite his height—or the lack of it—Lieutenant Porter appeared to be a powerful man. His sleeves were torn off at the shoulders, and he had huge biceps and forearms. His shoulders were wide and his waist thin. His arms were covered with cuts and lumps, the emblems of the veteran of hand-to-hand combat.

"Have a seat," Colonel Hutchins said.

"Thank you, sir!"

Lieutenant Porter sat with his back straight and his chin tucked in, the upper portion of his body at attention. He had the air of the regular Army professional soldier about him, and Colonel Hutchins liked that. He fingered through the papers in Lieutenant Porter's file and saw that Porter was thirty years old.

Colonel Hutchins smiled. "Good evening, Lieutenant Porter."

"Good evening, sir."

"How've you been getting along?"

"Can't complain, sir."

"Sure you can complain. You know the old saying: If the troops aren't complaining, they're not happy."

"I got nothing to complain about, sir."

"Well, I have."

Lieutenant Porter appeared ill at ease. He wasn't accustomed to sitting around in tents with full bird colonels, shooting the shit. His discomfort made Colonel Hutchins uneasy. Colonel Hutchins preferred soldiers who weren't too awed by him. But Colonel Hutchins didn't have much to choose from. Half of his regiment had been put out of the war during the past thirty-six hours.

Colonel Hutchins folded his hands on Lieutenant Porter's records and leaned forward. "We might as well get right down to business, Lieutenant. Do you know anything about my recon platoon?"

"A little."

"What do you know?"

"They do most of the regiment's reconaissance and patrolling."

"Do you know where they are right now?"

"No, sir."

"They're all missing in action."

Lieutenant Porter was surprised and raised his eyebrows.

"Yes," Colonel Hutchins said. "Not one came back."

Lieutenant Porter didn't reply. He knew Lieutenant Breckenridge vaguely, and had seen the recon platoon pass through the George Company area. They didn't have a very good reputation in the regiment. Some said they were a bunch of crooks, and others said they brown-nosed the colonel all the time. Lieutenant Porter always thought Lieutenant Breckenridge was okay, although he was sort of a wise guy.

"Anyway," Colonel Hutchins continued, "I need a new recon platoon. Would you be interested in heading it?"

Lieutenant Porter was surprised. He was a career soldier and would have to think about whether or not the job would be good for him in the long run. "How much time do I have to think about it?"

"About a minute."

Lieutenant Porter knew Colonel Hutchins would be angry if he turned down the job, so on the basis of that he said, "I'll do it."

"Good. I want you to pick about twenty good men and organize them into units of four or five each. I want you to send out the men here, here, here, and here," he said, pointing at spots on the map. "Have them probe forward toward the Driniumor River, if they can get that far, or if they can't get that far, have them go as far as they can and then return here and report to me or Major Cobb. And I want you to lead one of the patrols. Is that clear?"

"Yes, sir."

"Think you can handle it?"

"Yes, sir."

"How soon can you leave?"

"About an hour, sir."

"Any questions?"

"Yes, sir. Exactly what kind of information are you looking for, sir?"

Colonel Hutchins didn't like that question. An infantry officer should know what to look for. Lieutenant Breckenridge and Sergeant Butsko would never have asked a question like that.

"You don't know what to look for, Lieutenant?" Colonel Hutchins asked. "How can an officer have the experience you have and not know what to look for?"

Lieutenant Porter blushed. "I know what to look for in general, sir, but I wondered if you had any specific objectives."

"If I had, I would have told them to you. In the absence of my having told you, you are to report anything and everything of military intelligence value. Do you know what I mean by that, or do I have to explain further?"

"I understand, sir."

"And you're not to get into any fights out there if they're avoidable."

"Yes, sir."

Colonel Hutchins looked at his watch. "It's now eighteen-thirty hours. I'll expect you to be crossing into no-man's-land no later than twenty-thirty hours."

Lieutenant Porter glanced at his own watch. "Yes, sir."

"You're dismissed."

"Yes, sir."

Lieutenant Porter snapped to attention, saluted smartly, executed a flawless about-face, and marched out of the office. Colonel Hutchins closed Lieutenant Porter's personnel files and sighed, wishing he had his good old reliable recon platoon back.

It was dark in the jungle, and the Driniumor River surged and rippled along, carrying coconuts that had fallen in, branches, leaves, dead animals, rotted planks, dead soldiers, articles of military equipment, and occasionally even a live soldier.

"Over here!" said Lieutenant Breckenridge, holding on to a branch overhanging the riverbank.

He looked out into the murky darkness and saw the heads and shoulders of his men bobbing up and down in the river. Eddies swirled them around, and whirlpools sucked them under, but the current was not so strong that they couldn't fight it. The sky was black without a star shining, and all shapes were indistinct. The jungle on the far side of the river could

105

be perceived only as a mass of blackness a few shades darker than the sky.

The men kicked their legs and paddled toward the riverbank where Lieutenant Breckenridge was. Each hung on to his piece of debris, his log or something he'd grabbed from the Japanese truck that had driven into the Driniumor. Frankie La Barbara hugged his seat cushion with both arms and kicked his legs in the cascading current. His wavy hair was slicked down by the water; his helmet was long gone. Approaching the riverbank, he saw a clear stretch of beach and went aground, his knees scraping the rocks on the river bottom. He stood, staggered toward dry land, tripped on a rock, and fell, scraping his knees on the rocks.

"Son of a bitch!" he yelled.

"Not so loud!" said Lieutenant Breckenridge.

"Fuck you," Frankie mumbled, raising himself up. He stepped forward carefully, nearly losing his balance again, his arms and legs exhausted, and collapsed on the riverbank, rolling over onto his back, his tongue hanging out of his mouth.

The others made their way to the shore, and they, too, were badly fatigued. They'd traveled approximately a mile on the Driniumor, fighting the current every foot of the way, and there was always the possibility that they'd pass a platoon of Japs who'd shoot the shit out of them.

Sergeant Snider hung on to a log, and he was damn near dead from loss of blood. The Reverend Billie Jones stayed near him, helping him along, his hand grasping the shoulder of Sergeant Snider's shirt. The Reverend Billie Jones pulled Sergeant Snider to the spot on the riverbank where Frankie La Barbara had gone ashore.

"You okay, Sarge?" Billie Jones asked.

"I need a drink," Sergeant Snider said weakly.

Sergeant Snider's toes and knees touched bottom. He let go of the log and stood up, but his head spun so swiftly, he lost his balance and collapsed into the water with a big splash. The Reverend Billie Jones lifted him by his armpits and dragged him to the shore, letting him down beside Frankie La Barbara, whose chest was still heaving.

"Oh, this fucking war," Frankie wheezed. "This goddamn fucking shitty war. I can't take this goddamn fucking war anymore. I gotta get outta this goddamn fucking war somehow.

I don't know how I'll do it, but I'll do it."

Pfc. Morris Shilansky came to the shore on his hands and knees like a dog. "The only way you'll get out of this war will be in a fucking pine box."

"Fuck you," said Frankie.

Lieutenant Breckenridge raised his voice. "Keep it down over there!"

Frankie pointed his thumb over his shoulder at Lieutenant Breckenridge. "Listen to that fucking asshole, willya?"

The other men came ashore one by one. Private Victor Yabalonka's hands were so ravaged, he could barely move his fingers. The water had caused the edges of the wounds on his hands to puff up, but the bleeding had stopped. He dropped to the muck and rolled over onto his back, breathing heavily.

Pfc. Craig Delane crawled toward the riverbank and stopped moving when his head and shoulders were out of the water. His cheek lay on the mud and he sucked in air through his nose and throat. His chest hurt and he thought he was going to have a heart attack.

Pfc. Gotbaum, the tubby little medic, had lost his eyeglasses when he'd jumped off his tree trunk, and now he stumbled toward the others, following the sounds of their voices because he couldn't see much. He had not lost his haversack full of medicine, though. It dripped water but still was slung crossways over his back and chest. Pfc. Gotbaum fell to the ground and lay still, his jaw hanging open.

"Hey, pill-roller," said Private Yabalonka, "looks like you need a medic."

Gotbaum didn't answer. His strength was gone. The other men shuffled ashore and collapsed in the tiny clearing on the riverbank. Lieutenant Breckenridge pulled himself branch by branch toward the clearing and climbed up the riverbank, his .45-caliber submachine gun hanging from his back. He unslung the submachine gun, sat, and lay it across his lap, wondering if it would fire when he pulled the trigger.

He let the men rest, because he knew he couldn't do much with them as they were. He wasn't that tired himself. He could have moved into the jungle, but not them. He pulled out his map to see how badly the water had damaged it. The map was encased in a zipper oilcloth envelope, but water had seeped through the zipper. The map was soaking wet, but the colors hadn't run. Lieutenant Breckenridge unfolded the map carefully, lay it on the ground, and bent over to examine it.

Visibility was poor, but he could make out a few salient details. He could see the Driniumor River and estimate where he and his men had come ashore. But the map couldn't tell him who held the land he was on, the Japs or his own army. He had no way of knowing how much ground the Japs had captured in their morning attack.

He glanced at his watch: The hands told him it was six-thirty in the evening. Holding the watch closer to his eyes, he perceived that the face was half covered with water. He pressed the watch against his ear and heard no clicks. The watch was waterlogged. Six-thirty was the time he'd hit the water. He estimated that at least an hour had elapsed since then.

"Sergeant Cameron?" he asked.

"Sergeant Cameron's dead," replied Pfc. Morris Shilansky.

"He's dead?" Lieutenant Breckenridge asked, astonished.

"That's right."

"You're sure?"

"He got shot in the neck. I saw it with my own eyes."

"Me too," said Craig Delane.

Several other GIs indicated that they'd seen Sergeant Cameron get hit too. Lieutenant Breckenridge stared at them in disbelief. It was difficult for him to accept the fact that Sergeant Cameron was dead. Sergeant Cameron had been in the recon platoon even before Lieutenant Breckenridge, and he'd always been one of the most durable, reliable members of the platoon.

"Anybody get his dog tags?" Lieutenant Breckenridge asked.

"Who had time?" Shilansky replied.

Lieutenant Breckenridge wished he had a dry cigarette to smoke. Sergeant Cameron's death made him more aware of his own mortality. If Sergeant Cameron could get killed, so could he. Death could come suddenly, from out of nowhere. One moment you were alive and the next moment you were gone forever.

Lieutenant Breckenridge didn't have time to wonder about life in the hereafter. He had to appoint somebody to be second in command. Who should he appoint? He didn't have much to choose from. Sergeant Snider was the highest-ranking man under Lieutenant Breckenridge, but Sergeant Snider was a mess sergeant; he knew nothing about basic tactics and fighting in the jungle.

Lieutenant Breckenridge glanced around at the men clustered in the tiny clearing as the Driniumor River roared past. He didn't think any of the survivors from the recon platoon were worth a damn, and the three stragglers from Headquarters Company who'd come this far weren't even real infantry soldiers. Corporal Froelich was a signalman, Pfc. Wilkie had been a clerk on Major Cobb's staff, and Pfc. Gotbaum was a pill-roller. It was a ticklish situation, but according to Army regulations, the ranking enlisted man should be appointed second in command.

"Well," Lieutenant Breckenridge said, "I've got to have somebody to take Sergeant Cameron's place. The next ranking man is Sergeant Snider, but you don't know anything about being a platoon sergeant, do you, Sergeant Snider?"

Sergeant Snider was a squat man with a blubbery mouth and a short growth of thick black beard. "I don't know anything about anything," he said. "And on top of that, I'm wounded." He held up his right hand, showing his bloody handkerchief wrapped around his wrist. "I ain't good for nothing."

Except for making white lightning, Lieutenant Breckenridge thought. He looked around at the others, and his eyes fell on Corporal Froelich. "You're the next ranking man after Sergeant Snider," Lieutenant Breckenridge said. "Think you can handle the job of acting platoon sergeant?"

Corporal Froelich had an egg-shaped body and a scraggly mustache. "The only thing I know about is communications."

Lieutenant Breckenridge nodded in appreciation of Corporal Froelich's honesty. Now he was down to pfcs., and he didn't think he had much to choose from. Frankie La Barbara couldn't take orders, so he certainly shouldn't be giving them. Shilansky wasn't very bright. Craig Delane had no leadership ability whatever. Jimmy O'Rourke was an utter fool. The Reverend Billie Jones was a religious screwball who liked to kill Japs.

Lieutenant Breckenridge was perplexed. He wished he had Butsko around, but he didn't. *Which of these guys would make a good acting platoon sergeant?* he wondered. It was a tough choice, but he narrowed them down to Frankie La Barbara and Jimmy O'Rourke. He didn't like the idea of either one. Frankie was uncooperative in every way all the time, and O'Rourke was obviously half crazy. The former movie stuntman thought he was Clark Gable.

Neither one of them is any good, Lieutenant Breckenridge decided. *Maybe I should get along without a platoon sergeant.* But he knew he couldn't do that and still have a smooth-running, efficient team. He also knew that sometimes the man who was the biggest fuck-up turned out to be the best soldier when the shit hit the fan. The big question was, could Frankie La Barbara or Jimmy O'Rourke rise to the occasion?

He thought it over and decided Jimmy O'Rourke couldn't rise to any occasion that required clear objective thinking, because he was too subjective, too narcissistic; O'Rourke lived in a weird Hollywood dreamworld and was striking poses all the time. That left Frankie La Barbara, the former mob knee-cracker from New York City.

"Well," said Lieutenant Breckenridge, "Private First Class Frankie La Barbara is the new acting platoon sergeant until further notice."

Everybody looked stunned, but nobody was more surprised than Frankie La Barbara himself.

"Why me?" he asked.

"I want to talk with you alone, La Barbara. Let's go into those woods over there and figure out what we're going to do."

Frankie frowned. "I don't want to be no fucking platoon sergeant."

"Let's go into those woods over there and talk about it."

"I got nothing to talk about," Frankie said. "Fuck you."

Lieutenant Breckenridge groaned. Already Frankie was giving him trouble. "I just gave you an order, La Barbara."

"Shove your orders up your ass."

"I'm going to tell you one more time to go into those woods over there, and if you refuse again, I'll just have to go over there and kick your worthless ass."

"You and who else?"

"Get into those woods over there."

"Fuck you where you breathe."

Lieutenant Breckenridge now realized he'd made a mistake. Frankie La Barbara could never be a platoon sergeant. But Lieutenant Breckenridge couldn't let Frankie make him back down.

110

"I just changed my mind," Lieutenant Breckenridge said. "Pfc. La Barbara is a fuck-up and could never make a platoon sergeant."

Frankie grinned. "I toldja."

"But I'm going to kick your fucking ass anyway."

"You are?"

"That's right."

"Don't make me laugh."

Lieutenant Breckenridge got to his feet. He knew he'd have to kick the shit out of Frankie La Barbara, otherwise Frankie wouldn't respect him and would argue every time Lieutenant Breckenridge gave an order. That defiance would spread among the other men, and the unit would lose its cohesiveness. They'd never make it back to safety if everybody did what he wanted to do.

Frankie looked up at Lieutenant Breckenridge. "You're not serious, are you, Lieutenant?"

"On your feet, fuck-up."

"Not me," Frankie La Barbara said, "because even if I win, I lose. If I kick your ass, I'll get court-martialed afterwards."

"No you won't. This is between you and me. Nobody else has to know. And besides, you couldn't kick my ass even if you had ten more fuck-ups just like yourself with you."

The right corner of Frankie's mouth turned up. "Oh, yeah?"

"Yeah."

"The bigger they come, the harder they fall," Frankie said, pushing his hands against the ground, getting to his feet.

The others pulled back to the edge of the clearing, to give Frankie La Barbara and Lieutenant Breckenridge some fighting room. Frankie unbuckled his cartridge belt and let it fall to the ground. Lieutenant Breckenridge rested his Thompson submachine gun against a tree. He raised his fists in the air.

"Let's go," he said. "No rules."

"No rules?" asked Frankie.

"That's right. Anything goes."

"Anything?"

"Anything."

"Suit yourself," Frankie said.

Frankie knew everybody was watching him, so he danced a bit on the balls of his feet to impress the other guys. He punched the air, threw his shoulders around, bobbed and weaved.

111

Lieutenant Breckenridge looked at Frankie through narrowed eyes, measuring him. He knew he was bigger and stronger than Frankie, but he also knew that Frankie was tough and mean, a skilled fighter. Frankie wouldn't have survived two years in the South Pacific if he weren't a skilled fighter.

Lieutenant Breckenridge advanced sideways, holding his right fist near his jaw and his left fist in front of his left shoulder. He knew he had to vanquish Frankie, otherwise he'd look like a fool. The men would never respect him again. He'd lose all credibility.

Frankie settled down and waited for Lieutenant Breckenridge to come within punching range. He hated officers and was happy for the opportunity to beat up on Lieutenant Breckenridge. He knew that Lieutenant Breckenridge was bigger and stronger, but he was the dirtier fighter. He'd even up the odds and clean up the jungle with Lieutenant Breckenridge.

"C'mon," he said to Lieutenant Breckenridge. "C'mon."

Lieutenant Breckenridge's arms were longer than Frankie's, and he now was within punching distance, but Frankie wasn't. Frankie realized he'd have to counter off Lieutenant Breckenridge's punches, bobbing and weaving so that he could get inside and do damage.

Frankie moved his head from side to side as he danced on his toes, holding his fists underneath his chin so he could protect his head. Lieutenant Breckenridge shot a jab to Frankie's face, and Frankie wiped it away with his left hand. Lieutenant Breckenridge threw another jab, and Frankie ducked underneath it, then danced two steps to the side and launched his own jab, connecting with Lieutenant Breckenridge's cheek, snapping his head back.

"How'd that feel?" Frankie asked, dancing from side to side.

"My grandmother hit me harder than that," Lieutenant Breckenridge replied.

Lieutenant Breckenridge jabbed Frankie's head again, and Frankie blocked the blow with both his hands, but Lieutenant Breckenridge followed with a right hook to Frankie's left kidney. Frankie couldn't get out of the way in time. The blow landed, and Lieutenant Breckenridge's fist sank into the soft meat that covered the sensitive organ. Frankie's face became a mask of pain, but he danced to the side and threw an overhand right at Lieutenant Breckenridge's head. Lieutenant Breckenridge ducked and Frankie's fist flew over Lieutenant Breckenridge's head. Lieutenant Breckenridge advanced and threw another hook to the same spot as before, connecting again with the soft meat. Frankie grunted, grabbed Lieutenant Breckenridge's head, and pulled it down, kneeing Lieutenant Breckenridge in the face.

Lieutenant Breckenridge was dazed for a moment, and Frankie saw his big chance. He lashed out with his foot to kick Lieutenant Breckenridge in the head, but Lieutenant Breckenridge wasn't that dazed, and twisted to the side, avoiding the blow.

Frankie danced backward, annoyed that his kick had done no damage. Lieutenant Breckenridge's mind cleared quickly, and now he was mad. He jabbed at Frankie's head, and Frankie blocked the punch with both his hands, then shot back a jab of his own, which hit Lieutenant Breckenridge on the nose, breaking the flesh inside. Blood trickled out of Lieutenant Breckenridge's nose, and Frankie was elated, because he thought he was winning.

Emboldened by the sight of blood, Frankie jabbed again, but Lieutenant Breckenridge moved his head to the side, slipping the punch. Frankie threw a right hook, but Lieutenant Breckenridge leaned backward and watched Frankie's hand fly past harmlessly. Frankie threw a left hook to Lieutenant Breckenridge's kidney, but Lieutenant Breckenridge caught the blow on his elbow.

Lieutenant Breckenridge took a step back and jabbed Frankie on the nose; a second later blood leaked out. Lieutenant Breckenridge jabbed again, mashing Frankie's lips against his teeth. Then Lieutenant Breckenridge threw an overhand right to follow up, but Frankie was already on the move, ducking and charging at the same time, hammering Lieutenant Breckenridge's right kidney with his left fist, hooking up to Lieutenant Breckenridge's head with his right fist, and then pummeling Lieutenant Breckenridge's stomach with a flurry of blows.

The punches hurt, but Lieutenant Breckenridge was tough. He hopped backward, and Frankie kept charging. Lieutenant Breckenridge timed him coming in and threw a hard uppercut that struck Frankie underneath his jaw.

Frankie went flying backward, and Lieutenant Breckenridge

lunged after him. Frankie kicked his left foot toward Lieutenant Breckenridge's stomach, and Lieutenant Breckenridge reached out, grabbing Frankie's ankle in both of his mighty hands. Frankie's kick was stopped in midair, and Frankie lost his balance. He fell backward, and Lieutenant Breckenridge pulled hard, yanking Frankie off from the ground.

Lieutenant Breckenridge spun to the side and swung Frankie through the air. He pivoted again and swung Frankie around. Continuing to pirouette, he whizzed Frankie through the air again and again. Frankie held out his arms, hoping to grab on to something solid, but nothing was there.

Frankie became dizzy. He knew he was in deep trouble. Lieutenant Breckenridge stepped to the side, took aim, and slammed Frankie's head against a thick jungle tree.

The collision was incredible. It was a miracle that Frankie's head didn't split wide open. Frankie was knocked out cold, and Lieutenant Breckenridge let him fall to the ground, where he lay in a clump at the base of the tree.

Lieutenant Breckenridge wiped his bloody nose with the back of his hand. "That's one down," he said. "Who's next?"

Nobody said a word.

"C'mon," Lieutenant Breckenridge said. "One of you guys must think you can whip me."

Nobody made a move.

"This is your big chance," Lieutenant Breckenridge said. "Kick my ass if you think you can do it."

Frankie La Barbara moaned at the base of the tree. The other soldiers crouched in the darkness, intimidated by Lieutenant Breckenridge, who spit blood onto the ground.

"Okay," Lieutenant Breckenridge said. "From now on I'm not taking any more baloney from you guys. From now on there'll be no more back talk. When I say go, I want you to go, and when I say shit, I want you to say how much, what color, and where. Is that clear?"

Nobody answered.

"I said is that clear?"

"Yes, sir," said Craig Delane.

"Uh-huh—you bet," said Private Victor Yabalonka.

"Yowza," said Morris Shilansky.

All the others indicated that everything was clear to them. Next to the tree, Frankie shook his head and pushed himself up from the ground. Lieutenant Breckenridge turned and walked to him. Frankie rolled around and sat heavily on the ground, resting his back against the tree, his mouth wide open, breathing hard. Lieutenant Breckenridge raised his foot and touched the toe of his combat boot to Frankie's nose.

"If I get any more trouble from you, I'll kick your god-damned head into horseshit," Lieutenant Breckenridge said. "Do you get my drift?"

Frankie didn't say anything. Blood dribbled out of his nose, and his mouth hung wide open as he looked up at Lieutenant Breckenridge.

"I just asked you a question," Lieutenant Breckenridge said.

"Fuck you," Frankie replied.

Lieutenant Breckenridge drew his combat boot back eight inches and then snapped it forward, connecting with Frankie's mouth, and Frankie La Barbara saw stars. The back of his head smacked against the tree and he saw more stars.

Frankie's surliness was making Lieutenant Breckenridge mad. He felt like kicking Frankie to death, and that became a greater temptation with every passing moment. Frankie was a rotten, stinking troublemaker who never did anything you told him and always talked back.

"I hate you," Lieutenant Breckenridge said. "I ought to fucking kill you."

"Go ahead," Frankie said. "I dare you."

Lieutenant Breckenridge felt a terrible pressure building up inside his head. He realized he should never have started fighting with Frankie, because now there'd be no end to it.

Frankie laughed, blood oozing from his split lip. "Go ahead," he said, taunting Lieutenant Breckenridge. "You don't have the guts to kill me, you big fucking lump."

The pressure grew hotter inside Lieutenant Breckenridge's head. His hands trembled and his heart pounded like a tom-tom. He hated Frankie with every fiber in his body. Frankie represented to him every vile antisocial, antihuman element in the world. Frankie was an ex-criminal, a bully, a liar, and a completely sleazy son of a bitch. He had no honor and no loyalty, and couldn't be trusted at all.

"What're you waiting for?" Frankie asked. "What're you afraid of?"

Lieutenant Breckenridge knew he'd be in hot water if he

killed Frankie. Somebody would rat on him sooner or later, and he'd be court-martialed. It would be ugly and disgraceful. They might drum him out of the Army, and that wouldn't be such a bad idea; but they also might put him before a firing squad.

Frankie spit onto the ground. "I always knew you didn't have any guts," he said. "I always figured you had piss in your blood."

Lieutenant Breckenridge clenched his teeth. "I'm going to kick your fucking head in," he said.

"Suck my dick," Frankie replied.

Lieutenant Breckenridge drew back his foot and kicked Frankie in the face with all his strength. Frankie couldn't get out of the way and received the blow on his nose, which was already bent out of shape, having been broken before. Now it was broken again. Frankie's lights went out and he sagged sideways to the ground.

Lieutenant Breckenridge looked down at Frankie. He felt a hand on his arm and turned around. It was Pfc. Gotbaum, the little roly-poly medic.

"Easy, now, sir," said Gotbaum. "Maybe you'd better sit down for a spell."

Lieutenant Breckenridge looked at his men and saw their eyes glowing at him in the darkness. He realized he'd gone a little too far. He should never have got into a fight with Frankie. He'd have to do something about his temper.

Pfc. Gotbaum knelt beside Frankie to check him out. Lieutenant Breckenridge wished he had a cigarette, but he didn't. He needed something to settle him down and thought of asking Pfc. Gotbaum for a pill.

"Have a drink," said Sergeant Snider.

Something struck Lieutenant Breckenridge in the gut, and he clutched it to him like a football. It was Sergeant Snider's canteen. Lieutenant Breckenridge unscrewed the lid, touched the lips to his mouth, and tilted his head back.

He expected water, but it was Sergeant Sniders' special white lightning, the same brew he concocted for Colonel Hutchins out of potato peels, coconut rinds, and anything else he could get his hands on. The white lightning burned all the way down Lieutenant Breckenridge's throat, warming his stomach and enlivening his mind. Lieutenant Breckenridge clicked his teeth and tossed the canteen back to Sergeant Snider.

"Thanks," he said.

Sergeant Snider nodded. Lieutenant Breckenridge sniffed the air. He looked up at the sky and could see no moon and no stars. There was no way he could get a fix on where he was. The only thing to do was move out quietly and try to break through the Japanese lines, but he didn't even know where the Japanese lines were. He had only a vague idea of where the American lines were. Turning around, he looked at Pfc. Gotbaum, who was examining Frankie La Barbara.

"How is he?" asked Lieutenant Breckenridge.

"Out cold."

"Good. The rest of you guys saddle up. We're moving out."

"What about Frankie?" Pfc. Gotbaum asked.

"We're going to leave him here," Lieutenant Breckenridge replied, "unless some damn fool wants to carry him."

"But, sir," said Gotbaum, "we can't just leave him here!"

"Why not?"

"Well . . ."

"Sure we can leave him here," Lieutenant Breckenridge declared. "He's nothing but a pain in the ass, always arguing whenever I give an order, constantly insubordinate. He's a detriment to all of us. We're better off without him."

Pfc. Morris Shilansky took a step forward. "The more men we got, the better," he said.

"You can carry him, Shilansky, if you want to."

"I'll do that, sir."

Lieutenant Breckenridge heard the resentment and rebellion in Shilansky's reply. *What've I got here, a mutiny?* Lieutenant Breckenridge asked himself. He turned toward Frankie La Barbara and felt the anger return. *That son of a bitch is screwing up my life. I hope the Japs shoot him.*

Then Lieutenant Breckenridge heard something and he froze. At first he thought it might be a normal jungle sound, such as branches rubbing against each other or leaves rustling in the breeze, but then he realized it wasn't an ordinary jungle sound. It was a gasoline or diesel engine coming closer.

"Uh-oh," said Pfc. Jimmy O'Rourke.

"What the hell's that?" asked Pfc. Morris Shilansky.

"Sounds like a motor boat," replied Private Victor Yabalonka.

Lieutenant Breckenridge turned his head. That was what it was—a motorboat. The Japs were patrolling the river, probably looking for them.

"Take cover!" he said.

The men scrambled through the jungle, finding depressions in the ground to lie in, or trees to hide behind. Pfc. Gotbaum dragged Frankie La Barbara behind a bush. The sound of the motor became louder. Lieutenant Breckenridge lay behind a log and cursed himself for getting into the big hassle with Frankie, because he'd neglected important business. He should have ordered somebody to hide their footprints in the mud on the riverbank after they'd come ashore, but instead he'd let the men rest awhile, and then the trouble had started with Frankie. He'd forgotten all about the footprints. He had never dreamed the Japs would send a motorboat to search for them.

The motor went *put-put-put*, reverberating through the jungle. In the distance the jungle became lighter, then dimmed again. *They've got a searchlight*, Lieutenant Breckenridge realized. He wiped blood off the end of his nose and wondered what to do. If he and his men turned tail and ran, would the Japs come after them? How many Japs were on that motorboat?

He looked down to the river, only twenty yards away, and figured out what to do. He'd go down close to the riverbank and take cover. If the Japs spotted the footprints on the riverbank and steered closer, he'd throw a grenade at the boat. Then they'd try to run for it. He wished Sergeant Cameron were alive to help out, but he wasn't.

"Pfc. O'Rourke!" he shouted.

"Yo!"

"C'mere, and the rest of you guys open fire at my command, but only at my command. Got it?"

The men rose up and moved through the jungle, finding positions of safety from which they could fire at the boat. Lieutenant Breckenridge pushed through the leaves and branches, making his way toward the opening in the jungle where he and his men had come ashore. Behind him came Pfc. Jimmy O'Rourke, holding an Arisaka rifle in both his hands. O'Rourke couldn't help thinking that the situation would be great in a war movie, with him starring as Lieutenant Breckenridge.

Lieutenant Breckenridge lay on the top of the incline that

led down to the river. A boulder was to his right and a tree to his left. Vines hung down from the foliage over his head, and a spider dropped onto his bare head; he smacked it with the palm of his hand and felt a sudden stinging sensation in his palm. He pointed to a spot a few feet away, and Jimmy O'Rourke got down. Lieutenant Breckenridge removed a US Army hand grenade from his lapel, and Jimmy O'Rourke did the same. They pinched the ends of the pins together so the pins could be pulled quickly.

A shaft of bright light shone around the bend in the river, illuminating the mists and gasses arising from the water. A fish jumped in the beam of light that swung from side to side, scanning the riverbank. Lieutenant Breckenridge knew who the Japs were looking for.

The sound of the boat's engine became louder, and then the boat came into view, an old, decrepit wooden vessel that the Japanese evidently had commandeered. Its outline reminded Lieutenant Breckenridge of American fishing boats. It was thirty or forty feet long, and Japanese soldiers were gathered on the deck. Lieutenant Breckenridge counted ten of them in the darkness and figured the boat probably carried twice that many.

The boat turned the bend and motored along with the current, its searchlight darting over the riverbank first on one side of the river, then the other side. Lieutenant Breckenridge wondered what the visibility would be like on the boat, and whether the Japanese would be able to see the footprints left by him and his men.

Again he cursed himself for not obliterating the footprints. Taking care of little details, or not taking care of them, could spell the difference between life and death. There was always something new to learn. His men were in trouble, and it was his own damn fault.

The boat motored nearer, moving more slowly than the river. Lieutenant Breckenridge realized it must have its engine in reverse, to slow it down. The engine had no muffler and made a horrendous racket. The boat's mast had been cut off, presumably to prevent it from being caught in the tops of the trees. The searchlight was mounted on the bow of the boat, and its halo illuminated the boat's hull, which had long streaks of rust running down its side.

The boat was so close, Lieutenant Breckenridge could see the faces of the Japanese soldiers standing near the searchlight, their faces glowing in the scattered light. The boat was being steered down the center of the river, and Lieutenant Breckenridge wished it would hit a submerged rock. The searchlight danced on the bank of the far side of the river, and Lieutenant Breckenridge hoped the Japanese soldiers were bored, losing interest in their mission. Sometimes on guard duty your eyes glazed over and you went into a trance. He hoped that was happening to the Japanese soldiers on the boat.

Then the beam of light emanating from the searchlight swept across the river, moving to the side where Lieutenant Breckenridge hid with his men. The boat was thirty yards upriver, and Lieutenant Breckenridge saw the searchlight make the riverbank as bright as day, then plunge it into darkness as it moved along.

The boat moved downriver quickly, and the searchlight flashed along the bank. It was approaching the spot where Lieutenant Breckenridge and his men had come ashore, and he gritted his teeth, hoping they wouldn't notice the footprints. The circle of bright light came closer to the spot, and Lieutenant Breckenridge held his breath. Sweeping along quickly, the circle of light landed on the spot where Lieutenant Breckenridge and his men had come ashore; then the light passed on. Lieutenant Breckenridge exhaled with relief. He'd made a mistake, but it didn't matter. The Japs hadn't spotted the footprints anyway.

But then suddenly the shaft of light jerked back to the spot, and Lieutenant Breckenridge's heart sank. He heard shouting on the boat, and the boat slowed in the current. Its stern swung toward the middle of the river and the boat pointed to the footprints on the shore. Lieutenant Breckenridge knew the Japs had seen the footprints. Now the only thing to do was fight. He and his men would have the element of surprise, but the Japs had superiority of numbers and probably even a machine gun on the boat.

Somebody on the boat shouted an order in Japanese. The searchlight rose up and the beam roved through the jungle. Lieutenant Breckenridge ducked his head and hoped his men had the good sense to do the same thing. He hoped the searchlight wouldn't reflect off a shiny bit of gunmetal or somebody's eyeballs.

The boat motored closer to the spot where Lieutenant Breckenridge and his men had come ashore. Lieutenant Breckenridge wondered whether to grenade the boat while it was still in the river or wait until it touched the riverbank. He'd have a better chance of hitting it if he waited, but there was such a thing as waiting too long.

He decided to try to disable the boat while it was still in the grip of the river's current. He raised his right hand, which held a grenade, and pulled the pin. Jimmy O'Rourke saw what he did and pulled the pin of his grenade too. Lieutenant Breckenridge swung his arm back and aimed for the searchlight on the bow of the boat. He took a deep breath and let the grenade fly. Jimmy O'Rourke threw his grenade a second later.

Lieutenant Breckenridge's grenade sailed into the shaft of light projected from the searchlight, and Japanese soldiers on the boat shouted hysterically. The grenade flew over the searchlight and bounced off the head of a Japanese soldier, stunning him. He dropped to his knees as other Japanese soldiers tried to grab the hand grenade, but it was dark and round. It rolled over the deck and then exploded, shredding the Japanese soldiers nearby and blowing a hole in the deck.

A few seconds later Jimmy O'Rourke's grenade exploded. It, too, had landed on the deck, but it rolled off and detonated near the waterline, ripping a two-foot gash in the hull. Water poured into the engine compartment. The Japanese officer in charge of the boat screamed orders. The Japanese machine gun opened fire, spraying the jungle with death. One of the first bullets hit Pfc. Gotbaum in the head, killing him instantly. The GIs raised themselves up bravely and returned the fire. Morris Shilansky shot out the searchlight. Frankie La Barbara hit the officer who was screaming. Craig Delane shot another Japanese soldier. Victor Yabalonka, who had a BAR, blew down a bunch of Japanese soldiers. Lieutenant Breckenridge threw another hand grenade, which landed on deck, in the midst of the Japanese soldiers there, blowing them to smithereens. A second grenade from Jimmy O'Rourke also landed on deck, blasting Japanese soldiers over the side.

The remaining Japanese soldiers on the boat didn't know

what to do. The attack had been sudden and their boat was sinking. There was no place to run and no place to hide. The only thing they could do was jump over the side, and the GIs shot them in midair. Some of the Japanese soldiers landed unscathed in the water, and the GIs fired at their bobbing heads, but visibility was poor and the Japanese soldiers were carried off by the swift current.

The boat turned around in the water, listing to the left. It went aground, and Lieutenant Breckenridge threw another hand grenade, which landed on the afterdeck, exploding and sending the steering wheel into the air. The current pulled the boat away from the shore and carried it downstream. The boat sank more deeply into the water and went aground again. The burgeoning current pushed it over the bottom, and it bounced over submerged rocks and debris, its deck and cabin awash, bumping and grinding toward the river's mouth and the sea beyond.

The current was swift, and the Japanese soldiers who'd survived the fight were on their way to the sea. There were five of them, and two couldn't swim. They drowned, but the other three made it ashore four hundred yards downstream of Lieutenant Breckenridge and his men.

EIGHT . . .

Lieutenant Breckenridge didn't know three Japs were four hundred yards away. All he knew was that he and his men had better get away from where they were as quickly as possible.

"All right, let's go!" he said as he stood. "Get ready to move out!"

Under ordinary circumstances he'd order Sergeant Cameron to tell the men what to do and Sergeant Cameron would follow up. But now there was no more Sergeant Cameron. Lieutenant Breckenridge would have to handle everything himself.

The GIs gathered around, waiting to be told which way to go. Lieutenant Breckenridge counted heads and discovered that somebody was missing. "Who's not here?" he asked.

"Gotbaum," Private Yabalonka replied. "He's dead."

"Where?"

"Over there." Yabalonka pointed toward shore.

Lieutenant Breckenridge moved in that direction and found Pfc. Gotbaum lying on his back, a neat hole between his eyes. Lieutenant Breckenridge didn't bother taking Gotbaum's pulse, because nobody could survive a shot in the head like that. He pulled Gotbaum's dog tags off his neck and stuffed them into his back pocket, then lifted the medicine bag off the ground and returned to the others. He tossed the bag at Shilansky.

"Carry that!"

Shilansky slung the bag over his shoulder.

"Everybody else all right?" Lieutenant Breckenridge asked.

Sergeant Snider raised his hand, showing the bloody handkerchief wrapped around his wrist. "My hand hurts."

Lieutenant Breckenridge looked at the others. "Anybody here know anything about being a medic?"

Nobody said anything.

"Jesus Christ," Lieutenant Breckenridge said, "I gotta do everything around here. Gimme the medicine bag back."

Shilansky threw it to him.

"Lay down," Lieutenant Breckenridge said to Sergeant Snider.

Sergeant Snider dropped to the ground and flattened himself out on his back. Lieutenant Breckenridge knelt beside him and untied the bloody bandage on Sergeant Snider's wrist. Lieutenant Breckenridge looked closely and could see blood oozing out. He sprinkled sulfa powder on, and then coagulant powder. The blood caked and stopped oozing.

"How's that?" Lieutenant Breckenridge asked.

"Still hurts," replied Sergeant Snider.

"I'll give you a shot."

"You sure you know what you're doing, sir?"

"I think so."

Lieutenant Breckenridge tied a fresh white bandage around the wrist and then took a morphine ampule out of the bag. He removed the covering and jabbed it into Sergeant Snider's arm.

"That ought to fix you right up," Lieutenant Breckenridge said.

"I hope it don't kill me."

"You're not that lucky. Lay there for a while."

Lieutenant Breckenridge looked up at the sky; clouds still covered the moon and stars. There was nothing he could get a fix on. All he could do was take out his map and make a rough estimate of where he thought he was. He put his finger on the spot and knew that if he moved in a general westerly direction, he should reach the American lines sooner or later.

He still had his compass and opened it up. The luminous dial glowed ethereally. Those tiny phosphorescent dots would keep him moving in the right direction when the river was out of sight, he hoped. The next decision to make was who would be the point man for the tiny unit.

It didn't take long to figure out. Pfc. Jimmy O'Rourke was the best woodsman of the lot. The ex−movie stuntman had been raised in the forests of northern California and had worked on ranches in Montana before going to Hollywood. O'Rourke wasn't sharp enough to be acting platoon sergeant, but he probably could be relied upon to do a good job as point man.

Lieutenant Breckenridge looked down at Sergeant Snider. "How's your hand?"

"Feels better."

"Think you can stand up?"

"Sure."

Lieutenant Breckenridge helped Sergeant Snider get to his feet. Sergeant Snider was a little woozy, and pinpoints of light appeared before his eyes. His wrist still hurt but the pain didn't bother him.

"I'm okay," he said.

Lieutenant Breckenridge tossed the medicine bag to Shilansky, then put his map and compass away. Looking around, he saw a narrow trail leading away from the clearing. It began at the open spot on the riverbank and headed inland. It had probably been used by natives in the years before war came to New Guinea.

"Everybody set to move out?" Lieutenant Breckenridge asked.

The men grunted or nodded. They were still wet and fatigued, and their morale was piss-poor. They knew they were in Jap-infested territory and couldn't be sure they'd get out alive.

"Okay," said Lieutenant Breckenridge, "move it out. O'Rourke, take the point."

"Me?" asked O'Rourke, surprised to have been chosen for the job.

"There aren't any other O'Rourkes around here, are they?"

"No, sir."

"Get the fuck going."

"Yes, sir."

O'Rourke ran forward, elated to be given such a responsible, crucial job. He felt as though he'd won something and that somebody should applaud. He imagined a camera crane swooping down at him from the treetops, taking his picture, recording his every move as he trotted along the narrow winding jungle trail. Stopping when he was twenty yards ahead of the other men, he unslung his M 1 rifle and held it in both his hands, slowing down to a walk, hunkering down and examining the jungle ahead of him, looking for Japs.

He wore a black mustache like Clark Gable and narrowed his eyes like Clark Gable, feeling heroic and handsome as he moved along the jungle trail. If he survived the war he knew he'd return to Hollywood and become a big star, because he had so much talent.

The cameras followed him as he crept along in the darkness. His makeup was perfect and the hair on his head was mussed; the hair on his chest was visible because his shirt was unbuttoned to the waist. Jimmy O'Rourke was always intensely aware of how he looked. It was very important for him to look right for his roles. You could never be sure when somebody might come along and discover you.

Farther back, Lieutenant Breckenridge led the nine men left in his command. He tried to keep Jimmy O'Rourke in sight, but sometimes the trail would twist and cause Jimmy to pass from his line of vision. The night was hot and humid, with insects chirping everywhere. Lieutenant Breckenridge's mind churned with speculation about where he was, where the American lines were, and whether there were Japs in the vicinity. He hoped Jimmy O'Rourke would see Japs before Japs saw him.

Behind Lieutenant Breckenridge, the rest of his platoon trudged through the jungle. Pfc. Frankie La Barbara looked at Lieutenant Breckenridge's back, feeling the strong temptation to shoot Lieutenant Breckenridge down.

Frankie La Barbara wasn't a good loser. Never in his life had he been graceful in defeat. He hated the people who'd beaten him, and often he'd exacted revenge in a multitude of sneaky shitty ways. Frankie La Barbara wasn't a nice guy. His nose was smeared all over his face and throbbed painfully. Every throb made him hate Lieutenant Breckenridge more.

But Frankie couldn't shoot him then and there. The other men would see what he was up to and stop him before he could pull the trigger. He'd have to bide his time and wait.

On top of that, Frankie didn't want to do something rash that might imperil his own life. Although he hated Lieutenant Breckenridge, he thought Lieutenant Breckenridge was a smart officer. Lieutenant Breckenridge might be able to get them all out of the mess they were in. If Lieutenant Breckenridge was killed, Frankie didn't know how they'd get back to their lines in one piece. A brawl would break out over who would command them, and they'd probably kill each other off.

Frankie felt nauseous and exhausted as he put one foot in front of the other and made his way over the trail. He hated the war, hated the Japs, hated Lieutenant Breckenridge. He even hated Butsko, although Butsko wasn't even around. Butsko had kicked Frankie's ass many times, and Frankie had wanted to kill Butsko, but he'd never been able to do it.

A bug flew toward Frankie out of the night and bit Frankie on the neck. Frankie slapped the bug, but it got away. Frankie's feet hurt and his boots were rotting apart. He had a case of crotch itch and was constipated. His stomach felt as though a ball of concrete the size of a grapefruit were lying in it, weighing him down. The bug bit him on the ear and Frankie slapped himself, but the bug got away again.

Frankie was frustrated and angry, and when he got that way he wanted to kill somebody or beat somebody up. He felt like punching somebody in the mouth, but that would be inappropriate then. Somehow he'd have to keep going and stay under control. He cursed the day he'd been drafted into the Army. He should have hid in somebody's cellar until the war was over.

At the rear of the formation Sergeant Snider reached for his canteen so he could drink the last of his white lightning. He had only a few swallows left, and there was no reason to save it. He unsnapped the canvas case and withdrew his canteen, gulping the remaining liquid down. It just took a few seconds, and then his canteen was empty.

But he felt better. He put his canteen back into its case and shrugged his shoulders, following the others into the jungle. Occasionally he staggered to one side or the other, but he always managed to right himself and stay on the path. He'd been a cook throughout most of his military career, and didn't know much about soldiering in the jungle, behind enemy lines. He didn't think they'd get out alive, but that didn't particularly

127

bother him. When he had a snootful of white lightning, nothing bothered him much.

Midway in the formation, Craig Delane carried an M 1 rifle slung over his shoulder and followed Victor Yabalonka. Craig Delane was a pessimistic, cynical young man, and he was sure he and the others would never make it back to safety. The odds were too much against them. He could understand why Lieutenant Breckenridge wanted to try to return to their lines, because Lieutenant Breckenridge was an officer and officers had to keep up appearances. Craig Delane was laboring under no such delusion. He felt like falling out at the side of the road and finding a place to sleep. He'd probably get killed anyway, so what was the difference? They'd probably have a better chance if they all split up anyway. Individually, on their own, they'd be less conspicuous than moving through the jungle together.

Delane wished he'd proposed that idea to Lieutenant Breckenridge, but he hadn't thought of it. Maybe he'd mention it at the next break. It annoyed Craig Delane that he always had his best brainstorms after it was too late to put them into effect. He thought he had a slow mind and that he wasn't as intelligent as he'd been before he'd been drafted into the Army.

The fucking Army's ruined me, he thought. *I can't even think straight anymore, and I'll probably get killed out here in the jungle before the sun comes up in the morning.*

The three Japanese soldiers who'd made it to shore sat cross-legged in a circle and tried to figure out what to do. They were in a tiny clearing surrounded by bushes, and their uniforms were soaking wet. They'd lost their hats, but each still had his Arisaka rifle.

"To begin with," said Pfc. Muguruma, "I think we must determine which one of us is in charge so that we can operate efficiently here." He turned to Pfc. Goto. "How long have you been a private first class?"

"Since March of 1942," Pfc. Goto replied.

"Ah. Then I am the senior man here, since we are the only two pfcs. I became a pfc. in 1940."

The others nodded. They accepted what he said because it was inconceivable that he would lie, and in fact he wasn't lying. He actually had been a private first class since September

128

of 1940, but the other two men thought Muguruma couldn't be much of a soldier if he hadn't made corporal in the nearly three years since he'd become a pfc.

They were right. Pfc. Muguruma was a dimwit with delusions of grandeur. He'd always wanted to be in charge of something, and now he had his big chance.

"Well," Pfc. Muguruma said proudly, a skinny little man with a long flimsy black mustache, "I think the only thing for us to do now is find out where those Americans have gone, and follow them."

"What for?" asked Private Kawasaki, only eighteen years old, who had graduated from high school at the top of his class only a bit more than a year earlier. "We don't know how many Americans are there. Perhaps there are a great many of them."

"He's right," said Pfc. Goto, a former farmer. "We might find ourselves in a fight that we will not be prepared for."

Pfc. Muguruma flared out his nostrils in anger. "Japanese soldiers are always prepared for battle," he said. "The mission of Japanese soldiers is to kill American soldiers. It does not matter if they outnumber us, because we have Japanese spirit and they don't. We will win in the end."

"I think," said Private Goto, "that we should try to find our way to one of our units and forget about the Americans."

Pfc. Muguruma scowled. "What a cowardly thing to say! What kind of soldier are you? Forget about the Americans? How can we forget about the Americans, when it is our duty to kill Americans?"

"I don't think we should undertake this mission by ourselves. I think we should find one of our units and take orders from whoever is in charge there."

"And let these Americans roam around behind our lines? You can't be serious, Goto."

"I am serious, Muguruma."

"Well, I am in charge here and I have made my final decision. We are going after the Americans." Pfc. Muguruma looked at his watch. "You have five minutes to get ready."

Private Kawasaki got up and walked behind a tree, where he took a piss. He'd been drafted and wasn't very enthusiastic about being a soldier. Moreover he was tired of taking orders either from men he considered crazy, like most officers and noncoms, or from men who were stupid, like Pfc. Muguruma. But there was nothing he could do about it. He was fatalistic and believed he'd be killed before long anyway.

He finished and returned to the little clearing. Pfc. Muguruma and Pfc. Goto watched him approach. They appeared ready to go. None of them had any food, because it had been thought that they'd eat with their units when they returned from the boat patrol.

"Are we all ready?" asked Pfc. Muguruma, puffing out his chest.

Pfc. Goto and Private Kawasaki muttered that they were ready.

"Follow me."

Pfc. Muguruma pushed into the jungle. A branch snapped back, striking him on the cheek, nearly putting out his eye, but he didn't cry out because he was a leader now and couldn't show pain or fear. He continued to bull his way through the thick foliage as branches scratched his face and arms. He was headed toward the last known positions of the Americans. He and the others had heard the Americans leave the area, so they didn't have to crawl on their bellies and be quiet. Pfc. Muguruma stepped over a log and steered around a big puddle. He ducked under a thick, low-hanging branch and then stepped on the head of a gigantic crocodile.

The crocodile had been asleep and now suddenly awoke. It was angry at having its rest disturbed, and saw figures above it in the darkness. Opening its mouth wide, it heard screams and confusion. It chomped its mouth shut on Pfc. Muguruma's leg and bit it off.

Pfc. Muguruma shrieked at the top of his lungs and hopped up and down on his one good leg while the stump of his other leg gushed blood. Pfc. Goto and Private Kawasaki fled in two different directions, and the crocodile whipped out its tail, lunging toward Pfc. Muguruma, opening its mouth and clamping it shut again on Pfc. Muguruma's other leg, severing it below the knee.

Pfc. Muguruma blacked out and fell into the bushes. A shot rang out, and blood spouted out of a hole in the crocodile's back. The crocodile hooted in pain and swished its tail and turning around, looking for somebody else to bite. Another

130

shot was fired, and a bullet pierced the crocodile's neck. A third bullet hit it in the tail, and a fourth bullet put a hole in its head.

The crocodile moaned and stopped moving. It was still alive, but not by much. Pfc. Goto approached the crocodile cautiously, a wisp of smoke trailing up from the barrel of his rifle. He aimed the rifle carefully and pulled the trigger, blowing off the top of the crocodile's cranium. The crocodile sighed, and that was the end of it.

"I think it's dead now," Pfc. Goto said.

"Are you sure?" asked Private Kawasaki.

"It's not moving."

"That doesn't mean it's dead. Maybe you should fire another shot."

"I'm not going to fire another shot. We shouldn't waste ammunition."

He turned toward the last known position of Pfc. Muguruma and moved in that direction. Pfc. Muguruma, minus both legs, lay in the bushes, a pool of blood underneath him. Pfc. Goto knelt and felt Pfc. Muguruma's pulse. There was none.

"I think he's dead," Pfc. Goto said.

"Nobody could live without two legs like that."

Pfc. Goto shook his head. "It's too bad."

"What'll we do now?"

"I don't know. What do you think?"

"I think we ought to try to find one of our units and report."

"That makes sense. Which way should we go?"

"I think we ought to cross the river," Private Kawasaki explained, "because Americans are on this side of the river, but there are no Americans on the other side of the river."

"I'm not crossing that river," Pfc. Goto said. "The current's too strong, and for all we know, there are crocodiles out there."

"That's right too."

"I think the best plan of action would be to find a trail and follow it until we come to one of our units. We hold this part of the jungle, I think."

"Maybe we should wait here and let one of our units find us."

"That might take too long. We don't have any food, and there are crocodiles in the area. I don't want to stay here."

131

Private Kawasaki recalled the horror of the crocodile biting off Pfc. Muguruma's legs. "Actually I do not wish to stay here either."

"Then let's go."

Pfc. Goto ducked low and walked into the bushes, pulling the branches away from his eyes with his hands. He examined the ground carefully because he didn't want to be crippled by a crocodile. The foliage was thick and he waded through, using the breaststroke. Private Kawasaki followed at a safe distance so that none of the branches would smack him in the mouth. Both soldiers were cautious, because they remembered what had happened to Pfc. Muguruma. Every log on the ground became a crocodile in their imaginations, and they circled them to make sure. Every branch appeared to be a snake. The river roared behind them, and visibility was poor. But no crocodiles or snakes attacked them, and after a while they came to a trail. Pfc. Goto looked both ways and they stepped out onto it, half expecting an American to shoot him.

No American shot him. Private Kawasaki joined him on the trail.

"This way," said Pfc. Goto pointing to the east.

"Are you sure our soldiers are in this direction?" Private Kawasaki asked.

"All this territory was taken in the attack this morning."

"Lead the way."

Pfc. Goto turned around and walked east on the trail, crouching over and holding his Arisaka rifle. Private Kawasaki followed him. Neither was much of a soldier, and they didn't bother to get down on their hands and knees to see if there were any footprints on the trail. If they had looked, they would have found many footprints, because this was the trail Lieutenant Breckenridge and his men were using.

Pfc. Goto and Private Kawasaki proceeded cautiously on the winding trail. They were only about a quarter of a mile behind Lieutenant Breckenridge and his men.

Sergeant Snider's legs were tired and his heart chugged in his chest. He was in terrible physical condition because he spent most of his time in mess tents, cooking and eating food and brewing and drinking white lightning. His chest heaved and his lungs were on fire. He couldn't keep up with the fast pace Lieutenant Breckenridge was setting, and fell behind the others. Mild alcohol withdrawal was afflicting him, and the morphine made him groggy. He didn't think he could go on.

He didn't even see the point of going on. What was the big rush? He wondered if maybe he could bug out. All he'd have to do was lag back and hide in the woods. Lieutenant Breckenridge and the others wouldn't even miss him. He'd find a comfy little spot in the jungle and lay low until the American army moved into the area in force. Then he'd come out and say "Hi, fellers, I was missing in action but you just found me."

Sergeant Snider slowed his pace even more and let the distance increase between him and the others. There was a bend in the road, and the others swung around it. Now they were out of sight completely. Sergeant Snider was all alone. With the silly grin of a drugged fool, he pushed his shoulder into the bushes, took a few steps, and sat down on the muck. A mosquito landed on his forehead and he slapped it away. Reaching into his shirt pocket, he took out a small bottle of citronella, poured some into the palms of his hands, and rubbed the foul-smelling stuff onto his face and neck.

Then he lay down in the muck and closed his eyes. It felt so good to rest. *Let the others knock themselves out*, he thought. *I'm just going to take it easy for a while. I'm a lover, not a fighter.*

He was thirsty, but his canteen was empty. He decided to take a short nap and then look for some water. He had halazone tablets in his cartridge belt, and they'd purify any water he found. Then he'd look for a place to hide.

He went limp on the ground. It wasn't long before he was sound asleep.

Lieutenant Breckenridge looked at his watch. It was nine-thirty in the evening. He heard an explosion in the distance; it sounded like a hand grenade. Then rifle shots reverberated across the jungle, followed by a machine gun. A fight had broken out someplace. Probably a patrol had been ambushed. The machine gun had the unmistakable chatter of a Japanese weapon, so evidently it was an American patrol that was receiving the fire.

Lieutenant Breckenridge turned around to see how his men

133

were doing. They were behind him in close formation, dragging their asses. It occurred to him that somebody was missing. He counted the men: There were only eight of them. Pfc. Jimmy O'Rourke, on the point, was number nine and he was ten. He'd left the riverbank with a total of eleven men, including himself. He raised his hand in the air.

"Hold it right here," he said. "Shilansky, run up ahead and get O'Rourke."

Shilansky raised his M 1 rifle and moved out on the double. Lieutenant Breckenridge looked the other men over.

"Sergeant Snider's missing," Lieutenant Breckenridge said. "Where the hell did he go?"

Nobody had an answer. Shilansky returned with Pfc. Jimmy O'Rourke.

"Whatsa matter?" asked Jimmy O'Rourke.

"Sergeant Snider's missing."

"What happened to him?"

"I don't know."

Lieutenant Breckenridge wondered what to do. He didn't think he had time to go back and look for Sergeant Snider, but didn't want to leave him behind either. What had happened to Sergeant Snider? Lieutenant Breckenridge knew that Japs hadn't got him, otherwise there would have been noise. The only possibility was that Sergeant Snider had fallen out by himself. He must have got tired. He was an older man with a big fat belly, and he couldn't keep up the pace.

He reached his decision. He couldn't jeopardize the safety of nine men for one. He'd let his men take a short break, and then they'd get moving again.

"Okay, take ten," he said to his men.

"What're we gonna do about Sergeant Snider?" asked Pfc. Jimmy O'Rourke.

"We're going to forget about him," Lieutenant Breckenridge replied. "We don't have time to go back. From here on in, any man who can't keep up with the rest of us will be left behind. Is that clear?"

The men nodded and grunted as they sprawled around on the jungle. They closed their eyes, some fell asleep immediately. Lieutenant Breckenridge sat with his back against a tree and took a drink from his canteen. He would have liked to bivouac all night in the area, but didn't dare take the chance.

He thought it very possible that Japanese soldiers would be dispatched to follow him and his men, once the Japs found out that their patrol boat had been demolished.

Not far behind Lieutenant Breckenridge and his men, Pfc. Goto and Private Kawasaki moved through the jungle, peering from side to side, very unsure of themselves. They'd never been alone in a combat zone without officers and NCOs around, and their training had never emphasized personal initiative.

"It seems to me," Private Kawasaki said, "that we should have found one of our units by now. Do you think we may be lost?"

Pfc. Goto slowed down. "I don't know. Do you?"

Private Kawasaki stopped. "Maybe."

Pfc. Goto stopped and faced Private Kawasaki. "Perhaps we should retrace our steps."

"What good would that do?"

"We could go back to the river and work our way along the shore until we reach our positions there."

"That would be awfully difficult to do," Private Kawasaki pointed out. "There is a tremendous growth of foliage along the riverbank, which would impede our movement."

Pfc. Goto wrinkled his brow. He knew Private Kawasaki was right and wondered which way to go. So did Private Kawasaki. They both stood in the middle of the trail, trying to think, when suddenly they heard a noise that startled them.

It sounded like a snarl of a ferocious wild animal, and the two Japanese soldiers were frozen with fear. They held their rifles tightly and turned in the direction of the sound, afraid of what they might see.

The sound came to them again, and this time it didn't seem so frightening. Pfc. Goto and Private Kawasaki turned to each other in amazement, because the sound was a snore! Someone was sleeping nearby!

Pfc. Goto and Private Kawasaki didn't know whether the person snoring was Japanese or American. If the person was Japanese, all their problems would be over; but if he was American, there might be other Americans in the area as well.

"Let's get out of here!" Private Kawasaki whispered.

"But it might be one of our units in the vicinity."

"One of our units would have a guard!"

"So would the Americans."

"I'm leaving," said Private Kawasaki.

"Coward!" replied Pfc. Goto.

"Who are you calling a coward!"

"You!"

Japanese soldiers didn't like to be called cowards, because to them nothing in the world was lower than a coward. Even a relatively nonaggressive person like Private Kawasaki didn't want to be called a coward, and as the two Japanese soldiers quarreled they didn't realize the snoring had stopped.

The person who had been snoring was Sergeant Snider, and he'd just been awakened by the voices of the Japanese soldiers and the shuffling of their feet on the gravel of the path. Sergeant Snider's instincts were dull, but not that dull. He narrowed his eyes and looked at the Japanese soldiers only a few feet away from him.

Sergeant Snider didn't know two important facts. The first was that he'd been snoring, and the second was that the Japanese soldiers had heard him snoring. He'd just awakened suddenly to find two Japanese soldiers nearby, having an argument.

If I just lie here quietly, Sergeant Snider thought, *they won't even know I'm here.*

Meanwhile the two Japanese soldiers continued their discussion. "I'm going to see who's there," Pfc. Goto said. "I am senior in rank here, and I am ordering you to come with me."

"But he's not even snoring anymore!"

Pfc. Goto wrinkled his brow as he realized that Private Kawasaki was right. He wondered if the person who'd been snoring had awakened. If so, the person was probably watching Pfc. Goto and Private Kawasaki at that very moment!

"Get down!" said Pfc. Goto.

Both Japanese soldiers dropped to their bellies on the path, turning and pointing their rifles in the direction of Sergeant Snider, whose hair stood on end. Now at last he knew the Japs were aware of his presence in the bushes nearby. His hands shaking, he reached for a grenade on his lapel.

"Something's moving in there!" Private Kawasaki shouted.

"Who's there?" demanded Pfc. Goto.

Sergeant Snider didn't understand Japanese, but he knew he was in trouble. He pulled the pin of the grenade, but it wouldn't come loose. He hadn't thrown a hand grenade since basic training at Fort Campbell ten years ago, and forgot that pins don't come out easily. Pfc. Goto raised his rifle to his shoulder and fired a shot in Sergeant Snider's direction. The flash, the muzzle blast, and the bullet slapping into the muck next to Sergeant Snider's elbow scared the shit out of him, and he dropped the grenade.

Then Private Kawasaki fired his rifle, and Pfc. Goto pulled his trigger again. One bullet whistled over Sergeant Snider's head and the other hit the ground a few inches in front of his face. He scrambled to pick up the hand grenade.

"I can hear him moving in there!" Private Kawasaki shouted.

"Charge!" screamed Pfc. Goto.

The Japanese soldiers jumped to their feet. Sergeant Snider scooped up the hand grenade, grabbed the ring fastened to the pin, and pulled with all his strength. The pin came loose.

"Banzai!" hollered Pfc. Goto.

The two Japanese soldiers charged into the bushes beside the road. Sergeant Snider's hands shook violently as he chucked the hand grenade at the two Japanese soldiers, but it was a bad move. Sergeant Snider wasn't a combat soldier and didn't know what the right move would have been.

The hand grenade bounced off Pfc. Goto's stomach and fell to the ground. Pfc. Goto was so excited, he barely felt the grenade touch his stomach and ran right over it. Private Kawasaki was beside Pfc. Goto and fired his rifle into the bushes, squinting his eyes, looking for whatever was there.

"I see him!" Pfc. Kawasaki yelled as he aimed his rifle from the waist and shot down at Sergeant Snider.

The bullet hit Sergeant Snider in the shoulder. Pfc. Goto saw Sergeant Snider and pulled the trigger of his rifle. That bullet smashed into Sergeant Snider's big buttock.

The hand grenade exploded five feet behind Pfc. Goto and Private Kawasaki, flinging them into the air like rag dolls. Shrapnel tore into their bodies, and they were dead before they hit the ground. They landed on either side of Sergeant Snider, who was unconscious and hadn't even heard the grenade go off.

Although he was unconscious, Sergeant Snider was not quite dead. Blood oozed out of his bullet wounds, and bugs landed on the blood to drink it up. Crickets chirped, and a rat poked its head out of a hole to see what all the excitement had been about. That part of the jungle returned to normal, as if no human beings had been fighting each other to the death only a few moments before.

Lieutenant Breckenridge jerked his head around when he heard the first shot. He looked backward on the trail as the next shots were fired, and then came the grenade explosion.

"What the hell was *that?*" said Frankie La Barbara.

"I think we'd better get out of here," Lieutenant Breckenridge replied. "O'Rourke, take the point!"

Nobody argued, because the shots and explosion hadn't been very far away. The GIs didn't want any trouble. O'Rourke ran forward to take the point and the other men got to their feet, slinging their rifles, adjusting their cartridge belts. All were bareheaded, having lost their hats and helmets when the truck plunged into the Driniumor. Lieutenant Breckenridge looked back along the trail. There were no more shots or explosions. He wondered what had happened back there. It occurred to him that maybe Sergeant Snider had been involved in it, but he had more important things to worry about.

Lieutenant Breckenridge faced front again. Jimmy O'Rourke should be where he was supposed to be. "Move it out!" Lieutenant Breckenridge said to the others.

They hooked their thumbs under the slings of their rifles and shuffled down the trail, wondering if they'd ever get out of the mess they were in.

NINE . . .

"Sir?" said Major Cobb in the darkness.

Colonel Hutchins opened his eyes. "What is it?"

"Bad news, I'm afraid. Maybe I'd better put the light on."

Major Cobb flicked his Ronson lighter and set aflame the wick of the kerosene lamp on Colonel Hutchins's desk. Colonel Hutchins sat up on his cot and swung his feet around to the ground. The interior of the tent became bathed in soft yellow light. Colonel Hutchins reached for the package of Chesterfield cigarettes on the little ammo box beside his cot. He wore only khaki skivvie shorts, and the skin on his belly and legs was as pale as the belly of a fish. Major Cobb flicked his Ronson again and lit Colonel Hutchins' cigarette, and Colonel Hutchins took a drag, filling up his lungs, and then he exhaled.

"Well?" he asked.

Major Cobb sat on one of the folding chairs in front of the desk and moved the chair around so he'd face Colonel Hutchins. "It's about that patrol you sent out earlier in the night. Evidently the Japs got them."

"How do you know that?" Colonel Hutchins asked.

"Well, it seems that a listening post from M Company heard

139

something going on near the barbed wire. A few soldiers went out to see what it was, and they found four heads. One of them was the head of Lieutenant Porter, and the others were the men he took with him."

"Shit," said Colonel Hutchins.

"The Japs cut off their heads and threw them over the barbed wire. It was a pretty gruesome sight, I'm told."

"Them fucking Japs. They're lower than savages."

"At least we know that no-man's-land is crawling with Japs."

"Nah, we don't know that," Colonel Hutchins said. "A more experienced patrol might've gone out and come back without any trouble." He looked up at Major Cobb. "You always criticized my recon platoon. You used to say they were a bunch of criminals and troublemakers and that I should disband them, but they always came back from patrols with good, hard information. Of course, some of them didn't make it back sometimes, but in general their patrols were successful. I wish I still had them."

"Lieutenant Porter was a very fine officer," Major Cobb said. "He had a very good record."

"Maybe his record was too good. Maybe that's why he's dead. I tell you, Cobb, the kind of people you want for a good reconnaissance platoon aren't necessarily the kind of people who are good soldiers in other ways, and soldiers like Lieutenant Porter, who are good in ordinary situations, aren't worth a shit in the dark in no-man's-land. I wish Butsko was here."

There was silence in the tent. Colonel Hutchins smoked his cigarette and thought of Lieutenant Porter, the nice, upstanding Mormon who'd won a battlefield commission. *One hour you're alive and the next hour you're dead. That's war.*

"Well," said Colonel Hutchins, "I'm gonna need me a recon platoon. When things settle down, I want you to meet with Major Stevens, the personnel officer, and comb military records for the most ornery, stubborn, rotten sons of bitches in the regiment. They'll be the new recon platoon."

"But, sir, we already pulled all those men for the old recon platoon. I don't think there are any left."

"Then I'll go to the nearest stockade to get them."

"I don't know," Major Cobb said shaking his head in dismay. "I think you could build a good recon platoon out of men who aren't criminals. Lieutenant Porter and his men might have run into an unusual situation that even Butsko couldn't have handled. We shouldn't shoot all the dogs just because a few of them have fleas. We have a lot of good soldiers in this regiment. Why don't you let me send out another patrol?"

Colonel Hutchins inhaled his cigarette and thought about what Major Cobb was saying. Colonel Hutchins decided that maybe he was being unreasonable and that Major Cobb was right. Just because one patrol of good, ordinary soldiers didn't come back, it didn't mean all of them would fail.

"All right," Colonel Hutchins said, "you've convinced me. Send out another patrol, just like the last one: twenty men split up into groups of five. We'll see what happens, all right?"

"Yes, sir."

Major Cobb stood and headed toward the exit. He pushed aside the tent flap and was gone. Colonel Hutchins sat on the edge of the cot and puffed his cigarette. Fatigued and still heavily medicated, his mind fell into macabre thoughts. He found himself wondering about Lieutenant Porter's head. *What happens to a head that doesn't have a body attached? Do the Graves Registry people send the head back to the soldier's family in the States? Or do they just list the soldier as missing in action?*

Colonel Hutchins shook his head. *War is a fucking nightmare,* he thought as he stood and stumbled across the ground toward the kerosene lantern so he could snuff it out and go back to bed.

Lieutenant Breckenridge looked up at the sky and saw patches of stars. That meant the weather was clearing. The sun might even shine tomorrow. But the sky still wasn't clear enough for him to see any important stars that would enable him to determine whether he was headed in the right direction.

He looked around. The jungle was a shade lighter. Behind him he heard the boots of his men as they slogged through puddles and patches of mud. Crickets chirped and fireflies danced among the branches. Clouds of insects surrounded the men, peeling off like fighter planes on a strafing run, coming in close to bite the men and suck up delicious red blood.

Lieutenant Breckenridge smacked bugs on his arms and

neck. He looked at his watch: It was nearly midnight. His men had been on the move for an hour and a half. Maybe it was time to give them a break.

He raised his hand. "All right, take ten! La Barbara, go up ahead and tell O'Rourke to get his ass back here."

Frankie La Barbara opened his mouth to say "Fuck you," but his vocal cords wouldn't warble and the words didn't come out. He knew that if he said "Fuck you," Lieutenant Breckenridge would charge him and there'd be another brutal, bloody fight. Frankie La Barbara didn't feel up to another brutal, bloody fight. His nose was extremely tender, and he didn't even want to touch it, never mind punch it.

However, he just couldn't follow the order without at least a minimum show of defiance. So he looked at Lieutenant Breckenridge and hesitated for a moment, to show Lieutenant Breckenridge that Frankie La Barbara wasn't a pushover. Frankie La Barbara wanted everybody to know that he didn't take any shit from anybody and that he'd just decided to cooperate with Lieutenant Breckenridge because he wanted to, not because he felt that he had to.

He unslung his rifle and jogged over the trail, feeling pain in his ribs where Lieutenant Breckenridge had slammed him. The air was humid and smelled of rotting vegetation. Mosquitoes buzzed past his ear. In the darkness the forest looked eerie and foreboding, like a bad dream. He turned the bend in the road and saw O'Rourke up ahead. O'Rourke stopped and turned around when he heard Frankie approach.

"What's going on?" O'Rourke asked.

"Lieutenant Asshole wants you back there."

"What for?"

"How should I know?"

Jimmy O'Rourke walked back on the trail, but Frankie didn't move.

"Aren't you coming?" O'Rourke asked.

"I gotta take a piss. I'll be back in a few moments."

Jimmy O'Rourke disappeared around the bend. Frankie La Barbara stepped into the jungle to take a piss. Nobody had to tell him not to piss beside the road, because he knew some smart Jap might come along, smell the piss, and start thinking that maybe GIs had been in the area recently. Frankie had been on many patrols and understood the basic precautions.

He raised his hands and pushed branches away from his face as he plodded into the jungle. The foliage was extremely thick, and he had to duck to get underneath a stretch of it. Then he straightened up and took a few more steps. *This is far enough from the road,* he figured. *No Jap would ever come here.*

He took out his dork and let the liquid flow, thinking of how nice and peaceful it was in the jungle. It was as if he'd walked away from the war. It occurred to him that a man could get lost in the jungle of New Guinea and no one would ever find him. All he'd have to do was find an inaccessible spot that no one would ever want to explore, similar to the spot he was in just then.

At that moment the moon came out, bathing the jungle in a warm yellow glow. Frankie looked up at the sky and saw a half-moon through a break in the clouds. It made the jungle appear enchanted, like an illustration in a book of fairy tales.

Jesus, Frankie thought, *maybe I shouldn't go back. Maybe I should just stay here in the jungle and hide. I'll live off the land, and when the Army takes over this part of New Guinea, I'll come out and say "Hi, guys, it's me—Frankie La Barbara." What're they gonna do, court-martial me? I'll just say I got lost.*

Frankie buttoned his fatigue pants and wiped his nose with the back of his hand. He wished he had a cigarette to smoke. He also wished he had something to eat, like a nice Coney Island hot dog with french fries. *Should I do it?* he asked himself.

He looked around at the jungle. A bug bit him on the neck. Clouds passed in front of the moon, plunging the jungle into darkness. Frankie's visibility became greatly reduced. A whole battalion of Japanese soldiers might be three feet away and he'd never see them. Frankie began to wonder if going AWOL in the jungle was such a good idea. Maybe it would be better to stay with the other guys. There was safety in numbers. Suddenly, Frankie didn't feel so confident about being alone in the jungle. What if he fell asleep and woke up next to a snake?

Frankie returned to the road and walked back toward the others. He was glad to be out of the jungle, because it had been scary in there when it suddenly got dark. He walked stealthily along the road, and when he rounded the bend he stopped, because he saw Lieutenant Breckenridge's back in front of him.

Lieutenant Breckenridge was sitting on the ground, not more than ten yards away, and evidently he hadn't heard Frankie La Barbara's approach. Frankie thought that all he had to do was raise his rifle and shoot Lieutenant Breckenridge in the back, but a moment later he rejected the idea. He'd have to put a round into the chamber of his M 1, and Lieutenant Breckenridge would hear that. Maybe some other time.

Frankie walked back among the other men and sat down. Lieutenant Breckenridge looked at his watch. "Saddle up," he said.

"But I just got here," Frankie complained.

"I said take *ten* and I meant take *ten*," Lieutenant Breckenridge replied. "Nobody told you to take a vacation in the jungle."

"But I had to take a piss."

"Too fucking bad. On your feet, gentlemen. O'Rourke, take the point."

The GIs got up, and some of them stretched. They milled around and waited for O'Rourke to reach his position.

"Let's go," Lieutenant Breckenridge said.

He stepped out with his left foot, and the other men followed him over the narrow trail that wound its way through the hot, smelly jungle.

Twenty yards in front of the others, Pfc. Jimmy O'Rourke felt like a star. Every time Lieutenant Breckenridge said "O'Rourke, take the point," his chest filled with pride. He felt important, needed, necessary. The whole bunch of them were depending on him. He felt that at last he'd won a leading role in a major production.

He walked in a crouch, holding his M 1 rifle at port arms, and his eyes roved back and forth over the jungle, darting to the treetops to detect the possible movements of snipers while his ears listened for unusual sounds. Pfc. Jimmy O'Rourke wanted to do a good job, because that's what leading roles called for. The hero of a movie was the most incredible person in the movie. He always did the right thing and never did the wrong thing.

144

Suddenly he heard a sound in the distance and stopped suddenly. The sound had been faint, and he'd barely detected it above the ordinary sounds of the jungle, but he'd heard it: a metallic sound like the ones commonly heard in bivouacs where there was so much military equipment lying around. It could be somebody closing the bolt of a rifle, or a mortar being stacked on top of another mortar, or maybe a shell being loaded into the chamber of a howitzer.

Jimmy O'Rourke dropped to one knee. He turned around and saw the others catching up with him, moving cautiously because they knew he'd seen or heard something. Lieutenant Breckenridge knelt beside him.

"What is it?" he asked.

"I heard something out there."

"What?"

"I don't know exactly, but it wasn't a natural jungle sound. It was more like a rifle or something like that."

"How close?"

"Not very close."

"Tell me in yards."

"A few hundred yards."

Lieutenant Breckenridge wondered what to do next. He'd thought that if he followed that trail far enough, he might get back to his own lines. For all he knew, the sound Jimmy O'Rourke heard had come from the American lines, but it might have come from Japs also. Somebody would have to go forward to check it out, but who?

Lieutenant Breckenridge didn't feel as though he could rely on Jimmy O'Rourke or anybody he had with him. There was only one person he could rely upon, and that was himself.

"I'm going ahead to see what's there," Lieutenant Breckenridge said. "You guys hide in the bushes around here and be quiet. If I don't come back in an hour, it'll mean the Japs got me and you're on your own. Everybody understand that?"

Nobody said anything. Lieutenant Breckenridge assumed they understood.

"Okay, get in the bushes," he said. "Stay together, but keep your mouths shut."

The men moved into the bushes on the right side of the road, and Lieutenant Breckenridge stepped forward, setting his feet down on the ground softly. He didn't want to make any

145

unnecessary sound, because the area might be infested with Japs. He held his Thompson submachine gun in both his hands and searched the trail ahead for enemy soldiers. Minutes passed, and the distance increased between him and his men. Soon he was on his own, moving silently over the muddy trail, his eyes bouncing around in their sockets, his ears straining for the sounds that Jimmy O'Rourke had reported.

Then he heard something that sounded like a piece of wood being struck against the trunk of a tree, and he stopped, moving his head from side to side, trying to home in on the noise. The jungle became silent again, so he advanced. After several paces he heard another sound, this one metallic, like the hatch on the turret of a tank being battened down.

The sounds were in the distance, a few hundred yards away, as Jimmy O'Rourke had indicated. It was clear that a bivouac was there, but was it American or Japanese? Lieutenant Breckenridge wished he could hear voices, because that would give him the answer.

The only thing to do was get closer so he could hear or see better. He'd have to be careful, because the bivouac would have stationary guards and he'd be on the move. They'd most likely see him before he saw them. *Maybe I'd better get off the road and go the rest of the way in the jungle,* he thought.

He realized it would take him a long time to reach the bivouac via the jungle, and he'd make more noise that way. Maybe the best thing to do would be to hide in the woods with his men and wait to see what might happen. If he was in Jap territory, the American army would take it over sooner or later, and if he was in American territory, all he had to do was wait until they saw some other GIs.

Yes, that's what I'll do, he thought. He turned around and walked back down the road to where his men were, then cut into the jungle. He found them lying around in the weeds.

"See anything?" asked Jimmy O'Rourke.

Lieutenant Breckenridge knelt down. "No, but I heard a few things. There's a bivouac up ahead, but I don't know if it's ours or the Japs'. If it's the Japs', we'll have to stay clear of them. I think we'd better hide out for a while. Sooner or later our people will come this way, and then we'll be okay. I think we'd better move deeper into the jungle, and then I'll look around for a safe place. Let's go."

146

Just then, as the last word passed his lips, he heard something.

"Wait a minute," he whispered.

Silently he lay on his stomach. The sound came from the trail and consisted of footsteps. A fairly substantial group of people was moving on the trail from the bivouac up ahead toward the Driniumor. All the GIs could hear it, and they flattened out on the ground.

"I'm going to see whether they're ours or theirs," Lieutenant Breckenridge whispered. "Don't make a sound while I'm gone."

Lieutenant Breckenridge crept through the underbrush, heading toward the road. He wanted to get close enough so that he could see who was coming, but not so close that they'd see him. Stopping, he parted some leaves with his fingers and looked at the road. The footsteps drew closer. He hoped American GIs would come into view. Then he and his men would be safe. They'd be able to smoke cigarettes and have a decent meal. The tension and fear would be over. Ordinarily, Lieutenant Breckenridge wasn't a religious man, but he gritted his teeth and prayed that the soldiers would be American.

The footsteps became closer. Lieutenant Breckenridge peered to the right and saw figures moving in a single file on the road. It was too dark to see what kind of uniforms they wore. He held the leaves away from his line of vision and strained his eyes. The soldiers trudged toward him, and then he noticed the funny peaked caps and leggings on the soldiers. His heart sank as he realized they were Japanese. Now he knew for sure that he was behind enemy lines.

The Japanese soldiers came abreast of him and walked by. He was tempted to throw a hand grenade at them, but then he'd have every Jap in the vicinity chasing after him. He moved the leaves in front of his face so the Japanese soldiers wouldn't notice him lying there. The Japanese soldiers passed him; he counted twenty of them. He waited until their footsteps receded into the distance, then turned around and crawled back to his men.

"I guess you know by now that they were Japs," he said to them, "because if they weren't Japs, I would've said something to them. Okay, now we know for sure where we are and what we've got to do. Let's move deeper into the jungle and find a good place to hide."

• • •

It was a half hour later, and Lieutenant Breckenridge was alone in the jungle, looking for a permanent place for him and his men to set up camp. He'd left them behind in a little clearing a safe distance from the trail, and he hoped they wouldn't get into any trouble. He knew that was asking for a lot, because they were a nasty, quarrelsome bunch. They couldn't do anything right.

Lieutenant Breckenridge crept through the jungle, and suddenly it brightened. The half-moon had come out again. Lieutenant Breckenridge looked up and saw the iridescent semicircle floating in the sky, wisps of clouds blown past its surface by the wind.

It was a beautiful sight, and it forced Lieutenant Breckenridge to pause. The night sky was like heaven, and the earth like hell. Lieutenant Breckenridge couldn't suppress the wish that he could live up there in the sky somehow instead of in the New Guinea jungle, which was full of bugs, Japs, snakes, and dozens of terrible tropical diseases.

He lowered his gaze and saw a hill not far away. He hadn't noticed it in the darkness, but now he could see it quite well in the moonlight. It was rocky and lined with ridges, a good place to hole up. There might even be a cave up there. It wasn't too high and could be scaled easily. He thought he'd check it out since it was so close.

He pushed through bushes and vines. His left leg sank into muck up to his knee and made him fall forward, nearly breaking his leg, the same leg that had been wounded earlier. He pulled his leg out and resumed his trek toward the hill. The moon became covered by clouds again, and he walked into a huge spider web that covered his face. The spider bit him on the forehead, and he squashed the spider with the palm of his hand. Then he picked the web off his eyebrows and lips, but it fragmented and he didn't want to take the time necessary to get all of it off his face.

He ducked underneath a branch and kept going. Finally he reached the base of the hill and climbed up its side. It was steep, and stretches of smooth rock made progress difficult. He had to search for toeholds and handholds, ascending a few feet at a time. He reached a ridge and rested for a few moments

148

while looking down. The more he thought about it, the more he thought the hill would be a good place for him and his men to hide. It would be easy to defend, and he couldn't imagine why Japs would ever want to climb it in the first place. The Japs would never know that he and his men were on top of it.

Having caught his breath, he continued to climb. He skinned his knees and bruised his fingers as he advanced up the side of the hill. Near the summit he came to another ridge and an opening that looked like the mouth of a cave. He tiptoed toward the cave and saw that the opening was about five feet tall and four feet wide. He was tempted to go inside, but thought he should look at the top of the hill first.

He climbed around the side of the cave and made his way to the top of the hill. It was a plateau covered with boulders, and a few hardy trees grew out of cracks in the rock. Lieutenant Breckenridge was pleased. It was an excellent place to hide out, and when the sun came up, the visibility should be good. He could send Jimmy O'Rourke up one of the trees to look around. Perhaps Jimmy O'Rourke could see where the Japs weren't, so all of them could return to their own lines.

Lieutenant Breckenridge decided to go back and see what that cave was like. He slid down the side of the hill and landed on the ridge next to the cave. Unslinging his submachine gun, he rammed a round in the chamber, because he didn't know what kind of toothed creature might be living in the cave. He wished he had a flashlight to shine inside, but his only source of light was his trusty old Zippo cigarette lighter.

He ducked his head and stepped inside the cave. It smelled musty and old, but there was also a peculiar additional odor like raw wood alcohol or medicine. He thought that maybe a peculiar chemical reaction inside the cave was causing the odor—maybe a small mineral spring or decaying limestone.

Something moved inside the cave and he stopped suddenly, dropping down to one knee. Was it a rat back there or a fucking Jap? Lieutenant Breckenridge wanted to make sure. Holding his submachine gun in his hands, he walked in a crouch to the side of the cave and stood, pressing his back against the wall. He took out his Zippo, flicked off the top part of the case, and spun the wheel. Sparks erupted and then the wick caught flame. Shadows danced against the walls of the cave, and then he saw something big move deeper inside the cave.

149

He ducked down just as a bullet was fired. He saw the muzzle blast, and the bullet struck the rock where his head had been.

Then a voice came to him from inside the cave. *"Hold your fire!"* it said, and Lieutenant Breckenridge's hair stood on end, because it was a *female* voice! *"He's one of ours!"* the voice added.

Lieutenant Breckenridge blinked. *"Who the hell's back there?"* he shouted, holding his submachine gun ready.

"American nurses!"

"Well, I'll be damned," Lieutenant Breckenridge said.

A kerosene lantern was lit back in the cave, and Lieutenant Breckenridge saw four figures in Army fatigues rise from behind boulders and crags. They advanced toward Lieutenant Breckenridge, one of them carrying the kerosene lantern, and he walked toward them.

The nurse carrying the lantern had short, curly brown hair and a chubby figure. She was in her late thirties at least. The nurse to her left was tall and skinny, with pinched features and a long pointy nose. The nurse to the right of the one with a lantern was petite and Italian-looking, sort of cute. The other nurse had short straight blond hair and looked like a washed-out ex-showgirl.

"You're lucky we didn't shoot you," said the nurse with the lantern.

"You're lucky I didn't throw a hand grenade," Lieutenant Breckenridge replied. "What the hell are you doing here?"

"We got ourselves surrounded when the Japs took over this area, and we managed to find this place to hide in. What are you doing here?"

"Some of my men and I got surrounded also, and we're trying to find our way back to our lines."

"Well," said the nurse with the lantern, "this area is crawling with Japs. I don't know how you're going to make it through."

"Maybe my men and I'll have to hide up here with you." He grinned. "By the way, I'm Lieutenant Dale Breckenridge from the Twenty-third Regiment."

"I'm Captain Doris Stearns from the Eighty-first Division Medical Headquarters, and this is Lieutenant McCaffrey, Lieutenant Jones, and Lieutenant Pagano."

"Hi," said Lieutenant Breckenridge.

The women said hello. Lieutenant Breckenridge looked them over and couldn't help making a few sexual judgments, despite the dilemma all of them were in. Captain Stearns and Lieutenant Jones were pooches, but Lieutenant Pagano and Lieutenant McCaffrey, the one who looked like a faded ex-showgirl, weren't so bad.

"My men and I have had some bad scrapes," Lieutenant Breckenridge said, snapping back into his official mode. "In fact, I've only got eight men left out of a platoon that numbered forty men two days ago, and I've also picked up a few stragglers from other units along the way. We need someplace to hide out, and this looks like a good place. We also could use some medical attention."

Lieutenant McCaffrey, the blonde who looked like a faded ex-showgirl, stared at Lieutenant Breckenridge's leg. "That bandage should be changed."

"You can change it when I return with the others. I hope you've got medicine here."

"We do," said Captain Stearns, "and we've got food and water too. Our headquarters was near here."

"I'll be right back with my men. Make sure you don't bring that lantern too close to the mouth of the cave, otherwise you'll have every Jap in the territory climbing this hill."

"No Japs have noticed us yet," Captain Stearns said. "We know what to do."

"Glad to hear that," Lieutenant Breckenridge said. "Be back in a little while."

Lieutenant Breckenridge turned and walked toward the mouth of the cave, stepped onto the ridge, and moved out of sight.

TEN . . .

Lieutenant Breckenridge thought he'd be real slick. He decided to sneak up on his men to see if they were sleeping without having posted a guard. Butsko used to do that all the time, with good results. He kept the men on their toes. Lieutenant Breckenridge crawled through the underbrush, approaching the place where he'd left his men. He moved slowly and carefully, because that was the only way to move silently.

Finally he reached a point where he knew his men were only a few feet away. They were quiet, and he thought that part was good. But they'd better have somebody awake. If they didn't, he'd really get tough with them. They had to learn to take care of themselves when he wasn't around.

He reached forward to part the leaves in front of him so he could look at his men. Holding one branch in one hand and another branch in his other hand, he pulled the foliage apart. Just then the moon came out again, illuminating the tiny clearing where he'd left his men, and Lieutenant Breckenridge saw eight gun barrels pointing at his nose.

He smiled. "Glad to see you're all alert."

"You're lucky you're still alive," said Shilansky.

"That's right," agreed Pfc. Craig Delane. "I was just about to squeeze off a round."

Lieutenant Breckenridge pushed his way through the bushes and rose to one knee. He realized he'd just had a close call. "Okay," he said, "I've just found us a good place to hide, but there's just one problem: Somebody's already there."

"Japs?" asked Private Yabalonka.

"No," replied Lieutenant Breckenridge. "Nurses."

"Our nurses?" asked Frankie La Barbara.

"Yes, from division headquarters. They got trapped behind enemy lines like we did."

"No shit!" said Corporal Froelich, the signalman from Headquarters Company.

"No shit," replied Lieutenant Breckenridge.

"How many of them?" asked Frankie La Barbara.

"Four."

Frankie La Barbara scratched his balls. "Whatta they look like?"

"What does that have to do with anything?"

"I just wanna know."

"You'll find out when we get there, and when we get there, I don't want any trouble. Keep your fucking hands off the nurses. Got it?"

"What if they wanna put their hands on us?" asked Shilansky, licking his full lips.

"Who'd want to put their hands on you?"

"You'd be surprised."

"That kind of surprise I'm not interested in. Okay, let's saddle up, gentlemen."

"Holy shit!" Frankie La Barbara said excitedly. *"Cunt!"*

"Keep your voice down, you stupid son of a bitch," Lieutenant Breckenridge said. "I'll take the point, since I'm the only one who knows where we're going. O'Rourke, you take charge of the others."

"Yes, sir."

Frankie didn't like that decision. "Why him?"

"Why not him?" replied Lieutenant Breckenridge. "Are you volunteering for the job?"

"I don't volunteer for anything," Frankie La Barbara replied.

"Then keep your mouth shut." Lieutenant Breckenridge looked around. "Everybody ready? Okay, let me get a head start on the rest of you."

Lieutenant Breckenridge turned sideways and pushed into the foliage. High up in the sky, the clouds covered the moon once more.

The four nurses lay around the cave in the darkness, each full of her own thoughts. They were glad they'd have soldiers to protect them, but on the other hand, they knew problems could develop. They were afraid the men might get a little out of control. Horny men sometimes went over the line that divided ordinary sexual advances from outright rape.

A scraping sound came to them from the cliff outside.

"This must be them," said Captain Stearns. "McCaffrey, go take a look."

Lieutenant Beverly McCaffrey, the blond nurse who was perhaps a little too pretty for her own good, crawled to the mouth of the cave and looked down, holding an M 1 carbine in her small, delicate hands. She was tall and slim underneath her baggy fatigues, and her long, languid curves didn't show. Squinting her blue eyes, she saw Lieutenant Breckenridge climbing the cliff, and below him was a group of other men.

"It's them," she said.

"You're sure it's not Japs?" asked Captain Stearns.

"I'm sure."

Lieutenant McCaffrey returned to the rear section of the cave, next to the crate of medicine and crate of C rations they'd brought with them. She sat on a blanket beside her friend, Dorothy Pagano, and lit a cigarette in the darkness. Lieutenant McCaffrey was from Missouri, and Lieutenant Pagano was from River Rouge, near Detroit. Captain Stearns was from California, and Lieutenant Laura Jones from Connecticut.

Lieutenant Breckenridge entered the cave and brushed himself off. "I'm back," he said. "The others will be here in a few moments." He saw somebody smoking in the rear of the cave. "Anybody got an extra cigarette by any chance?"

All the women said yes at the same time. Lieutenant Breckenridge homed in on the voice of Lieutenant McCaffrey and knelt down beside her. She held out her package of Camels and he took it in the darkness, their fingers touching. Lieutenant Breckenridge placed a cigarette in his mouth and lit it with his Zippo, then handed back the pack.

"Thanks," he said.

"You're welcome."

They heard a crunch at the mouth of the cave, and Frankie La Barbara climbed in, peering back into the darkness, scratching his balls. "Where is everybody?" he asked.

"Back here," replied Lieutenant Breckenridge.

Holding out his arms so he wouldn't bump into something, Frankie La Barbara moved toward the back of the cave. He hadn't even seen any of the nurses yet, but he already had a hard-on. Jimmy O'Rourke and the Reverend Billie Jones appeared at the mouth of the cave next, followed by Victor Yabalonka and then the rest of the men. Frankie La Barbara sat down next to Captain Stearns, barely able to see her features.

"Hi," he said.

"Hello," she replied pleasantly.

Her voice sounded nice. His hard-on got harder. He wondered how he could get her alone and stick his dick between her legs.

"We're back here," Lieutenant Breckenridge said to the men who were arriving.

The GIs shuffled across the floor of the cave, thoughts of romance fluttering through their minds. Lieutenant Pagano lit the lantern in the back corner of the cave and turned the wick low so the light wouldn't carry outside. Morris Shilansky sat next to her and winked. She smiled faintly, because she was used to GIs flirting with her.

Captain Stearns looked the men over. "I'd say that some of you need medical treatment," she said.

Frankie La Barbara inched away from Captain Stearns. Her voice had been pretty, but she wasn't a very attractive woman. His dick shriveled up in his filthy fatigue pants.

"What's wrong with your nose, soldier?" she asked.

"My nose?" Frankie asked.

"Yes. Is it broken?"

"I'm pretty sure it is, and this isn't the first time either."

"You'd better let me look at it."

Frankie would have preferred to let one of the other nurses

look at his nose, but it was too late for that now. "Should I lie down?" he asked.

"Yes—right here will be fine."

Frankie lay down. Nearby, Lieutenant Pagano examined the cut on Morris Shilansky's shoulder. Lieutenant Jones peeled the dirty bandage off Victor Yabalonka's chest. Lieutenant Breckenridge sat with his back against the wall of the cave, and Lieutenant McCaffrey touched the bandage on his leg with her long, dainty fingers.

"That hurt?" she asked.

"A little."

"It's going to hurt a lot when I take the bandage off. Would you like to get a shot first?"

"No."

"A tough guy, huh?"

"Yep."

"Hang on to something."

Lieutenant Breckenridge balled up his fists on the ground beside his legs and clenched his jaw. Lieutenant McCaffrey took the edge of the bandage in her fingers, inhaled, and pulled with all her strength. Lieutenant Breckenridge was barely able to suppress the scream that threatened to explode out of his throat. The bandage came off, revealing a big ugly red gash. Blood oozed up and out of the wound.

"It's not infected," Lieutenant McCaffrey said. "You're lucky."

"*Ouch!*" yelled Frankie La Barbara.

Lieutenant Breckenridge jerked his head around. "Shut up over there, you stupid son of a bitch!"

Frankie touched his fingers to his nose. Captain Stearns had just removed the bandage from his nose, and it felt as though someone had rammed a burning spear into his head.

"Sorry," said Frankie.

"It's my fault," Captain Stearns said. "I didn't realize it was so tender there."

Lieutenant Breckenridge took a deep breath. "Listen, folks, we have to bear in mind at all times that we're behind enemy lines and have to be quiet. It's not likely that Japs are nearby, but you never know."

Lieutenant Jones, the pinch-faced nurse, looked at him.

"Everything was quiet here until you guys showed up."

Everything's going to be quiet again," Lieutenant Breckenridge replied. "I personally guarantee it. You hear that, gentlemen?"

"Yeah," replied Frankie La Barbara and all the others.

"Good."

Lieutenant Breckenridge closed his eyes as Lieutenant McCaffrey poured sulfa powder onto his open wound.

Lieutenant Breckenridge's warning came too late. Down in the jungle near the base of the hill, Corporal Kozo Tsukuda of the Imperial Japanese army was reconoittering the area for the possible placement of a field howitzer. He heard Frankie La Barbara's shout and stopped in his tracks, looking around, wondering what was going on. Then he heard other voices speaking in the English language.

Corporal Tsukuda looked up and saw the hill. All was quiet now, but that was where the voices had come from. American soldiers were up there, evidently. He decided to break off his reconnaissance and return to headquarters to report the incident to his superiors.

He looked around for landmarks so that he could return to the area. Then he headed toward the road as fast as his legs would carry him.

ELEVEN . . .

"Sir?" said Major Cobb.

Colonel Hutchins opened his eyes. "What is it?"

"One of the patrols is back, sir. Would you like to speak with Sergeant Plunkett?"

"What time is it?" Colonel Hutchins asked.

"Nearly midnight."

Colonel Hutchins realized that the patrols had been gone for more than three hours. All of them should have been back.

"No word at all from the others?" asked Colonel Hutchins.

"No, sir."

"What does Plunkett have to say?"

"He said he ran into Japanese fortifications about a hundred yards from our front lines. He tried to work around them, but he just kept running into more fortifications and Japanese troops. Finally he returned."

"That's basically his report?" Colonel Hutchins asked.

"Yes, sir."

"I don't think I have to speak with him. Relay the information to General Hawkins."

"Yes, sir."

"Wake me if any of those other patrols come back."

"Yes, sir."

Major Cobb walked out of the dark tent area. Colonel Hutchins rolled over and fell back asleep.

At division headquarters General Hawkins wasn't sleeping. He sat behind his desk, drinking coffee and studying maps, worrying about the attack that would begin in just a few more hours.

He knew that his entire career was on the line. He'd fucked up the day before, and if he fucked up again, he'd be relieved of command. There were no two ways about it. He'd become one of those pathetic officers you see in Washington, pushing papers around in a dark corner office someplace.

He couldn't let that happen. He was the son of a general and the grandson of another general. Tremendous pressure was on him to succeed and live up to the proud traditions of his family. He actually thought that death would be preferable to failure.

He wished he could go out and lead the attack personally, because the sight of a fighting general inspired the men. MacArthur did it all the time when he was a division commander in the First World War, and he'd become one of the most famous American officers in the Army as a result.

But General Hawkins had to stay in his headquarters and move pins around on maps. He had to make sound military decisions and anticipate what the enemy would do. He couldn't make any mistakes whatever, because he knew General Hall would be watching him like a hawk.

General MacWhitter pushed aside the tent flap and showed his head. "Busy?" he asked.

"What's going on?" General Hawkins replied.

"Reports from patrols have been coming in. The Japs are lined up in strength in front of us."

"That's good," General Hawkins replied. "Our artillery will blow them to shit."

"I know," said General MacWhitter, sauntering into the office, "but we don't know how much depth the Japs have in their defense."

"Not much, I don't think. It's my opinion that they've just

160

got a thin crust out there, and they're tired. We shouldn't have much trouble."

General MacWhitter shrugged. "I hope you're right," he said.

Lieutenant Breckenridge sat near the mouth of the cave, peering down at the jungle below. The moon was shining and few clouds were left in the sky. The weather was clearing, and that meant the US Air Corps would be able to fly in the morning. Lieutenant Breckenridge hoped the American planes would bomb and strafe the Japs ferociously and kill them all.

His eyes roved back and forth over the jungle. He'd elected to take the second tour of guard duty himself, so his men could get more sleep. Jimmy O'Rourke had taken the first tour and hadn't reported anything. Lieutenant Breckenridge didn't expect any trouble, because he didn't think the Japs had any idea that Americans were hiding out in the area.

He heard footsteps deeper in the cave and turned around. It was Lieutenant McCaffrey approaching. "I have to go to the latrine," she said, a little embarassed.

"Be careful."

She climbed out of the cave and walked to the area on the leeward side of the mountain, where she and the other nurses had set up their latrine. Insects sang love songs all around her as she took down her pants and squatted over the stinky, smelly hole in the ground. The breeze rustled leaves around her, and she looked up at the moon in the sky. Something clumped on the ground in the distance behind her, but she assumed it was just another jungle sound. She picked up her pants, fastened the buckle, and walked back to the cave.

Meanwhile, inside the cave, Frankie La Barbara approached Lieutenant Breckenridge.

"I gotta take a piss," Frankie said in a whisper.

"Wait," Lieutenant Breckenridge replied, also in a whisper.

"What for?"

"Because somebody's out there."

"Somebody's out there?" Frankie asked. "Oh, I didn't know that."

"The hell you didn't."

"Whataya talkin' about?"

161

"You know very well what I'm talking about, you lowlife."

Frankie looked deeply wounded. "You got me wrong, Lieutenant Breckenridge. I really don't know what you're talking about."

"You weren't following that nurse out to the latrine, right?"

Frankie stuck his thumb into his chest. "Me?"

"Sit down and shut up. I'm tired of talking to you."

Frankie didn't sit down, but he did shut up. The expression on his face suggested that he was unjustly accused by Lieutenant Breckenridge, even though Frankie knew Lieutenant Breckenridge was right. Frankie had intended to follow the pretty blond nurse out to the latrine and maybe put his hand into her drawers. If nothing else, maybe he could have snuck a peek at her while she was doing her business.

Lieutenant McCaffrey returned, throwing her long leg over the natural barricade at the opening of the cave. Lieutenant Breckenridge turned to Frankie.

"You can go now."

Frankie didn't reply. He still pretended that Lieutenant Breckenridge had made an unfair accusation. He passed Lieutenant McCaffrey without saying anything and climbed out of the cave.

"What's wrong with him?" Lieutenant McCaffrey asked.

"He's an imbecile," Lieutenant Breckenridge replied.

"How's your leg?"

"It's okay."

"Is any blood showing on the bandage?"

"I haven't noticed."

"Let me see."

She knelt down beside him and brought her eyes close to the bandage, because the light wasn't good.

"It looks like we stopped the bleeding," she said.

"I didn't stop it; you did."

She looked back toward the section of the cave where everybody was sleeping. He examined her profile in the moonlight and decided she had nice features. If it weren't for the lines of fatigue in her face and the bags under her eyes, she'd probably be quite pretty.

"Mind if I smoke a cigarette here?" she asked.

"Just stay down so the lit end can't be seen."

She dropped down on her stomach so that her face would

162

be below the wall at the opening of the cave, then took out a cigarette and lit it up. She filled up her lungs with smoke and blew it into the air.

"I'm exhausted," she said, "but I can't sleep. I don't know what's the matter with me."

"Why don't you take one of your pills?"

"Because then I'll be even worse the next day."

"You're probably a little tense because of where you are. We'll all be out of here pretty soon."

"Do you really think so?" she asked.

"Sure. This ground belonged to our side, and our people will come back before long and take it back. They might even attack this morning—who knows?"

"I hope they do. I don't like this at all."

"Neither do I. Say, have you got another cigarette?"

"Sure."

She reached into her shirt pocket and took out her pack of Chesterfields, holding them out to him. He picked out a cigarette, placed it between his lips, and lowered his head so he could light it. He flicked the wheel of his Zippo, and the sparks shone in her eyes. He touched the flame to the end of the cigarette and looked at her face, deciding that she really was quite pretty. Their eyes met and a silent, intimate communication passed between them that was so subtle they doubted it really had taken place.

He closed his cigarette lighter and dropped it into his pocket. Her face was shadowy in the moonlight.

"Well," he said, "maybe if we get out of this mess alive, we can go to a movie together sometime or have a drink or something."

"Maybe," she replied. "But first we've got to get out of this mess alive."

Frankie La Barbara didn't have any trouble finding the latrine. All he had to do was follow the stink. He shuffled over the rocky ridgeline, furious at Lieutenant Breckenridge for foiling his plan. *That son of a bitch would have to be on guard,* he thought. *If it weren't for him, I could be putting it to that blond bitch right now.*

I just know she wants me, Frankie told himself. *I could see it in her eyes. When she went outside she knew I'd follow her.*

She wanted me to stick my pepperoni up her ass, but that fucking Lieutenant Breckenridge had to mess everything up. I hate that son of a bitch. Someday I'm going to kill him.

Frankie arrived at the latrine, its contents glistening in the moonlight. A swarm of flies arose to meet him. He waved them away from his face and spit them off his lips. He really didn't have to take a piss, but since he was there, he thought he might as well drain his vein anyway.

He whipped it out and proceeded to pour his waste liquids into the hole. The foul odor rose to his nostrils and he wrinkled his nose. He looked around, brushing flies away from his face with his free hand.

The jungle below was illuminated by the half-moon in the sky. He thought he saw something move on the edge of the cliff, but he told himself that he must be mistaken. His eyes were playing tricks on him. Nobody could be climbing up the side of the cliff, right? He finished taking his leak and buttoned his fly, gazing in the direction of the movement he thought he'd seen. At infantry advanced basic training at Fort Ord, California, they'd taught him never to look directly at the object he wanted to see in the night, but to look slightly to the left or right of it. That was because the center of the retina saw during the day, but the edges of the retina saw during the night.

Frankie thought he perceived something like a head bob up and down at the edge of the cliff. Then he saw another one. Were they boulders coming into his vision and fading away? That could be the answer, because night vision was tricky. Too many latent images glowed on the retina.

Frankie was enough of a combat soldier to know he'd better check out the images to be sure. Maybe his eyes weren't playing tricks on him. Maybe Japs were climbing up the hill, although he figured that was unlikely. Why would Japs want to climb up the hill? There were no Japs in the area anyway.

Unslinging his M 1 rifle, Frankie stalked toward the edge of the cliff. He realized it would make sense for Japs to come that way if they wanted to attack the cave. The Japs would approach the cave on its flank, instead of head-on.

He drew closer to the edge of the cliff but couldn't see anything moving now. He smiled, because he realized he'd been seeing things. There was no point going all the way to check, and he paused, turning back toward the cave.

He stopped. Something told him he ought to go to the edge of the cliff and look down to be sure. Perhaps Japs were clinging to the side of the cliff, where he couldn't see them. He thought he might as well go all the way to make certain. If Japs were there, he'd better get ready for them.

Frankie thought he was being overly cautious and silly, but he knew from bitter combat experience that it was better to be overly cautious and silly than to be dead. If Japs were climbing the side of a cliff, the best way to get them would be with a hand grenade.

Frankie felt ridiculous as he crouched down and pulled a grenade from his lapel. There were no Japs on the side of the cliff; yet, he felt as though he had to go through the motions. He pinched together the ends of the pin so it would come out easily, and then he thought, *Fuck it, I'll pull the pin and hold the lever in, to really be on the safe side*.

He pulled the pin and stepped softly toward the edge of the cliff, the grenade ready to explode in his right hand except for the arming lever, which he held down. He carried the pin in his left hand, because he was sure he'd have to replace it as soon as he looked down the cliff and saw nobody there.

Silently he moved toward the edge of the cliff. He raised his size-ten-and-a-half combat boots slowly and brought them down as if they were feathers. Closer he came to the edge of the cliff. It was only a few feet down now, and he bent forward, but couldn't see anything.

He took the last step and leaned over the edge. His eyes goggled out at the sight of a Japanese soldier pointing a pistol directly up at him! Frankie leaned back, and the pistol fired. The bullet soared past Frankie's face and came so close he could feel its heat. He turned the lever loose on the hand grenade and it popped away as he dived to the side. He rolled over as he hit the ground, then rolled over again as a bullet ricocheted off the rock where he'd been. Then he stopped and rolled the grenade toward the heads of the Japanese soldiers sprouting up all over the edge of the cliff.

The Japanese soldier with the pistol fired at Frankie again. The bullet struck the ledge directly in front of Frankie, blowing rock splinters into his face, bringing forth dots of blood. Then the hand grenade exploded a few feet behind the Japanese soldier with the pistol, at about the level of his ankles. The blast plastered the Japanese soldiers in the vicinity against the cliff and filled their bodies with scraps of shrapnel. Four Japanese soldiers were killed instantly, and five were wounded severely. The wounded ones relaxed their hands and rolled down the side of the hill.

Frankie leaped to his feet and ran in a zigzag toward the mouth of the cave. *"Japs!"* he screamed. *"Watch out!"*

He carried his M 1 rifle in his right hand and plunged into the mouth of the cave, sailing over the heads of all his buddies and all the nurses, who were assembled there. Landing on his stomach, he scrambled around and faced the front of the cave.

Everybody looked at him. He looked back at them. The eyes of the nurses were full of terror.

"Where are they?" asked Lieutenant Breckenridge.

"They were coming up the side of the hill near the latrine! I got a bunch of them with a grenade, but I don't know how many more are there!"

Lieutenant Breckenridge realized the Japs were trying to assault the cave from the side. The only thing to do was fight the Japs from inside the cave. There was no rear entrance, and he and the others were trapped like rats. Sooner or later the Japs would lob a hand grenade into the cave, and that would be the end of the road for him and the others.

"Well," Lieutenant Breckenridge said, "all we can to is try to hold them off as best we can. We have room for five men here at the front of the cave. The rest of you stay back and throw out any hand grenades that land in here. I want La Barbara, Yabalonka, O'Rourke, and Shilansky to man the front of the cave with me. Let's go!"

The four men Lieutenant Breckenridge named took positions at the front of the cave, while the rest lagged back. Captain Stearns told the nurses to get their medicine and bandages ready in case somebody got wounded. The nurses crawled to the rear of the cave to prepare the materials. Lieutenant Breckenridge felt naked without a steel helmet on top of his head. He was reluctant to raise his head and take a look, but it had to be done.

He raised his head and looked outside, then ducked quickly. He'd seen nothing, and no one had fired at him, so he felt emboldened to take a longer look. Raising his head again, he squinted and tried to see Japanese soldiers, but couldn't spot

166

any. He poked his head out of the cave to examine his right flank, and didn't see anything there either. Then he turned to the left. No Japs could be seen from that direction. He ducked down behind the natural rock barricade.

"Can't see them," he said, "but that doesn't mean they're not there."

A second after the last word was out of his mouth, a machine gun opened fire in the jungle below, and bullets ricocheted off the roof of the cave. The nurses in back of the cave dived to the ground as bullets whistled over their heads. The machine gun in the jungle lowered its sights, and the bullets ripped into the rock barricade. Other bullets flew over the barricade and bounced off the rear walls at the rear of the cave.

Lieutenant Breckenridge held his head low and clicked his teeth in anger. He had no way to put the machine gun out of commission except by backing it down with his Thompson submachine gun and Yabalonka's BAR, but he couldn't afford to waste the bullets, and he wouldn't be able to silence the Japanese machine gun for long anyway.

"Listen to me," he said to the others. "Keep your heads down and wait until they get close. Then we'll stop them."

Frankie La Barbara snorted cynically. "For how long?" he asked.

"As long as we've got bullets," Lieutenant Breckenridge replied.

The Japanese machine gun continued to fire in bursts, and its bullets whacked into the stone wall in front of the cave or ricocheted off the ceiling and walls inside the cave. The GIs and nurses lay on the floor, and everybody was scared, but not so much that they couldn't function or think straight.

The combat veterans knew pretty much what to expect, because they'd all attacked Japanese bunkers at one time or another and knew the scenario. The first step was to pin down the people inside with machine-gun fire, as the Japs were doing then. The second step was to assault the bunker from the sides. The machine gun would stop firing when the Japs got close to the mouth of the cave, and then the Japs would try to throw grenades into the cave. The GIs were glad the Japanese army didn't have flame throwers, because it was better to be blown up than roasted alive, if you had to make the choice.

TWELVE . . .

"Sir?" said Major Cobb.

"I'm awake," replied Colonel Hutchins, lying on his cot.

"It's oh-three-thirty hours."

"Light the lamp on my desk, will you Cobb?"

Major Cobb walked to the tent and lit the wick of the lamp with the flame from his Ronson. Colonel Hutchins reached for his shirt on the chair beside his cot and took out his pack of Camels. Major Cobb rushed toward him with his lighter. Colonel Hutchins took his first nicotine puff of the day, and it made him dizzy.

"Those other three patrols come back?" Colonel Hutchins asked as the light in the kerosene lamp made shadows flicker on the walls.

"No, sir."

"I guess we'll have to presume that they were killed out there."

"We've heard sporadic gunfire throughout the night. You can hear some right now."

Colonel Hutchins yawned. "Where is my old recon platoon, now that I really need it? See if you can scare me up a cup of coffee, will you, Cobb?"

"I'll tell Lieutenant Harper, sir."

Major Cobb walked out of the tent. Colonel Hutchins stood and put on his pants, the cigarette dangling out of his mouth. He walked barefoot to his desk and sat down, pulling out the top drawer. His bottle of GI gin was there, and he unscrewed the top, taking a big swig.

The GI gin warmed him up and banished the shitty morning taste from his mouth. He screwed the top back on the bottle and closed the drawer. On top of his desk was the map of the Eighty-first Division's location and the territory in front of it. At four-thirty the artillery bombardment was supposed to begin, and Colonel Hutchins wanted to visit his front line, to make sure his men were ready for the attack that would follow the bombardment.

Lieutenant Harper marched into the office, carrying the cup of coffee. "Good morning, sir."

"What's so good about it? Wake up Bombasino and tell him to bring my jeep around. I'm going to troop the line, and you're coming with me."

"Yes, sir. Should I bring you some breakfast?"

"Yes, and you'd better get something to eat too. It's going to be a long morning."

The machine-gun fire stopped.

"Now!" screamed Lieutenant Breckenridge.

He and the others rose up and looked around for Japs, but they couldn't see any in front of them. Lieutenant Breckenridge leaned out of the cave and aimed his submachine gun to the right. Something moved and he saw an object flying through the air at him. He jumped up and caught it with his right hand, then threw it with all his strength and ducked behind the wall.

The grenade exploded thunderously, and shrapnel cut into the rock that surrounded the front of the cave. Lieutenant Breckenridge raised his head and saw Japanese soldiers attacking the cave from both sides, and then a bunch of Japanese soldiers jumped down from the part of the hill above the cave, landing directly in front of the opening.

"Banzai!" screamed the Japanese soldiers.

Lieutenant Breckenrdige opened fire with his Thompson submachine gun, and Victor Yabalonka pulled the trigger of his BAR. The other GIs fired their M 1 rifles, and the Japanese

170

soldiers fell before the hail of bullets. The GIs maintained their fire, blowing the Japs away, but more Japs continued to charge. Two of them threw hand grenades that sailed over the heads of the GIs behind the front wall of the cave.

Farther back, the Reverend Billie Jones caught one of them and threw it out of the cave. At the same time Craig Delane caught the other and hurled it back. Everybody hit the deck. A Japanese soldier leaped over the barricade, and the two grenades detonated almost simultaneously, shredding the Japanese soldiers in the vicinity.

The Japanese soldier landed inside the cave, carrying his rifle and bayonet, and the first thing he saw was the light-complected face of Lieutenant Susan McCaffrey farther back in the cave. The Japanese soldier blinked, because he didn't expect to see a beautiful western woman in the cave, and then the Reverend Billie Jones rose up in front of the Japanese soldier.

The Reverend Billie Jones had a big boulder in his right hand, and he smashed it into the face of the Japanese soldier, who raised his rifle and bayonet to defend himself but was too late. The Japanese soldier fell to the ground, and Billie Jones bent over to strip him of his weapon and ammunition. Blood oozed out of the busted skull of the Japanese soldier. The nurses in the back of the cave were horrified, because they'd never seen somebody get killed at close range.

Lieutenant Breckenridge raised his head and saw dead Japanese soldiers littered around the front of the cave, but more Japanese soldiers were charging from the left, right, and front of the cave, screaming at the tops of their lungs, shaking their rifles and bayonets and baring their teeth. Lieutenant Breckenridge raised his submachine gun and pulled the trigger.

Click!

He was out of ammo and didn't have time to reload. Three Japanese soldiers jumped into the cave; one was an officer brandishing a samurai sword. The Japanese officer saw the Reverend Billie Jones and swung the samurai sword at his head. The Reverend Billie Jones dodged to the side, avoiding the blow, and then lunged forward, grabbing the officer's wrist. The Reverend Billie Jones was the biggest, strongest man in the recon platoon, and he was mad. He held the officer's wrist tightly and kicked him in the balls.

171

The officer's eyes rolled up into his head, and Billie Jones tore the samurai sword out of his hands. He looked around and saw Craig Delane lying on the ground, blood pouring from his stomach and a Japanese soldier standing over him. The Japanese soldier turned toward the Reverend Billie Jones, who swung his sword with all his might. The Japanese soldier raised his rifle and bayonet to protect himself, and the sword clanged against the barrel of his rifle, sending sparks flying in the air. Then the Japanese soldier closed his eyes and dropped to his knees. Standing behind him was Pfc. Wilkie, who had clobbered the Japanese soldier with his M 1 rifle. The Reverend Billie Jones raised his samurai sword in the air and drove it downward, chopping off the Japanese soldier's head to make sure he was dead. At the rear of the cave Lieutenant Doris Pagano passed out from the horror of it all.

The Reverend Billie Jones looked around and saw the third Japanese soldier lying on the ground. Pfc. Shilansky stood over him, the bayonet on the end of his M 1 rifle dripping blood.

Craig Delane groaned, trying to hold his intestines in with his hands. Captain Stearns rushed toward him and dropped to her knees. She removed his hands from his stomach and unbuttoned his shirt. Lieutenant Jones brought over sulfa medicine and blood coagulant. Lieutenant McCaffrey knelt on the other side of Craig Delane and felt his pulse.

Meanwhile, at the front of the cave, Lieutenant Breckenridge and the four GIs with him threw hand grenades and fired their weapons at the Japanese soldiers swarming toward them. The grenades exploded in a violent crescendo, blowing Japanese soldiers into the air; American bullets tore into other Japs, but still they continued to surge toward the mouth of the cave. Hand grenades flew into the cave, and the GIs inside threw them back. Pfc. Wilkie caught a grenade but bobbled it, and it fell to the ground. In his frenzied mind he realized it was going to explode, and he did the first thing that came to his mind: He fell on top of it, hoping to smother the blast with his body.

The grenade exploded, and Pfc. Wilkie was killed instantly. His heart was blown to bits, along with his lungs and most of his stomach, which burst out of his back, splattering blood everywhere, but he did muffle the worst of the explosion. The shrapnel passed through his body and was spent before it could harm anybody else.

The nurses worked feverishly on Craig Delane, trying to stop his bleeding. Private Yabalonka's BAR stopped firing; he didn't have any more ammunition. Jimmy O'Rourke was also out of ammunition, and he didn't have any more hand grenades. Lieutenant Breckenridge had only one clip of ammunition left, and he was out of hand grenades too.

Japanese soldiers leapt over the barricade and spilled into the cave. The Reverend Billie Jones attacked them, swinging his samurai sword to the side. He slammed the blade against the arm of one Japanese soldier, chopping it off just below the shoulder. A shot rang out and it whistled past the Reverend Billie Jones's ear as he raised the samurai sword again and brought it straight down, chopping a Japanese soldier's head in two. The Reverend Billie Jones yanked the gory blade loose and smacked the next Japanese soldier on the hip, cracking his pelvic bone. The Japanese soldier roared like a wild bull as he dropped to the ground, and the Reverend Billie Jones jumped over him, swinging the blade of the samurai sword again and connecting with a Japanese soldier's face, lopping off the side of his head.

Private Victor Yabalonka turned away from the barricade and saw a Japanese bayonet streaking toward his heart. He parried the thrust with his big heavy BAR and then slammed the Japanese soldier in the chops, breaking the Japanese soldier's jaw loose from its hinges. The Japanese soldier fell down and Yabalonka lashed out with his foot, kicking another Japanese soldier in the balls. A Japanese bayonet slashed down at his head and Yabalonka danced to the side, then pushed his rifle butt forward, ramming the Japanese soldier in the face, flattening his nose. The Japanese soldier fell down and Private Yabalonka spun around in time to parry a thrust that had been aimed at his back. The Japanese soldier in front of him tried to kick him in the balls, but Yabalonka pivoted to the side, catching the blow on his outer thigh, then hammered the Japanese soldier in the head with his rifle butt. The Japanese soldier's head cracked apart and brains oozed out of the fissures as he fell to the ground.

Victor Yabalonka looked around and saw dark, shadowy

173

figures locked in close combat all around the interior of the cave. He decided to hold his BAR by the barrel and use it like a baseball bat. He turned the BAR around and grasped the barrel. It was hot, but the bandages on his hands were like potholders. He charged the soldiers fighting a few feet away and saw the backs of two Japanese soldiers emerge out of the darkness. Raising his BAR in the air, he brought it down with all his strength on the head of a Japanese soldier. The Japanese soldier's head burst apart, blood and brains flying into the air. Then Yabalonka swung sideways at the head of the next Japanese soldier, caving in his skull. The Japanese soldier sagged to the ground at Yabalonka's feet. Yabalonka stepped forward, looking for another Japanese soldier to kill. A group of Japanese soldiers burst through the melee and charged toward the rear of the cave, where the four nurses were working on the supine body of Craig Delane. The nurses heard the Japanese soldiers coming and picked up their carbines. The Japanese soldiers saw the figures on the ground and angled their bayonets downward. The nurses gritted their teeth and fired their carbines on automatic at point-blank range.

They couldn't miss. Each Japanese soldier was hit by bullets and fell to the ground.

"Make sure they're dead!" shouted Captain Stearns.

The nurses aimed at the bodies, which were squirming and writhing on the ground, and continued to fire until the bodies stopped moving. The nurses lowered the barrels of their carbines and stared at the dead Japanese soldiers, aghast at what they'd done.

Lieutenant Breckenridge was in the middle of the fight, holding his Ka-bar knife blade up in his hand; he punched it into the stomach of the Japanese soldier in front of him, then pulled the blade out and slashed to the side, severing the windpipe of the next Japanese soldier. The Japanese soldier collapsed onto his back, and Lieutenant Breckenridge spun around in time to see a Japanese rifle and bayonet zooming toward his stomach. Lieutenant Breckenridge darted to the side and jabbed the blade of the Ka-bar knife into the Japanese soldier's arm. The Japanese soldier's forward motion caused the blade to rip open his arm from his elbow to his shoulder.

The Japanese soldier screamed horribly, but he didn't drop his rifle. Lieutenant Breckenridge swung the Ka-bar knife at the Japanese soldier's neck and cut open his jugular vein. Blood spurted out like a geyser into Lieutenant Breckenridge's face. Lieutenant Breckenridge spat blood out of his mouth and wiped it away from his eyes as he rammed the knife between the ribs of a Japanese soldier who'd been trying to stick his bayonet into Private Yabalonka. Lieutenant Breckenridge pulled the knife out, and blood spurted after it.

Lieutenant Breckenridge's hand was covered with blood and gore. A Japanese soldier lunged at him with his rifle and bayonet, and Lieutenant Breckenridge batted the rifle stock out of the way with his left forearm, then thrust the blade of his knife into the Japanese soldier's soft belly. The Japanese soldier shrieked as he fell backward. Lieutenant Breckenridge pulled the knife out, jumping to the side, drawing his arm back for another strike.

Lieutenant Breckenridge stopped, because the throat in front of him belonged to Frankie La Barbara, who rushed past Lieutenant Breckenridge and thrust forward his rifle and bayonet, jamming the bayonet between the ribs of a Japanese soldier who'd been creeping up on Lieutenant Breckenridge. Frankie yanked down on his rifle and bayonet, but the bayonet wouldn't come loose. Just then Frankie saw movement in the corner of his eye. He turned around and saw a Japanese soldier lunging toward him, thrusting his rifle and bayonet forward. Frankie timed him coming in, parried the rifle stock to the side with his left forearm, and kicked the Japanese soldier in the balls.

The Japanese soldier screamed and dropped his rifle and bayonet. He clutched his shattered balls in his hands and jumped up and down. Frankie bent over to pick up the rifle and bayonet, and noticed something coming at the side of his head. He ducked backward, but received the smack of a Japanese rifle butt against his forehead. It was a grazing blow, but it dazed Frankie and he fell onto his ass.

The Japanese soldier aimed his rifle and bayonet down and lunged toward Frankie La Barbara's chest. Frankie rolled out of the way, and the Japanese soldier took aim again, but was jostled in the fighting taking place beside him, and that gave Frankie time to jump to his feet.

Frankie kicked the Japanese soldier in the balls, but the Japanese soldier dodged to the side. The Japanese soldier leveled his rifle and bayonet at Frankie, when suddenly a samurai sword in the right hand of the Reverend Billie Jones swooped out of nowhere and cut off the Japanese soldier's left arm.

The Japanese soldier looked at his blood gushing out of the stump. Frankie snatched the rifle and bayonet out of the Japanese soldier's hand, and the Japanese soldier went into shock, collapsing onto the other bodies lying on the floor. Frankie turned to his right, and *wham*, he collided with another Japanese soldier.

Both men took a step backward and sized each other up for a moment, then charged each other at the same time. *Wham*—they collided again, and Frankie's rifle stock mangled the Japanese soldier's right hand. He dropped his rifle and Frankie whacked him in the mouth with his rifle butt. The Japanese soldier went down for the count.

Frankie was near the back of the cave, and he heard one of the nurses scream. He turned to the right and saw a Japanese soldier charge the nurses. Frankie held his rifle and bayonet in his right hand and threw it like a harpoon at the Japanese soldier. The rifle and bayonet stuck into the Japanese soldier's right kidney and hung there, the rifle butt bouncing up and down. The Japanese soldier shrieked horribly and fell backward. The butt of Frankie's rifle hit the floor and caused the Japanese soldier to pole-vault onto his face.

Another Japanese soldier ran toward the nurses, aiming his rifle and bayonet at them. Frankie ran two steps forward and dived onto the Japanese soldier, wrapping one hairy forearm around the Japanese soldier's neck.

The Japanese soldier crashed to the floor next to Lieutenant McCaffrey, and Frankie landed on top of him. The Japanese soldier's head struck the floor and he saw stars for a moment, letting his rifle and bayonet go. Frankie pulled the Japanese soldier onto his back, scrambled around, and grabbed the Japanese soldier by the throat.

Frankie placed his thumbs on the Japanese soldier's throat and squeezed hard. The Japanese soldier's eyes popped out and his tongue extended its full length into the air. He tried to claw Frankie La Barbara's face with his fingernails, but Frankie leaned back and kept squeezing. The Japanese soldier grabbed Frankie's wrists and stuck his fingernails into them, but Frankie wouldn't let go. He gritted his teeth and tightened his grip on the Japanese soldier's throat, and the Japanese soldier coughed

176

and gagged as his windpipe throttled. The Japanese soldier's face became purple, and his grasp on Frankie's wrists weakened. Frankie increased the pressure and felt something snap inside the Japanese soldier's throat. The Japanese soldier went limp on the ground. He was dead.

Frankie took a deep breath and removed his hands from the Japanese soldier's throat. Lieutenant McCaffrey stared at the dead Japanese soldier, sick to her stomach. The fight had been so brutal, so elemental, so grim. She shook her head because she couldn't believe her eyes. She didn't want to believe them. Looking up toward the front of the cave, she saw soldiers grappling in the narrow, confined space. It was difficult to distinguish the GIs from the Japs. Frankie La Barbara rose wearily, picked up a Japanese rifle and bayonet, took a deep breath, and charged into the melee.

Lieutenant McCaffrey saw him wind up and push the rifle and bayonet into the back of a Japanese soldier, then yank the rifle and bayonet loose, step to the side, bash a Japanese soldier in the face with his rifle butt, and advance into the center of the fight.

Out of nowhere a Japanese soldier appeared behind Frankie and aimed his rifle and bayonet at Frankie's back.

"Watch out!" screamed Lieutenant McCaffrey.

Frankie heard her but didn't know she was speaking specifically to him. The Japanese soldier thrust his rifle and bayonet forward, when suddenly a shot rang out and the Japanese soldier's head exploded from the impact of the bullet. The Japanese soldier collapsed onto the ground, his head a mass of twisted bone and gristle.

The shot had been fired by Pfc. Jimmy O'Rourke, who carried a Nambu pistol in his right hand; he'd just taken it from the holster of a Japanese sergeant he'd killed with his rifle and bayonet. He swaggered into the thick of the fighting like John Wayne, held the pistol close to the back of a Japanese soldier, and pulled the trigger. The pistol fired, and a red splotch appeared on the back of the Japanese soldier, who pitched forward onto another Japanese soldier. That Japanese soldier turned around to see what was happening, and Jimmy O'Rourke advanced toward him, shooting him in the face.

Jimmy squinted his eyes, because it was hard to see who was who in the cave. A Japanese soldier charged him, rifle and bayonet aimed toward Jimmy's chest, and Jimmy took aim with the Nambu pistol, squeezing the trigger. The pistol fired and the Japanese soldier was knocked off his feet by the impact of the bullet. He landed on his back, and the shirt of his uniform became soaked with blood.

Jimmy heard footsteps from his right and turned in that direction. A Japanese soldier lunged toward him, his rifle and bayonet streaking toward Jimmy's ribs. Jimmy raised the pistol and pulled the trigger. The pistol fired and kicked, and the bullet pierced the Japanese soldier's neck. His lips burbled blood as he tripped over his feet and fell to the ground.

Jimmy felt as though he were invincible with the pistol. It was as if he were the hero of a movie, destined to prevail and survive because the hero of a movie can't be killed. He saw a Japanese soldier fighting with Lieutenant Breckenridge, and Jimmy fired the Nambu pistol at the Japanese soldier, hitting him on the arm. He fired again and shot a Japanese soldier in the head. He saw another Japanese soldier fighting with Victor Yabalonka, and Jimmy jumped toward the Japanese soldier, pushed the Nambu pistol toward the Japanese soldier's ribs, and fired from a distance of one foot. The Japanese soldier was knocked to the side by the bullet and fell to the ground, and somebody stepped on his face as he died.

Jimmy O'Rourke turned to his right and saw a Japanese soldier standing a few feet in front of him, shoving his rifle and bayonet at him. Jimmy whipped the Nambu around and pulled the trigger.

Click!

It was out of bullets. A cold wave of fear swept over Jimmy O'Rourke. He realized he wasn't so invincible after all, and he wasn't the hero of any movie. The Japanese bayonet plunged into his chest, and Jimmy O'Rourke was overwhelmed by a horrible tearing pain. He bellowed like a wounded bull and went into shock. The Japanese soldier tried to pull his rifle and bayonet loose, but it was stuck in Jimmy's ribs. Dazed and numb but still conscious, Jimmy felt as though he were having the worst nightmare of his life as the tug of the Japanese soldier dragged him off his feet. He dropped to his knees, and the Japanese soldier pulled his rifle and bayonet again, but still it wouldn't come loose, and he dragged Jimmy forward a few feet.

Jimmy was as limp as a rag doll. The Japanese soldier pushed him onto his back, placed his foot on Jimmy's chest, and drew back his rifle and bayonet. Jimmy was aware of everything happening to him as blood bubbled out of his mouth. He heard a cracking, crunching sound, and then the Japanese bayonet broke loose from his chest. A surge of blood followed it, and now at last the merciful black curtains fell over Jimmy O'Rourke.

The Japanese soldier turned around and perceived figures kneeling on the floor at the back of the cave. He lowered his rifle and bayonet, the blade dripping with blood, and took a step toward the back of the cave, when *wham!* the samurai sword in the hands of the Reverend Billie Jones slammed him in the neck, chopping off his head.

The head flew into the air and landed in front of Lieutenant Pagano, bouncing forward and rolling toward her, coming to a stop when it touched her foot. Lieutenant Pagano didn't know whether to shit or go blind. She wanted to push the head away, but she also didn't want to touch it. The eyes in the head stared at her accusingly. She mustered up all her courage and pushed it away with the butt of her M 1 carbine.

Meanwhile, in the center of the cave, Lieutenant Breckenridge looked around and saw no more Japanese soldiers charging toward him. He narrowed his eyes and spotted Victor Yabalonka carrying a BAR soaked with blood. Then he saw the Reverend Billie Jones and his bloody, gory samurai sword. Frankie La Barbara lurched into his line of vision, looking for more Japanese soldiers. Morris Shilansky held a rock in his right hand, ready to throw it at the first Jap who moved toward him. The floor of the cave was covered with the bodies of dead Japanese soldiers.

Lieutenant Breckenridge drank the last swallow of water in his canteen. He and the others had somehow stopped the Japs, but more of them would return soon. The Japanese soldiers couldn't let the GIs remain at peace behind their lines.

"Gather up all the ammunition you can find," Lieutenant Breckenridge said wearily. "Take your positions in front of the cave."

Lieutenant Breckenridge bent over and picked up a Japanese rifle and bayonet. He knelt beside a Japanese soldier and looked into his haversack for hand grenades. Three Japanese hand grenades were inside, and Lieutenant Breckenridge put them into his pocket. The Japanese soldier lay on top of another soldier, whom Lieutenant Breckenridge assumed to be Japanese, too, but when he looked closer he saw that it was Pfc. Jimmy O'Rourke, his point man.

Lieutenant Breckenridge pulled the Japanese soldier off O'Rourke and felt for O'Rourke's pulse, but couldn't find it. "Are the nurses still here?" he asked.

"Yes," they replied more or less in unison.

"One of my men is hurt, here. I think he might be dead."

Frankie La Barbara's voice sounded on the other side of the cave. "Here's another one over here. Jesus, it's Froelich!"

"I think this is Wilkie," Shilansky said, kneeling beside a mangled, broken body.

The nurses moved forward to examine the bodies while the other GIs grabbed armfuls of rifles and bandoliers full of ammunition. Lieutenant Breckenridge carried his stack of weapons and bullets to the front of the cave and dropped them in front of the barrier. He looked down on the dark jungle below and could perceive figures moving around. A Japanese voice barked an order, and a second later a machine gun opened fire. The bullets flew into the cave and ricocheted around.

"*Yeeoooowwww!*" screamed Morris Shilansky, slapping his hand onto his leg, but he couldn't stanch the blood.

Lieutenant Jones crawled toward him, carrying a bag of medicine. Shilansky writhed and hollered as blood flowed in red ribbons around his fingers.

"Stay still so I can look at it," Lieutenant Jones said.

"It hurts!" Shilansky said, gritting his teeth.

"Let me see it!"

Shilansky took his hand away. Lieutenant Jones inspected the wound as blood welled out and Japanese machine-gun bullets continued to ricochet around in the cave. She took a scissors from her bag of medicine and cut away Shilansky's trousers.

"Let's get ready!" Lieutenant Breckenridge shouted. "They'll come back anytime now!"

180

THIRTEEN . . .

"This is as far as I can go, sir," said Pfc. Nick Bombasino from behind the wheel of the jeep.

"Stop anywhere around here," replied Colonel Hutchins.

Pfc. Bombasino steered the jeep to the side of the narrow trail and hit the brake. Colonel Hutchins climbed out of the jeep, followed by Lieutenant Harper and Pfc. Levinson, who carried a backpack radio with the long aerial whipping back and forth in the air.

All around them was thick jungle and foxholes. Colonel Hutchins wore his steel pot and carried a Thompson submachine gun in his right hand. He was full of codeine, alcohol, and caffeine, and his morale was high. His wounds hurt somewhat, but they only slowed him a little. His head was large and his steel pot rode high in the back and low over his eyes. He looked up at the sky and saw that it was full of stars, except for a few small patches of clouds. It would be a good day, and the Air Corps would fly missions.

Colonel Hutchins pushed through leaves and elbowed branches out of the way. He came to a foxhole where three men sat around a 60mm mortar, eating C rations. The men glanced up as Colonel Hutchins approached, and when they recognized him they jumped to their feet.

"As you were," Colonel Hutchins said with a grin on his face and a twinkle in his eye. "How's breakfast?"

"Just fine, sir," said one of the men, although the greasy cold sausage patties he was eating were dreadful.

"Are we all set for the big attack here?"

"Yes, sir."

"Glad to hear it."

Colonel Hutchins walked around the foxhole and moved forward, followed by Lieutenant Harper and Pfc. Levinson. Colonel Hutchins came to another foxhole, with two riflemen inside.

"Good morning!" said Colonel Hutchins in his deep booming voice.

The two GIs scrambled to attention; one was bare-headed.

"You'd better put your helmet on, son!" Colonel Hutchins said.

The GI bent over, picked it up, and placed it over his head. "Yes, sir!"

"How're you feeling this morning?"

"Fine, sir!"

"Ready to kill Japs?"

"Yes, sir."

"That's the way to be."

Colonel Hutchins turned to the left and approached a machine-gun nest with three soldiers in it, and they all snapped to attention as he approached.

"Is that gun ready to fire?" Colonel Hutchins asked.

"Yes, sir!"

"Lemme see."

Colonel Hutchins jumped over the sandbag and sat behind the machine gun. He pulled the bolt back and a round flew out of the chamber. The safety was on and it was ready to fire. Boxes of ammunition were stacked beside the machine gun.

"Who's in charge here?" asked Colonel Hutchins.

"I am, sir," said a freckle-faced soldier about nineteen years old.

"What's your name?"

"Private First Class John Ritter, sir."

"Where you from, Ritter?"

182

"Nazarath, Texas, sir!"

"Ranch country, ain't it?"

"Yes, sir!"

Colonel Hutchins slapped the soldier on his shoulder. "Keep up the good work!"

"Yes, sir!"

Colonel Hutchins climbed out of the machine-gun nest and walked around a bush. He came to a one-man foxhole with a soldier fast asleep in the bottom.

"Hey, what the hell you doing in there!" Colonel Hutchins shouted, standing at the edge of the foxhole, his hands on his hips.

The soldier opened his eyes, focused, recognized his regimental commander, and jumped to his feet, his heart accelerating. "Pfc. Morton Schrank reporting, sir!"

"What the hell you doing in there, Schrank?"

"I guess I was sleeping, sir!"

"Haven't you heard about the big attack!"

"Yes, sir!"

"Well, if you keep sleeping down in there, you're liable to miss it! You don't want that to happen, do you?"

"No, sir!"

"Get your gear in order and have breakfast. When I come by this way again, you'd better be up and at 'em."

"Yes, sir!"

Colonel Hutchins wandered through the J Company area, shouting orders and making certain the men were ready for the attack, but most of all he wanted them to see him, so they'd know he was interested in what they were doing and was sharing the dangers of the front lines with them. The CO of J Company, Captain Dixon, heard the colonel was in the area and went to see him. Colonel Hutchins gave him a pep talk and then returned to his jeep, followed by his entourage, so he could move on to another company. He wanted to visit all the companies in his regiment before the bombardment began.

Checking his watch as he approached the jeep, he saw that it was four o'clock in the morning. The bombardment would begin in just thirty minutes.

The cave was a bloody mess. Dead Japanese soldiers lay everywhere and were stacked up three high in places. Froelich and Wilkie were dead, and Craig Delane and Jimmy O'Rourke were unconscious, shot full of morphine and covered with bandages. The four nurses huddled around them, glancing apprehensively toward the front of the cave.

Lieutenant Breckenridge, Pfc. Frankie La Barbara, Pfc. Morris Shilansky, Pfc. Billie Jones, and Private Victor Yabalonka crouched behind the barricade as the front of the cave was peppered with machine-gun bullets, and mortar rounds exploded near the opening. Every mortar explosion reverberated inside the small cave, and everybody's ears were ringing. The explosions loosened rocks and clods of earth from the top of the cave, and the air was rank with the smell of gunpowder.

Everybody knew that the Japanese soldiers would attack again as soon as the machine gun stopped firing and the mortar rounds stopped falling. Lieutenant Breckenridge's submachine gun and Private Yabalonka's BAR were out of ammo, and they'd armed themselves with Arisaka rifles and bayonets. There was no more M 1 ammunition, either, and the other GIs held Arisaka rifles also. A samurai sword lay on the floor beside the Reverend Billie Jones. They all believed that the end was in sight, but no one suggested surrender. They all knew what Japs did to their prisoners, and they preferred to die clean, fighting for their lives.

Lieutenant Breckenridge felt somebody tap his shoulder and turned around. Captain Stearns was on her knees behind him, and with her were the other three nurses. All carried Arisaka rifles in their hands.

"We thought we'd join you," Captain Stearns said, her face dirty and streaked with sweat.

Lieutenant Breckenridge shrugged. "Do whatever you want."

The nurses took their places with the men as bullets zipped over their heads and chunks of shrapnel flailed the rock wall in front of them. Lieutenant McCaffrey positioned herself next to Lieutenant Breckenridge and smiled bravely at him. He winked back. There was nothing to say. Both figured they'd be dead within an hour. Lieutenant McCaffrey's lips trembled as she rested her shoulder against the wall and closed her eyes. Lieutenant Breckenridge placed his big hand on her shoulder and squeezed it gently, leaning toward her.

"Make sure you save one bullet for yourself," he said.

She nodded, trying to come to terms with the fact that she

184

was going to die. She was only twenty-five years old and had so much to live for, but it wasn't going to happen. It was difficult for her to believe that her life could end, and she wondered what would happen to her when she died. Was there a heaven and a hell, or would she just go out like a light bulb?

On the other end of the wall, Lieutenant Jones knelt beside Frankie La Barbara. She was the skinny one with the pinched face and long, pointed nose, and Frankie La Barbara smiled ruefully, because he'd chased beautiful women all his life, and now he was going to die next to an unattractive one.

She raised her arm and wiped her grimy forehead with the back of her hand. Her complexion was blotchy and she looked scared shitless, but she was trying to tough it out. Frankie La Barbara couldn't help feeling sorry for her. He figured a woman that ugly was probably still a virgin, and he wondered if there was a way that he could throw a good fuck into her before she died, because he thought everybody should have at least one good fuck in his or her life, and he always believed he was the best there was.

He leaned toward her and spoke out the side of his mouth. "Hey, why don't you and me go back in the cave there and screw?"

She stared at him, her eyes bugging out of her head. Frankie thought she was admiring his incredible good looks, when in fact she thought he must have gone totally stark raving insane due to the pressures of combat. He had a five-day growth of beard, his nose was covered with a white bandage, and he had a silly look in his eyes.

"Just relax, there, soldier," she said. "Everything's going to be all right."

Frankie raised his eyebrows. "What d'ya mean, everything's gonna be all right? Everything's not gonna be all right! We're gonna get fucking wiped out here, so why don't we go back in the cave and screw one last time?"

She shook her head. "Soldier, this is no time for that."

"This is the best time for that!" Frankie said. "I always wanted to die in the saddle, if you know what I mean, and I think it's about time you had a good one!"

"Calm down, soldier" was all she could say.

"Listen," Frankie implored, "you know you've been want-ing to have a good one all your life, because let's face it, you're

185

not exactly Betty Grable, so why don't we go back there and screw?"

She was so angry, she wanted to spit. All her life men had treated her like dirt because she was ugly, and now, on the hour of her death, she had to tolerate more of it. "We can't go back there," she said wearily. "A ricochet is liable to hit us."

Frankie fumbled for his fly. "But you can gimme a blowjob right here!"

She closed her eyes. "Oh, God!"

"C'mon."

He grabbed her hand and pulled it toward his fly. She drew back her other hand, balled it into a fist, and punched him right on his broken, mangled nose.

"Yaaaaahhhhhhhhh!" he screamed, holding both his hands to his face, but he didn't dare touch his nose.

Lieutenant Breckenridge leaned back and looked at Frankie. "Are you hit?" he asked.

Lieutenant Jones leaned into his line of vision. "Yeah, he's hit, and I'm the one who hit him!"

Lieutenant Breckenridge wondered what she was talking about. He got down on his hands and knees to crawl over and find out what had happened, when suddenly the Japanese machine guns stopped firing. He snapped back to his position at the barricade just as a mortar shell exploded on the ridge to the side of the cave entrance. A few seconds passed, and no more mortar shells fell. The machine guns weren't firing anymore. An eerie silence settled over the top of the hill.

"Get ready!" Lieutenant Breckenridge shouted.

He raised his Arisaka rifle, looked over the barricades, and saw Japanese soldiers in the jungle below, rushing in waves toward the base of the hill. Leaning over the barricades, he glanced left and right and saw Japanese soldiers advancing along the ridgelines. He spotted hand grenades in the hands of the Japanese soldiers in front.

Lieutenant Breckenridge leaned over the barricade, aimed his Arisaka rifle at the Japanese soldiers on the right, and pulled the trigger. The rifle kicked in his hands, and a Japanese soldier crumpled to the ground. The Reverend Billie Jones reached over the barricade and threw his last American-made hand grenade toward the Japanese soldiers advancing to the right of the cave entrance. He and Lieutenant Breckenridge ducked

186

behind the barricade, and a few seconds later all the grenades exploded, blowing apart Japanese soldiers, stalling the advance for a few seconds; but then more Japanese soldiers charged through the smoke, and they were ten yards from the front entrance of the cave. One Japanese soldier threw a grenade, but he was too far away and at a bad angle. The grenade bounced off the rock near the right side of the entrance to the cave and landed at the feet of the Japanese soldiers on the left side. Some of them dived on the grenade to throw it away, but they fumbled and stumbled, and the grenade blew up in their faces.

Japanese soldiers continued to attack on the right. The Japanese soldiers on the left jumped over their dead comrades and continued to charge. They swarmed toward the front of the cave, and the GIs and nurses fired their weapons at them as quickly as they could. Japanese soldiers fell to the ground, their bodies spurting blood, and other Japanese soldiers pressed forward, screaming and hollering, shaking their rifles and bayonets, anxious to get into the cave and impale the Americans on the ends of their bayonets.

The Japanese soldiers surged forward, and Lieutenant Breckenridge pulled the trigger of the Arisaka rifle as fast as he could, working the bolt like a maniac, but he knew he and the others didn't have a chance. There were so many of the enemy, and so few Americans. It was almost the end.

Japanese soldiers leapt over the barricade, shrieking *"Banzai!"* Lieutenant Breckenridge aimed the tip of the bayonet at a Japanese soldier's chest, and the Japanese soldier kicked the air with his feet as he tried to get away, but the force of gravity was inexorable and he landed on the bayonet, which pierced him from breastbone to spine.

Lieutenant Breckenridge threw the Japanese soldier on the ground, placed his foot on the Japanese soldier's chest, and pulled his rifle and bayonet loose. He turned to the front, slashing with the bayonet, and it caught another Japanese soldier on the face, peeling his skin away from his cheekbone, and before his feet touched the ground, Lieutenant Breckenridge smacked him in the nose with his rifle butt. The Japanese soldier collapsed and Lieutenant Breckenridge raised his rifle and bayonet again, pulling the trigger and shooting a Japanese soldier in the gut. He pulled the trigger again and shot another

187

Japanese soldier in the balls. Next to him, the other GIs shot and clubbed Japs, or stuck them with their bayonets, while the nurses fired their carbines as quickly as they could.

But it wasn't enough. The Japanese soldiers continued to rush forward, jumping into the cave. The GIs and nurses managed to kill some of them, but most got through. The GIs and nurses retreated back from the barricade, to fight the Japanese soldiers hand to hand. Captain Stearns was put down instantly with the thrust of a Japanese bayonet into her stomach. The Reverend Billie Jones had saved his captured samurai sword for the hand-to-hand fighting, and he chopped off the head of the Japanese soldier who'd killed Captain Stearns. Then Billie Jones spun around and swung the samurai sword, hacking off the arm of a Japanese soldier. He raised the samurai sword and swung down, cutting the head of the Japanese soldier in half. He swung sideways and buried the blade of the samurai sword in the rib cage of a Japanese soldier, but the blade wouldn't come loose. Billie Jones tugged, and just then a bayonet zoomed through the air, heading toward his massive chest. He turned to the side and the bayonet plunged five inches into his shoulder.

Billie Jones screamed and lunged forward, grabbing the Japanese soldier by the throat. A Japanese rifle butt slammed Billie Jones on the head, and he dropped to his knees, trying to clear the cobwebs out of his mind. A Japanese soldier kicked Billie Jones in the face, and Billie Jones dropped onto his back. He blinked and saw a Japanese bayonet on the end of a rifle coming at him; he reached up, catching the blade of the bayonet in his hands, slicing his palms like salami.

The Japanese soldier holding the rifle and bayonet closed his eyes and fell on top of Billie Jones, and there was a bullet hole in his back. It had been fired from the rifle of Lieutenant Beverly McCaffrey, who gritted her teeth, moved the rifle a few inches to the left, and shot another Japanese soldier in the back.

Out of the tangle of soldiers fighting hand to hand, grunting and cursing, a Japanese soldier charged toward her, readying his rifle and bayonet for a thrust toward her heart. She fired her rifle from the waist and the bullet struck the Japanese soldier on his chest. He tripped over his own feet and fell down in front of her. She kicked him in the face, stomped on his head, and stepped over him, firing her rifle, blowing down another Japanese soldier who'd emerged to confront her.

Japanese soldiers crowded around the front of the cave, elbowing each other, trying to get inside to kill the Americans, when suddenly they heard the roar of engines above them. They looked up and saw the sky filled with airplanes, and tiny objects fell out of the bellies of the airplanes. Then they heard the whistles of incoming shells. The Japanese soldiers dived to the ground as the area became blanketed with the explosions of artillery shells. Some of the shells landed on top of the hill, blowing apart the solid rock, filling the air with shrapnel and splinters.

The ground shook from the violence of the explosions. The American artillery barrage had begun, blasting the Japanese positions inside their salient on the west side of the Driniumor. Gigantic trees were sheared in half by incredible explosions. Bombs and artillery shells landed on Japanese troop concentrations, gasoline dumps, roads, ammunition dumps, and the bridge crossing the Driniumor. Japanese soldiers cowered in their holes as bombs and shells showered to earth all around them. The explosions tore up the jungle, blowing the Japanese soldiers to bits.

The US Army artillery and Air Corps really laid it on. Five minutes passed, and the bombardment became even more intense. Japanese soldiers went insane from the sound of the explosions. Others had busted eardrums from the concussion of the blasts, but they were the lucky ones. Hundreds of Japanese soldiers were blown limb from limb, killed instantly by the bombardment, while others were wounded horribly. Not enough medical supplies were available to save their lives.

Japanese soldiers retreated down the hill in front of the cave, so they could take shelter in the jungle, but the jungle was only marginally safer than the hill. American bombs and artillery shells convulsed the jungle and lacerated the Japanese soldiers. A few managed to take cover in the massive shell craters, and prayed to their gods that the bombardment would stop, but it didn't.

It just kept going on and on, and the Japanese soldiers thought the world was coming to an end.

• • •

A few miles away, Captain Yuichi Sato, the former decathlon athlete, lay on a cot inside the hospital tent and listened to the sound of the bombardment. The ground trembled as though an earthquake were taking place, and he was delirious with pain and fever. Gangrene spread throughout his bloodstream from the wound in his shoulder, and his magnificent athlete's body was wasting away.

There was a shortage of nurses, doctors, and medics. The wounded soldiers in the tent groaned in pain as American explosives devastated the jungle nearby. Captain Sato was dizzy and feverish. He knew the Americans would attack as soon as the bombardment ended, and he had to rally his men.

He sat up and looked around at wounded soldiers lying on cots or on the ground, but in his feverish eyes they weren't wounded at all. They were his men, waiting for him to give the order to charge.

"The Americans are coming!" he hollered hoarsely. "Follow me, men! Attack!"

He stood beside his cot, and everything spun around him, but he had to keep going. He reached for his samurai sword, but it wasn't there. Touching the spot where his Nambu pistol was supposed to be, he found that his holster was empty. He couldn't imagine what had happened to his weapons as he staggered toward the tent flap fluttering in the breeze. He went outside, and the jungle burst and churned all around him. Looking to the ground, he saw a branch that had been split in half by an artillery explosion. Captain Sato thought it was his samurai sword, and he picked it up. He looked at the branch and imagined he saw on the blade the trademark of the famous sword-maker in Kobe who'd fashioned it.

He raised the sword in the air and stumbled into the jungle. "Forward!" he said. "Attack!" He glanced behind him and hallucinated his company of soldiers holding their rifles and bayonets in their hands, following him, charging hard.

He ran into the jungle, jumped over a fallen log, and fell on his ass. Breathing heavily, his head spinning, he got to his feet and waved his sword over his head. "Onward!" he hollered. "Follow me!"

He charged forward again, and ahead, in the smoke and

190

flames of the jungle, he imagined he saw American soldiers running toward him.

"There they are!" he screamed. "Attack!"

He pointed his samurai sword at the American soldiers in front of him and shuffled forward. Bombs and shells crashed to earth all around them, but you never hear the one that lands on you. Captain Sato's eyes were glassy as he wobbled onward. His heart beat quickly and he licked his lips in anticipation of the hand-to-hand fight that he thought was about to begin.

A big bomb landed three feet away, and its explosion blew apart the gallant, once-great Olympic athlete. When the dust cleared it was as though he had been wiped off the face of the earth, except for a drop of blood here and there on the green foliage, or a length of bone or chunk of gristle lying on the ground.

FOURTEEN . . .

The bombardment lasted for an hour, and then its intensity slackened. One by one the big howitzers stopped firing, and the bombers in the sky closed the doors in their bellies. Silence came to the battlefield, and in the distance Colonel Hutchins saw a world of smoke and flames.

He was with Baker Company of his First Battalion, and he unslung his Thompson submachine gun from his shoulder. Checking the clip, and ramming a round into the chamber, he raised the submachine gun high in the air!

"Forward, Twenty-third!" he yelled. *"Charge!"*

Colonel Hutchins ran forward, aiming his submachine gun straight ahead at the vortex of smoke and flames. His belly bounced up and down over his cartridge belt, and his steel pot was low over his eyes. Behind him the men from Baker Company came out of their holes to follow their regimental commander into battle.

Meanwhile, up and down the regiment's line, all the other units were on the attack also. They swept forward into the jungle, screaming at the tops of their lungs, in accents that came from every nook and cranny in America.

193

Colonel Hutchins led the way, jumping over shell craters, dodging around trees. He came to the first line of Japanese fortifications; they had been devastated by the bombardment. Japanese machine guns were upside down, Japanese howitzers lay on their sides, and Japanese soldiers lay everywhere, many minus head and limbs. The ground was splashed with blood, and the dust settled on top of it.

Colonel Hutchins saw a head rise up from a hole, and he pulled the trigger of his submachine gun, blasting the head into lasagna. Then he saw movement in another hole and pulled a grenade from his lapel. He yanked the pin and hurled the grenade.

"Hit it!" he yelled.

All the GIs nearby dropped to the ground. The grenade exploded in the hole, and three Japanese soldiers flew into the air.

"Up and at 'em!"

Colonel Hutchins jumped to his feet and charged again. A dazed Japanese soldier raised his rifle and fired wildly. The bullet cracked over Colonel Hutchins's head, and he leveled a deadly stream of submachine-gun fire at Japanese soldiers. They ducked down, and a sergeant from Baker Company threw a hand grenade into a foxhole. The GIs hit the dirt, waiting for the big explosion. It shook the ground and sent rocks and clods of earth flying through the air, along with several Japanese soldiers.

The GIs didn't wait for Colonel Hutchins's command. They knew what to do. Before the Japanese corpses landed, the GIs were on their feet again, firing rifles and BARs from the waist as they advanced into the salient the Japanese had made in their lines.

Some Japanese soldiers stayed put and fought to the death, while others retreated back toward the Driniumor. Meanwhile, GIs from the Eighty-first Division's Fifteenth Regiment were crossing the Driniumor to the left of the Japanese salient as GIs from the Eighteenth Regiment crossed on the right of the salient. Their mission was to link up and cut off the Japanese retreat.

The GIs from the Twenty-third Regiment continued their headlong attack against the Japanese front. Resistance was light and they made steady progress. General Hawkins had been correct in his assessment: The Japanese presented only a thin crust on the west side of the Driniumor, and it wasn't difficult to break through. The American artillery and aerial bombardment had done most of the work.

Here and there the GIs came upon an intact Japanese bunker, which slowed down the advance. The GIs wiped out the bunkers cautiously, using the principles of fire and maneuver, and then continued to charge, killing all the Japanese soldiers still alive and pushing the rest back.

American casualties were light. Japanese casualties were heavy. In his headquarters General Hawkins smoked a cigarette and looked down at his map, smiling as reports from the front came in. He was winning a victory. His career was not ruined after all.

Meanwhile his GIs continued their rampage through the jungle, pushing their way toward the Driniumor.

Inside the cave they heard the fighting draw closer. They knew what was happening and were biding their time.

Heaps of dead Japanese soldiers lay outside the cave, where they'd been shot by nurses and GIs from the recon platoon or annihilated by bombs and artillery shells. The jungle below was torn apart, and bodies of dead Japanese soldiers could be seen from the entrance to the cave.

Craig Delane and Jimmy O'Rourke lay at the rear of the cave, wrapped in bandages, unconscious. Corporal Froelich and Pfc. Wilkie were lined up nearby, and beside them was Captain Doris Stearns, her uniform blouse soaked with blood, her eyes wide open and staring.

The other three nurses sat with the wounded, but they themselves also had been wounded, and wore bandages on their heads, arms, legs, and bodies. Lieutenant Pagano's nose had been broken, and Lieutenant Jones was missing a few teeth. Lieutenant McCaffrey's left arm was in a sling.

At the front of the cave the five survivors from the recon platoon also wore bandages. Exhausted, weakened from hunger and the loss of blood, they stared hollow-eyed at the jungle below, waiting for the US Army to arrive.

Lieutenant Breckenridge sat against a wall of the cave and lit a cigarette. The sun was bright and sent rays of light deep into the cave. He puffed the cigarette and looked at his bloody, mauled men. He could hardly believe that he was alive. If the fight had gone on for another five minutes, he and the others would have been wiped out.

The American bombardment had saved them all, but just barely. Lieutenant Breckenridge was cut and bruised all over his body. He felt more dead than alive. All he wanted to do was sleep, but he couldn't sleep until he was sure he and the others were safe.

His mind was too fatigued to think. He just puffed the cigarette and stared off into space. He hurt everywhere, but his leg provided the most pain. He'd probably need an operation before long.

"Hey, I see something down there!" said Frankie La Barbara, leaning over the barricade and pointing.

"Where?" asked Morris Shilansky.

"There!"

Lieutenant Breckenridge managed to drag his voice out of his throat. "Be careful!" he cautioned. "It might be Japs!"

"They ain't Japs," Frankie said. "They're our guys!"

Frankie stood up, tilted to one side and then the other, and waved his arms in the air. *"Halp! We're up here!"*

"Yeah!" replied Shilansky. *"We're Americans!"*

Victor Yabalonka stood up and showed himself. The Reverend Billie Jones clasped his hands together and murmured a prayer of thanks. Lieutenant Breckenridge knelt at the barricade and saw the green fatigue uniforms and steel pots of the United States Army. They looked better than a field of flowers resplendent with all the colors of the rainbow.

The GIs in the jungle swerved toward the hill. An officer stepped forward and cupped his hands around his mouth. *"Who are you up there?"*

Lieutenant Breckenridge pushed himself to his feet. *"Recon platoon, Twenty-third Infantry!"*

"What the hell you doing there?"

"We've been cut off for two days!"

The officer beckoned to them. *"Well, come on down, for Chrissakes! You ain't cut off anymore!"*

Lieutenant Breckenridge looked at the others and smiled. "Let's get the hell out of here," he said.

The GIs picked up their dead and wounded. The Reverend Billie Jones carried Jimmy O'Rourke over his shoulder, and

Victor Yabalonka cradled Craig Delane. The others carried Froelich and Wilkie. Lieutenant Breckenridge lifted Captain Doris Stearns, and Lieutenant McCaffrey came over to close Captain Stearns's eyes.

The GIs and nurses climbed over the barricades and descended the side of the hill. Some GIs in the jungle climbed up to help them out, and the rest stared at the bloody, mangled crew coming toward them, tripping and stumbling.

They reached the bottom of the hill and stopped, their mouths wide open, their dead and wounded on their shoulders or in their arms. The GIs in the jungle crowded around them, gazing at their bandages and wounds, their torn uniforms, and the glaze of horror in their eyes.

The officer was Captain Richard Swette, the CO of Easy Company, and he recognized Lieutenant Breckenridge.

"You all right, Dale?" he asked.

"I think so, but you'd better get us some medics."

Captain Swette turned to his runner and told him to call for medical assistance. Lieutenant Breckenridge set Captain Doris Stearns down on the grass and then sat beside her. He lit another cigarette and blew the smoke out the side of his mouth.

"Anybody got any water?" he asked.

Somebody handed him a canteen. More canteens were passed to the other GIs from the recon platoon, and to the nurses. Lieutenant Breckenridge gulped some water out of the canteen, then handed it back and lay down on the grass, closing his eyes. All the tension left his body as he went slack on the ground. His cigarette dangled out the corner of his mouth, and the other survivors dropped down around him, thinking of hot meals, clean uniforms, and someplace quiet where they could go to sleep.

Watch for

TOUGH GUYS DIE HARD

thirteenth novel in THE RAT BASTARDS series
from Jove

coming in July!

68